PROPHECY
GiRL

RAVIN TIJA MAURICE

Cover and Formatting

RMGraph

ALSO BY RAVIN TIJA MAURICE

THE AFFLICTED SERIES

Rebirth
Ikon

For all the little lost girls. If I got here, so can you.

"You can't save everybody. In fact, there are days when I think you can't save anyone. Each person has to save himself first, then you can move in and help."

- Laurell K Hamilton *Guilty Pleasures.*

1.

MY NAME IS CAMILLE BISHOP.
I MIGHT BE JUST LIKE YOU.

ONLY, I'M NOT.

Jane Lowry fidgeted nervously, twisting the brightly coloured beads on her Pandora bracelet. She would look at me, and then quickly look away like she was somehow not confident enough to speak to me. There was a thin sheen of sweat on her forehead by her hairline. She blinked a lot. I wondered if she thought it would stop her pupils from dilating.

All it did was make her look more nervous.

She couldn't have been more than eighteen years old.

"Why don't you tell me why you are here, Miss Lowry?" I asked. She turned her body towards me. My office was so small there wasn't much room. The sides of my desk each touched a wall, and the only way around it was to climb over it.

"I want to find my real father," she said, making eye contact then immediately looking away. "I believe the man who I've always thought is my father....isn't. But I have to prove it on my own. Can you help me?"

I started making notes. For my first case this seemed pretty standard.

"Well, we need to gather some DNA so we can run a test," I began. I made sure that I kept my eyes on her, regardless of if she turned hers away from me. She reached into her purse and pulled out four zip lock bags, two with toothbrushes and two with hair. All labelled.

"Oh. Well, you're efficient. Aren't you?" I continued. "Now, what can you tell me about the man you believe to be your father?"

She touched her face nervously. "I don't know anything about him except he's....."

She moved around uneasily, returning to fidgeting with the beads on her bracelet. I'd been around the P.I game since I was young and I'd heard a lot of craziness. I would be impressed if she shocked me.

"I think he's not of this world, you know? With these health issues I have it would explain a lot," she blurted out. She went from relaxed and looking around the room to nervous again when she looked at my face.

"You have to be more specific."

"I think he's a....creature of the night."

She couldn't be serious.

I started to wonder if Jane Lowry was a prank set up by my cousin to torture me. I tried to keep my expression level but prepared for this to turn shitty in an instant.

I cleared my throat. "Excuse me?"

"I think he's a creature. Part of a bigger network of creatures, actually."

I wrote it all down. I wasn't sure what she meant by 'creature'. Some people called prostitutes creatures of the night. I wasn't about to mock my first client, though. Besides, there was a time when something unexplainable consumed a large part of my life.

"Does he have a name?" I asked. She looked uncomfortable again, and my instinct said she had a name but didn't want to give it to me.

"No. That's another reason why I am here. I need a name and I want to know exactly who I am dealing with before I approach them - if I even can."

"Okay. Well, I will send these samples off and we should know in a few days," I said, "but with the info you gave me I can do some poking around. Now, we need to talk about fees. The DNA test is not cheap."

She pulled out a rolled up wad of cash a few inches thick. She smiled, clearly proud of her achievement.

She blushed. "I knew it wasn't cheap so I've been saving. I'm not sure if you can understand what it's like to know that something went on with your parents that regular minds can't grasp. You can't talk to anyone about it."

I smiled at her. My parents had been killed by the mob when I was thirteen years old. What I saw often haunted my thoughts. Visions of death and ghosts that took me years to suppress.

"Don't worry, Miss Lowry. You don't have to justify anything to me. Hopefully I can find you some information that will set your mind at ease."

When I was really little I wanted to grow up to be a Princess. My Mother told me the legend of King Arthur, and I thought I was destined to live in such a grand and exciting world.

As I got older and figured out Canada didn't have Princesses, I changed my goal to a crime fighting super hero. Which was sort of like what my Dad and most of the Bishop family did; for a long time the Bishops were the law. My grandparents, aunts, uncles, all cops of one flavour or another. And now most of their children.

But then, ten years ago, my parents were murdered. Mob hit was the official story; the crime remains unsolved. When I told them what I saw, they brought in the doctors. I didn't witness it directly, but I saw things.

In the house.

In my dreams.

Every time I closed my eyes.

I went to live with my Uncle Ted and stopped talking about it. I tried to settle into a somewhat normal existence. I learned to keep what I saw to myself.

The law loving Bishop's became rather jaded after what happened to my parents. Uncle Ted and his partner Chris Lewis quit the police force and started a P.I firm, Ted's wife, Cindi, didn't take it well and took off not long after.

Ted took me to work with him, and I started learning the P.I biz. It was actually kind of brilliant; no cheating spouse would suspect a teenage girl was running surveillance on them. It may not have been entirely legal but it worked, enough that I went and got my college degree in private investigation. Since I had so few friends my Uncle Ted became so much more than an uncle and friend. He's the best man I know.

Uncle Ted came in about an hour after Jane Lowry had left with two mugs of coffee. He handed one across my desk to me.

"How'd it go?" he asked.

"Good," I replied. "Seems like some simple paternity stuff."

"Really? Ramona said the girl seemed odd."

Ramona, the agency's long suffering receptionist slash assistant, was really good at reading people. She'd tried to teach me but I didn't have that level of talent. But I practiced; it was a tool I really wanted to master.

She and I had spent a lot of time together over the years, and she taught me a lot about people and the world.

I smiled at him. "People say I'm odd, Uncle Ted."

"You're not odd, Cas. The amount of therapy you've had, you're better equipped to deal with life than ninety five percent of the population," he made himself comfortable in the chair Jane had sat in, not bothering to adjust it.

"Thanks, I guess," I said. "She wants a paternity test done and she thinks her real father could be identified by strange medical issues she has."

"What sort of issues?"

"She didn't elaborate. She is probably just being paranoid and the DNA test will reassure her."

He smiled and nodded, his big hands enveloping his coffee cup as he wrapped them around it.

"Well, if you need any help," he began, but Ramona's appearance in the doorway stopped him from continuing. Her curly red hair with silvery streaks was especially bouncy today.

"Your next client is here," she told him, smiling at me before she disappeared. He sighed, waving as he walked out.

I got on the computer and started running background checks on Lowry and her family.

Her Facebook family photos were heartwarming. The man she called Dad was a leather- patches- on- the- elbows- of- his- jacket kind of guy; Thomas Lowry was a university professor and an all in all respectable dude.

He had never been in trouble, had no dirt that could be easily found.

Jane and her mother Benita were an interesting duo. Benita was a very thin, wiry woman who clearly took great pride in her appearance. Now, I had no issues with thin people but I could see that she was so thin as a direct reaction to spending much of her younger years heavy. And Jane, who was quite pretty, looked heavier than she was standing next to her.

Benita, maiden name Collins, wasn't as clean as her husband. An arrest for disturbing the peace in the 1970's was from some kind of protest....and some gaps.

Gaps in a standard background check could mean a variety of things. She could have been pardoned for a crime or crimes, she could have fallen off the grid, and she could have been a mole woman literally living underground.

But the timing was weird in terms of Jane's conception. There was no record of Benita from about a year after she finished college until Jane was almost two years old, which spanned about four years. Jane's birth certificate wasn't registered until then.

I thought about asking Ted but that seemed silly. I couldn't justify asking for help with the easy stuff. It was essential that he and Chris respected me as an investigator, and that they took me seriously. I wouldn't ask for help unless it was something major.

So I decided to call my cousin Kiera.

Explaining my relationship with my cousins wasn't easy. There are a lot of us, twenty one or so I think, and after my parents died they became really divided.

Those who believed what I saw made up one small group. Those who didn't believe me, but didn't hold it against me another and those who not only didn't believe me but decided to mock me at every opportunity made up the last group. I called them Team Poppy because they were led by Ted's daughter, Poppy.

Kiera was a non believer but didn't hold it over me. She was quite a bit older, eight or nine years depending on the time of year, and had no interest in the petty bullshit. This worked out great for me because I respected her as a person and a woman. Ted even said she was a pretty decent role model.

"Detective Bishop."

Hearing her answer her phone always made my heart sink. There had only been one other Detective Bishop in the family and that was my Dad.

"Hey Kiera. It's Camille."

"Hey kiddo, how's your first day of clients going?" she asked.

"Good. I have a question that I think you might be able to help me with," I began. "I'm running a background check and there are some gaps."

"It could be something unexciting. What's the name?" she asked.

"Benita Lowry, maiden name Collins. She had some priors, nothing too serious."

"Alright. Let me take a look and I will call you back. If it's after hours I will call your cell. I don't want to call the house because I might have to talk to Poppy."

I groaned loudly. "I haven't seen her yet today. She'll probably have a lot to say when I see her."

"Doesn't she always? Just ignore her. You're good at this. Do you think Chris would have taken you on just because you're Ted's niece? Fuck no. Chris Lewis is a serious hard ass. He wouldn't bring in a woman willy nilly, and especially another Bishop."

I couldn't help but smile.

"But I gotta go, Cas. I'll let you know what I find," she spoke quickly and hung up so I didn't have a chance to thank her.

She called me back about an hour before I was going to leave.

"You got quite the doozy on your hands Cas," she said, chuckling to herself. "Where did you say this came from?"

"The daughter wants a paternity test, and if that's not her father then she wants me to find the real one," I replied.

"Well, I'm glad you called me. Benita Collins was involved in a massive lawsuit against a man named Elliot Kinkaid, and the whole thing doesn't show up on a check because someone made it disappear."

I thought I should be honest. "I don't understand."

"Have you ever heard the name Elliot Kinkaid? Of course not, you're too young."

"Is he a mobster or something?"

She laughed. "He is not a mobster, he *is* the mob. Or was when this all went down. He has moved up the pyramid since then so he's under the radar. But Benita Collins was involved in a massive lawsuit against Kinkaid. Several women who worked for his corporation accused him of 'sexual misconduct', rape from Collins specifically. He was a prime suspect in a string of unsolved rapes that happened in the vicinity of his office and to a large number of his female employees."

"So he threw some money at it and it got wiped clean?"

"Looks like it. Interesting tidbit, these cases resulted in multiple pregnancies. Most of them ended up in the foster system. Four of the twelve stayed with their parents."

"Wow."

"Also? Benita Collins had the only girl."

I wrote everything down in my notes. There had to be some information about the cases somewhere.

"You might want to talk to Ted about how to handle this one, honey," she continued. "Because if it turns out that your client is this girl, and there is a chance she might not be, she might not take it so well. I cannot imagine how I would react if I found out I was the product of rape."

"Great. Thanks Kiera."

"Anytime kid."

2.

I won't say this out loud, but my friend circle is very small.

Having a cousin who was the same age at the same school who wanted to destroy you doesn't exactly help the cause. The few friends I did have were great.

But I did have Jesse.

Jesse was all kinds of wrong for me. I knew that. We met in the seventh grade, and I took one look at him and decided I wanted him with me.

He was a bad boy. He got in trouble, sold drugs, hung out with rotten people; I wanted to save him.

I love him, and have loved him since the first moment I saw him. And he loves me.

Having a guy like Jesse love you is interesting for a huge nerd like me. At school I got more second glances than I probably ever would have, and the torment stopped when he was around. I kept him in school and made sure he graduated. He took me away when I needed to go. Which was probably more than you might think.

Ted was gone when I was ready to leave for the day so I called Jesse as I walked out to the bus.

"Hey. How did it go?" His voice immediately put me at ease.

"Good. Weird, but good," I replied. "How are you?"

"Five by five. You home?"

"No I'm heading home from the office now. Ted is out so I'm heading for the bus."

"You look cute today. The office gear is hot."

I stopped and turned in a circle looking for his car. "Where are you?"

"You're the P.I. You tell me."

I smiled to myself. "You're two blocks back on my side of the street."

He laughed. "How'd you know?"

"Because that's where you always park."

"You want a ride home, love?"

I hung up as I started jogging back towards him and Jesse laughed when he saw me. My laptop bag was bumping into my leg and I hugged my purse to me so it wouldn't jangle. He leaned across the passenger seat to open the door for me.

"So were you just randomly sitting outside my office?" I asked. He pulled me to him and we kissed. My body instantly relaxed as he touched my cheek, brushing my hair back behind my ear. The warmth of the car and his smell enveloped me.

I couldn't help but smile as we separated.

He smiled back, his blue eyes sparkling. "No. I called the office earlier and you were on the phone. Ramona said Ted was gone and you would probably need a lift."

"Thanks. Taking the bus home would've been a bitch."

I curled up in his front seat as I normally did, Jesse put his hand on my knee and we started driving.

I watched him as we drove. He had the sleeves of his hoodie pulled up over his hands with his thumbs sticking out small holes in the sides. I loved his hoodies. When I wore one I felt like he was hugging me all the time.

"Hey, you ever heard the name Kinkaid?" I asked.

"Yep. They've been running shit for years. First it was the daddy; he's a pretty serious dude. From what I heard his sons are nuts. Like cut off your ear and dance around while doing it. They don't fuck around. Why?"

"Long story."

"Whatever the story is, love, you need to be careful. These people don't like games. Speaking of games," he continued, "I saw Lisa today."

Lisa was one of my only friends from high school and Jesse wasn't a huge fan. She was really good at attracting the wrong kind of attention and that worried him.

It wasn't her fault men liked her. She didn't go above and beyond to turn heads; she was way too absent minded. Space cadet was probably the right term.

"What did she do now?"

"I saw her at the mall with her latest geek of the week. I don't want you around that guy."

"What was wrong with him?"

"He looked like an extra in a 50 Cent video who chews glass for fun. Where does she find these guys? I don't want you around him or his friends."

I smiled and took his hand. "I don't spend that much time with her anyhow. Our schedules are too different. Besides, she knows I don't want to chill with her rando's and their buddies. She tried that before and it didn't go well."

She had tried to hook me up with one of her guy's cousins a while back when Jesse and I were on the outs. It was an absolute epic disaster. I don't think I have ever disliked someone so much on first contact in my life.

"And where was I?" he asked.

"It was one of those times you thought you wanted to be with someone else."

Jesse kissed his teeth, squeezing my hand tightly. He'd had one of those moments recently during a drug fueled rampage. It took me several months to accept him back.

"I don't know why you put up with me," he said, kissing my knuckles. I had finally stopped picturing the crack whore I had found him with whenever I closed my eyes.

"Because I love you way too much," I replied. He pulled the car over and parked, pulling me into his arms again.

"I promise you won't regret it," he told me, staring deep in my eyes. "I know how badly I fucked up, Cas. And I will do everything in my power to prove to you that I am devoted to you and this relationship. I love you so much Camille."

His eyes glossed up and he shed some tears. It wasn't a full out cry, but it was the start.

I wiped his cheeks with my sleeve and kissed him. When we were apart, I felt like I lost a limb. I couldn't imagine my life without him in it. I wouldn't be a doormat, but I wouldn't let him go without a fight.

We drove the rest of the way home in silence, my hands wrapped around his free hand.

There were no cars in my driveway when we pulled up to my house.

"Looks like Ted isn't back yet," Jesse said.

"Poppy isn't here either so I'm good," I replied.

"Why don't you move in with me?" He smiled, and leaned over to kiss my neck.

"Not yet," I told him. I liked the idea of living with him but I just wasn't ready.

"Do you want me to come in?" he asked as his phone started to ring. I knew he wasn't going to stick around unless I had a fit.

He ignored it for a few rings then said, "I have to get this."

He spoke quietly enough into the phone that I couldn't hear him, an art he seemed to have mastered. I tried to pretend like I wasn't interested in what he was talking about but I was. I was worried. I didn't want to be but I was worried.

I hadn't gotten to the point where I felt the need to snoop. I wasn't against it.

He sighed and hung up the phone.

"Let me guess. You have to go?" I smiled as warmly as I could even as that knot formed in my stomach. The same knot I got every time he left me.

He kissed me deeply and passionately, pulling me to him like he wanted to devour me. We hadn't had sex since we reunited, I wanted to know he was clean first and we hadn't got the results from the clinic yet.

"I'm sorry," he said.

I smiled and shrugged my shoulders. "Hey, it's okay. Thank you for coming to get me."

"I'll call you tomorrow and see if you need a ride again," he continued. "I love you, Camille."

"I love you too Jesse," I kissed him again then got out of the car.

I watched Jesse drive away, the street cloaking in darkness and total silence. That was the only problem with suburban Toronto in my mind, when it got dark it was alarmingly quiet.

I noticed a man standing by the street light. I had no idea how long he had been there. He was hidden by the darkness, almost like he was made from it. The wide brimmed hat wasn't helping either.

I stood and watched him back; I knew I was braver than I should be. Being a P.I, people got super pissed at you on occasion, stalkers were not unheard of. Cheaters getting caught, either the catcher or the busted, made people insane. I'd seen some super angry people go in and out of L&B; it wouldn't shock me if someone finally followed Ted home.

I smiled my best happy smile and waved. I was about to cross the street to introduce myself when the man disappeared in the shadows like a puff of smoke. I paused and stared, confused. Did I need glasses?

I shook my head really fast, and when I heard a car pulling away I decided to leave it.

The dark must be playing tricks on me.

Again.

I turned and went into the house. If that dude thought I was weird it's a good thing he didn't encounter Ted.

Or my bitch cousin.

3.

A lot of people hate mornings, but I am kind of indifferent. Some are good, some are bad. The ones where I don't see Poppy are usually better.

When I came down the stairs to the smell of bacon and eggs I was hoping it was just Ted.

My little cousin Cuddy smiled happily from behind a pile of food. "Morning."

Cuddy wasn't that little, he was eighteen and finishing high school, but I would always consider him my little cousin. He was wicked smart which allowed the fact that he was a huge pothead slide.

Cuddy got all the good personality traits his parents had, his big sister Poppy on the other hand didn't.

Ted was busy at the stove, and Poppy didn't look up from her plate. She was in her blue cop uniform and had her bottle red hair pulled back in a tight bun.

"We had a guest outside last night when I got back Ted," I told him as I poured myself some coffee and sat in my chair.

"Anyone we know?" Ted asked.

"Are you sure someone was there or were you tripping out again?" Poppy quipped without looking up.

"I waved but they left before I could cross the street," I replied.

"Don't engage the weirdo's, Cas," Cuddy chuckled.

Ted put a plate of scrambled eggs and bacon on the table in front of me. "Did you get a good look?"

"Nope, they were doing some cloak and dagger type bullshit. Had on a wide brimmed hat and everything to help hide his face. From the size and general vibe I'm inclined to say it was a dude," I sat and began shovelling food in my mouth. I was hungrier than I thought.

"Are you sure it wasn't a *demon*?" Poppy's condescending tone made my ears burn.

Ted paused for a brief moment then continued on with his cooking.

"Daddy, I need a hundred dollars," Poppy asked in her best 15 year old girl voice.

"You have a job. Not just a job, a good, well paying job. You have money," Ted answered.

"But I need it for something else."

"Why? So you can spend your paycheck on hookers and blow? Get a grip, little girl. I will only give you money in a life or death emergency."

She smiled. "How do you know this isn't one?"

"Get your own place Poppy. You're starting to annoy me," Ted grumbled. I took a sip of my coffee to hide my laughter. I wondered if Ted ever anticipated us sticking around like this after college.

Moving out was often on my mind. If it was only me, Ted and Cuddy it would be different. But Poppy sours everything.

"I gotta go," Poppy said, standing and gathering her things. "Hey Cas, if you see that 'dude' again give me a call. I'll send a meat wagon so they can finally cart you off to the loony bin," she laughed loudly, shaking her head, "which we should have done years ago."

"Fuck off, Poppy," Ted snapped at her. She stuck her tongue out at me and left.

Cuddy chuckled. "What a bitch."

"It might be time to force her out," Ted began, sitting down with his plate. "I could get that home office I always talked about. Write that detective novel."

"Is that what you're going to tell Poppy? 'Bye, sweetie. I need your room so I can write a book?'" I asked.

"How about 'you're annoying and I don't like you'?" Cuddy chimed in. He giggled proudly to himself.

"I love you Cuddy," I grinned happily at him.

"She'll bitch and whine about me letting you stay, Cas. I'm not into the idea of letting you live with Jesse yet," Ted continued.

"I could live alone. Or with a girlfriend," I said.

"But you wouldn't. You don't like any of them enough. And you barely talk to them."

"That's true," I replied. "Just make it sound like her idea."

"You mean manipulate my own child?"

"What? Like it's hard?"

He laughed, shaking his fork at me. "That persnickety attitude will get you in trouble one day."

"You trained me well, sensei," I said, doing a little fake bow.

"Now, now, you two. Hurry up. I need a ride," Cuddy reminded us between chews. Ted smiled at his son; he referred to Cuddy as the 'great white hope' of the family to other people, but never in front of him. It would be too much pressure.

I've always hoped he would go to medical school, or really shake up the Bishops and become a lawyer. He seemed to have no interest in law enforcement which made Ted happy.

"I'll clean up while you guys finish getting ready," I volunteered. They both bolted out of the room before another word could be said. I didn't even have a chance to ask them to clear the table.

I exhaled loudly, pulling the hair elastic I constantly kept on my wrist off and putting my hair in a loose bun. My freshly dyed black hair was slippery and didn't hold well. But I ignored it and rolled up my shirt sleeves and began to load the dishwasher.

Ted and Cuddy were both ready to go about 15

minutes later. I've always loved that about men; not so much doddling about. We loaded into Ted's Crown Vic, I had told him a million times he needed a non police cruiser like vehicle, and I sat happily in the back. It was a happy place. I loved Ted's car but Cuddy didn't like getting out of what looked like the back of an unmarked cop car in front of his school and I didn't blame him. He went to the same school Poppy and I had gone to, and it wasn't long enough ago that we had been forgotten. Being Poppy Bishop's little brother was bad enough.

I stared out the window at the awful brown building willing it to catch fire with my mind. I hated high school. The only good thing to come out of it was Jesse, same with grade school. If I hadn't had Jesse.....

"Isn't that Jesse's car?" Ted's voice brought me back to the moment. I followed his eye line and, sure enough, Jesse's car was in the school parking lot. Parked in the same spot he took when we went there.

I scowled. "Yes it is. It's too early for my brain to compute."

"It's probably nothing important. Maybe he's scaring some kids straight or something," he began. "Or he's teaching the chem class the finer points of meth cooking."

"Ha-ha. Let's talk about something else. Ever heard of Elliot Kinkaid?" I asked. I took out my phone and took a photo of Jesse's car in the lot, making sure his license plate was visible and it was clear where the picture was taken.

Ted swallowed hard, looking at my face for a brief second in the rear view mirror.

"I knew this day would come and I couldn't prepare myself," he said as we drove off.

"The day I would ask you for help with a case? A little dramatic much?"

His expression completely changed. "The girl has something to do with Kinkaid?"

"He could possibly be her father. She may be the only female child in those rape cases against Kinkaid from years ago. How do I tell her something like that?"

"Did you tell Ramona? Is that why you're asking me this?"

"Jesus H Christ, Ted! No! You're kind of like my mentor, dammit. Don't most students go to their mentor's for advice? Isn't that what you're bloody here for?"

He paused again, focusing on the road. I watched him, curious and confused. It was rare that Ted Bishop would get jumpy and Elliot Kinkaid made him practically twitch.

"I wouldn't tell her directly. I would lay out the facts for her and let her connect the dots," he said bluntly. I considered probing him about Kinkaid then decided against it. This was something I would save for later.

We did not speak again as we drove. Ted hustled off rather quickly when we got to the office like he was on fire. There were several people waiting when I walked through the reception area, Ramona smiled at me from behind her desk.

"Good morning! There is fresh coffee in the break room," she began, coming closer to me and saying, "and your first appointment is here."

"Give me a few minutes," I said. I went and grabbed a coffee, quite happy that my yellow Charlie Brown mug was clean and available, and headed for my office.

I put down my stuff and slid over my desk, trying to look as professional as possible.

Christ. I had to really work on my overall appearance. This desk thing was terrible.

I buzzed Ramona and she walked my client down the hall. A middle aged, grizzly looking man came in and sat down. By his fidgeting I could tell this was going to be good.

Then I got the smell. This guy took brushing his teeth with a bottle of Jack to a whole new level.

"You're the P.I.?" his leathery looking face wrinkled up like a rotten peach when he spoke.

"Yes sir. How can I help you?" I asked, spinning my pen in my fingers.

"I need you to recover some money for me," he began. It was hard to read his face with such thick and wrinkled skin.

"Well, depending on the situation I will see if I can help you. Please explain."

"You see, I'm a long time subscriber to a website and recently they took my money and locked me out. They continue to charge my credit card even though they locked me out, and when I report it they charge under a different name. But I know it's them."

"What is the site called?"

"The Dollhouse."

I paused. "And the URL?"

"The Dollhouse dot com."

"Ok. What sort of site is this?" I braced for the word 'porn'.

"It's a lifestyle site."

"Oh. Ok. Well, I don't think I can help you. You really need to get a lawyer. I can recommend one....," I opened my desk drawer and stuck my hand in. I liked to refer to it as my junk drawer, which is where I kept the stack of random lawyer business cards that we would pass on to a certain type of client.

He huffed loudly, stood up and snatched the card from my hand before storming out. I couldn't help but wonder if he had thought a P.I would be cheaper, or more discreet, then a lawyer. Or would ask fewer questions.

How did that guy get passed Ramona?

I didn't have another appointment until the afternoon so I decided to do a little research for my one case, and text my boyfriend.

I would normally ask Jesse why he was at the high school this early in the day but I decided against it. I wasn't worried. Some of the teachers genuinely liked him, he was very charming when he needed to be, and maybe he was getting a reference or help with something. He wasn't on drugs, I believed him about that. I had to trust him.

I sent him my usual good morning check in text. On a normal day I'd assume he wasn't awake yet, but I already knew he was. I added in a second message that I hoped he'd heard back from the clinic. Normally I wouldn't be so nit-picky but the girl I caught him with was brutal. Like the plague monkey that created super syphilis brutal.

Ramona knocked lightly at my door, drawing me out of my thoughts.

"How did the last one go?" she asked.

"What did that guy say he needed us for?" I asked. "He was super weird. And got pissed when I told him he needed a lawyer."

She chuckled. "I told him that too but he wouldn't listen. But if he wants to pay us so you can tell him the same thing that's his problem."

"Do you know anything about this Dollhouse site he was talking about?"

"No, but Ted or Chris might."

"What about Elliot Kinkaid?"

She paused, giving me the same look Ted had in the car. "Why do you ask about him?"

"Ted got all weird when I asked him this morning. He may be that girl from yesterday's birth father," I continued. "What is with you guys? What did this guy do?"

She smiled, that 'I know something but you shouldn't hear it from me' look on her face. You'd be surprised how often she does that.

"Ramona, why don't you just tell me?" I asked.

"This one you really have to talk to Ted about, kiddo," she told me in her best mother voice. The main door opened, signalling with a delightful chime that someone walked in and sending Ramona speeding for reception.

I opened up my laptop and started my search for some info about Elliot Kinkaid. He could bury certain things but thanks to the internet not everything.

The assault and rape cases were well documented. No pictures of Kinkaid anywhere but lots of Benita and her co defendants. I was right that she was heavier, and the resemblance to her daughter was much stronger.

I did find a picture I did not expect. A small article that surprised me enough that I left my desk and went right to Ted's office.

I walked in and closed the door behind me. "Dude! What the hell?!"

"'Dude'?" Ted looked startled. 'I'm your boss. 'Dude' is not the proper way to address me at the office."

"Why didn't you tell me Kinkaid killed my parents?" I snapped.

Ted sighed. "Calm down."

I did a double take and he raised his hand to silence me.

"There is no proof Kinkaid killed your parents, but your Dad was building a case against him when....," Ted began. "No one could prove who did it. But you already know that."

"What happened to his files?"

Ted didn't look up from his computer screen. I felt myself roll my eyes, putting my hands on my hips.

"Dude!" I yelled. "What the hell!? Where are my Dad's files?"

"They are not relevant to your case."

"Are you kidding me?"

"Camille, until you can prove to me that Kinkaid is part of your paternity case I won't tell you anything and even then it won't be much. Until I know you can look at this with a clear head you'll stay on a need to know basis."

I opened my mouth to object and Ted turned his eyes to me.

"This is not up for discussion," he growled. My anger bubbled up in my throat, leaving a sour taste in my mouth. I knew he was right, but any info he had on Kinkaid could be helpful.

"Fine. If you won't let me look will you check the files for anything about Benita Collins? I need to know if it's remotely worthwhile for me to try to talk to Kinkaid if there is a chance he's Jane Lowry's father," I said, and I stormed out of Ted's office.

I stopped in the hallway, turned around and went back to Ted's door. "Ever heard of The Dollhouse dot com?"

"You're not that broke, Cas."

"My first appointment, we'll call him Captain McDrunkie, is being sucked dry and wants someone to get his money back. I referred him to a lawyer but I was curious about why someone would be so touchy about a 'lifestyle' site."

Ted's eyebrows rose. "It's bordering. And it's weird. Throw up in my mouth kind of weird. Check it out when you have a chance."

I smiled and headed back to my office. I was in the mood for something strange.

The Dollhouse dot com was most certainly not porn.

I couldn't access much without a credit card so I used one of the firm's dummy cards we had set up for that exact purpose. Not that such things happen often but I wasn't about to put in a real card number knowing what they were doing to guys like Captain McDrunkie.

The essential premise was that the user got to watch a girl or guy of their choice live their lives on camera, like they were in a dollhouse. For a fee you could even make certain requests, within reason. I assumed sexual things were involved somewhere.

Yep, this was weird.

Scrolling through the list of girls, things like prom queen, cheerleader and executive came up. Farther down the list of relatively common things like fat girl and CEO I found something that surprised me a bit.

Vampire. The Dollhouse claimed to have a real vampire.

I had to click on it. While hoarder would have been mildly entertaining it had nothing on a real vampire.

Colour me shocked when I clicked on the screen and Jane Lowry's face appeared.

4.

I like to think I'm good at my job.

Not stellar, not Sherlock Holmes level but good, especially for someone my age.

I missed something they teach you first on background check day. The first thing they teach you when you think you're getting Catfished, for Christ's sake.

Why the hell did I not image search these people?

There was no mistaking that The Dollhouse dot com's vampire was Jane Lowry. She was going under an assumed name; perhaps she thought 'Jane' was too plain for a vampire. Unfortunately it was Bella. I hoped it was a Bela Lugosi reference but I was probably wrong. She even had a dark brown wig and brown contacts to complete the look.

When I clicked the 'Step In' button I was brought into a bedroom, an average teenage girl's bedroom, with

Jane/Bella sitting beside a boy, who was sprawled out awkwardly on the bed which made me think he had been drugged. She had cut open his ankle somehow, it was a bit unclear, and was draining blood into a chalice of some sort.

What the actual fuck.

This must be how she had that roll of cash. I could not imagine she did this solely to make money to pay for a DNA test. The set up was too elaborate; and the test wasn't *that* expensive. Doing this sort of work and leaving a trail online, even using an alias, isn't good for a kid who may want to go to a fancy college or get a job where a tie is involved. 'Bella' popped right up in the Jane Lowry image search, not just the Dollhouse but some modelling type photos.

This involved a level of commitment on her part.

Jane Lowry's 'creature of the night' comment made more sense now. If she could prove she was the product of a 'vampire' for real it would be good for business. But someone like Kinkaid would not want a random little girl running his name through the mud like that.

"So? Weird, right?" Ted's head popped up in my doorway.

I turned my laptop around to face him. "That is my client. So, yeah. Weird."

"How the eff....?" he bolted towards the computer for a better look.

"A random coincidence. I'm the dummy who forgot to do an image search."

He pointed at the screen. "This girl is the Kinkaid paternity issue?"

"Yepperoo. She also believes her 'real father' is a 'creature of the night'."

"Did she say that specifically?"

"You bet she did."

"Crap on a cracker, Cas. Do you want me to take this off your hands?"

"Fuck no. I will figure it out."

"Don't address what she thinks Kinkaid is or isn't. If she didn't tell you about her extracurricular activities you may not want to mention it until you really need to."

"I hadn't planned on it, Ted. It's not technically illegal so I don't have to. It just makes this more interesting. Why would she think Kinkaid is a vampire?"

He shrugged his shoulders, saying, "This job is generally kind of boring."

He smiled and left my office before I could say anything else. I decided I should take a little walk to clear my head.

Most girls would call their friends to chat when they had a free moment from work. Not me.

Jesse was the only person I really had to call. I still said Lisa was my friend but in reality we had drifted apart a long time ago. We had nothing in common and spoke only rarely. I was embarrassed that I had no friends, so I didn't speak openly about it very much.

But not having anyone to call gave me lots of time to think.

Jane Lowry had given me real DNA samples. The test was an expensive procedure for some stunt. I could build a case for fraud, depending on what she decided to do with the info. There was no reason for me to doubt her sincerity.

"Hey there, little girl," a gruff male voice pulled me away from my thoughts. "Want some candy?"

My father's old partner, Dorien Reid, was leaning on his unmarked cruiser smoking a cigarette. He had always given me the heebie jeebies; I thought he was dirty but had no proof and was not equipped to prove it. It wasn't directly said that he knew the truth of what happened to my parents but it was danced around enough that I made my own assumptions. With Ted having my Dad's files I didn't even know the truth of what he thought of his creepy ass partner.

"Do you use that line to pick up chicks? Because you may want to lead with something other than candy," I replied. I tried to smile but I didn't want to give him the wrong impression like I liked him or anything.

"You seen Lewis today, kid?"

"Nope. Why? You need some tips on being a real cop?"

He laughed loudly. "You got that Bishop mouth on you! You should spend some time with people outside your family, they could teach you some manners.......not that you're Mother didn't have them, God rest her soul."

Dorien Reid always talked about my Mother like she

was a saint, and barely a word about the man he spend most of his day with. What that could mean, I don't know. I could also be reading too much into the actions of a wacked out old drunk.

What's with the drunks?

"Ted probably knows where Chris is," I said. Reid finished his cigarette and squashed the butt.

"Not interested in your dear old Uncle, kid. The only Bishops I like to have conversations with are you and Detective Two."

I wondered how long he would get away with giving Kiera that ridiculous nickname. She probably didn't care anymore, the old boys club said things like that and if you couldn't deal you were in the wrong line of work. There was a reason Kiera Bishop was one of the youngest women to make detective. She was probably even better then my Father.

"Well go ask Ramona then. And we do have these magic boxes that you can use to communicate called telephones that would help you find out if someone is available or not."

He tousled my hair like he would a small child as he walked passed me towards the front doors. "I think I'll be alright. Good seeing you."

I watched him go inside before I turned to continue walking. Something bright caught my eye, my gaze travelling to a particularly shiny Jaguar hood ornament on a black car with blacked out windows. Not just a heavy tint but blackened so much it looked like a thick coat of paint.

I continued on for a little, crossed the street and crouched to look like I was tying my shoes, checking out the car in a side mirror.

First a man in black outside the house, now a black car?

I thought about going inside and telling Ted and decided against it. I stood and crossed the street again, heading back to knock on the window.

Before I could get there the car's engine started and it drove off. I pulled out my phone and took a photo of the back license plate, which I should have done when I crouched down across the street.

Boy, I am off my game today. Could this Jesse thing have thrown me off that much?

I went back inside to look up that plate number and have some more coffee. Hopefully some work would help straighten me out.

Jesse hadn't responded to my text by noon so I texted again, my usual sarcastic 'you dead?' text that I sent when he didn't respond. My stomach was in knots. I hated to admit how much I needed him. How much it hurt when he pulled away from me. I wasn't confident I would make it without him.

I got online and into my Kinkaid research to try to distract myself. I was tempted to GPS track Jesse's phone but I didn't want to be *that* girl. I wanted to trust him but the previous wounds were still too fresh.

I started reading about the rest of the Kinkaid family, biological and mob. It was like something out of a movie; I didn't know mob like that even existed in this day and age.

Oddly enough there were no pictures of Daddy Kinkaid or his progeny. Three boys and one girl. Jesse had been right about their brutality, even the daughter was connected to some remarkably violent unsolved crimes.

Apparently Lucia Kinkaid liked to beat people with a hammer.

I must keep that in mind if I have to approach them.

There was a stunning photograph of a woman called Labella, Elliot Kinkaid's wife, exiting an airport. I assumed she was still his wife as there was no mention of any other women, and I assumed she was the children's mother. She was a statuesque blonde, resembling 80's supermodel Christy Brinkley. I did not know if Labella was her real name.

So, why no photo's of the rest of them? No social media pics, no random snapshots taken by friends, nothing. They either did a stunningly good job at hiding themselves, or they just could not be photographed. But in 2017, how does that even happen? Especially in certain age groups, which most of them fell into.

My phone beeped letting me know I had a text. A huge wave of relief washed over me and I hadn't even checked to see who it was from.

I chuckled to myself. No one ever texted me other then Jesse. The very little that I did speak to Lisa it wasn't by text.

I grabbed it and quickly flipped to the message. It was Jesse, saying he'd not slept last night and was passed out when I had messaged earlier. Of course he apologised and offered to come pick me up after he went to collect his test results from the clinic.

I texted back in agreement. I had that photo of his car at the high school on my phone if I needed to question him, but the truth was I didn't even want to. We had just reunited, I couldn't take something else happening.

I quickly wrote down the black Jag's license plate number from the photo I took then put my phone away. I needed to focus.

Before I could continue there was a commotion out in the direction of the reception area. I was confident that Ramona could handle herself but as the voices got louder I decided to go out and see what was going on.

A man and a woman in their mid 40's were arguing right in front of the doorway. It looked like one had walked in and seen the other and that's how it started.

Ramona scooted towards me from her place against the wall. "Looks like we took on Mister and Missus as clients."

"A rare oversight, or was someone not too thorough in their background check before taking on one or the other?" I asked.

"More like she thinks he's a cheater and he thinks his

partner is embezzling funds from their company."

"Ah. Do you want me to intervene?"

She waved her hands out like Vanna White on Wheel of Fortune. "Be my guest."

I crossed the room and tried to get between the arguing couple. She looked like she was about to take a swing at him so I got in front of her. It might not have been wise, considering I'm not so big and can't fight unless I have a weapon.

"Excuse me, ma'am? Is there something I can help you with?" I asked her. Her red face and huge eyes made it looked like her head was going to explode.

"What the hell is he doing here? Can you help me with why my no good......," she began.

"Ma'am I think it would be wise if we spoke in another room," I said, attempting to usher her into the lunchroom.

"Oh, hell no! I am not going to be pushed aside by some kid...."

"I am a fully licensed and frankly quite underestimated investigator, ma'am, but that is beside the point. Please, consider it advice from L&B Investigations that you and I continue this discussion elsewhere. My office perhaps?"

She stopped when I mentioned the company's full name, as if she understood that meant I was being super serious. She nodded and followed me out of the waiting area.

"I apologise for the oversight, you should have been informed," I started. "Your husband is here on a very separate matter, regarding his business. Unless you want to completely compromise your investigation I advise you think of something to tell him when you go back out there that doesn't make you look suspicious."

She smiled at me then, she was actually kind of pretty. She just looked tired. My guess was that she'd had a couple kids with this guy and while she was busy being a Mom he'd lost interest. We all wished stuff like that didn't happen but it did.

"We have a teenager. I'm sure I can figure it out," she replied. "Can you tell me anything about his case?"

"No. I probably shouldn't have told you it was business related, so if Mr. Bishop or Mr. Lewis asks, tell them I only said it was a 'separate matter'. I wanted to put your mind at ease a bit."

She smiled again and put her hand on my shoulder, a motherly gesture. "I appreciate it, dear. I'll keep it between us girls."

She winked at me then headed back into the waiting room, smiling and laughing as she did. I didn't know if I would ever fully understand women. My mother had died when I was at the age where she would have taught me the *womanly ways,* if you will, so what I knew about dealing with women I learned from Uncle Ted. I didn't know if that was more helpful or a hindrance.

"She's fun, isn't she?" a voice said from farther down the hallway. I turned to find Chris Lewis standing in his doorway. He was in a well tailored blue suit and looked like something out of a men's magazine, his dark hair styled perfectly like a 1960's businessman. Leaving the police force had done wonders for him; he had always been an attractive man but the suave Phillip Marlow thing looked good on him.

"That type of an oversight is rather unlike you," I said.

"Well, it's a good thing you are here isn't it? It's nice to know it least one of you Bishop's is good at diplomacy."

"How was your meeting with Dorien Reid?"

Chris laughed and started down the hallway. "Hey kid, I need your help with something. That boyfriend of yours let you out at night?"

"Depends. You planning on pimping me out to the highest bidder?"

He laughed. "No, nothing like that. Come to my office before you leave."

He tousled my hair as he walked out.

Why did people keep doing that?

Running a license plate is not as easy as they make it look on television or in the movies. Maybe it was in the US but in Canada it wasn't. L&B had a cheat code, as I liked to call it. Someone at the Ministry of Transportation liked Ted enough to give him a pass code, one that changed on a monthly basis to avoid detection. Not that we ran enough plates for it to be a thing but hey, whatever works.

I typed the plate in the database and clicked search.

It seemed like it took days for the little swirl that meant it was thinking to stop.

I stared at the screen in disbelief. A sentence written in green flashed underneath the registration information. 'Please see supervisor for more info' was what it said, and the info simply stated 'for diplomatic use'.

I cleared the search history and logged out, hoping that would avoid it getting flagged. Ted and Chris would be mighty pissed if I messed up their cheat code.

But then they would have to answer questions about why a dark car with diplomatic plates was chilling out front of the office.

I spent my afternoon continuing to look for photographic evidence of the Kinkaid's with no luck. It boggled my mind that Lucia Kinkaid, who I believed to be in her mid 20's, had no photos of herself anywhere. She didn't even have a Facebook profile I could find. It all seemed fishy to me.

The end of the day rolled around and I started to pack up my stuff. Ted was gone again so after texting Jesse to tell him I was almost done I headed to Chris's office.

The door was open a crack and he waved me in. He was on the phone so I sat down in front of his enormous desk and waited.

Chris Lewis's office was like something out of Scarface; a massive dark wood desk took up a large portion of the room, which was decorated in red and gold. I found it to be an assault on the senses but it didn't seem to bother the clients so I said nothing.

He sighed loudly as he hung up the phone. "Thanks for coming to talk to me Camille. I have a case that I'm working on that I need your help with."

"What sort of case?"

"A club owner has a few 'things' going on in his club that he wants us to keep an eye on."

"What sort of things?"

"Well, that's the issue. Some of it is not legal."

"Define not legal?"

"Camille, you've known me your entire life. Have I ever been one to dance around things? When I say not legal I mean not legal."

"Oh," I replied. "What would I be doing at the club?"

"Waitressing, of course. I wouldn't ask you to dance, you're far too...."

"Far too 'the niece of your partner'? Far too exquisite?"

"You're too soft. Strippers are hard, that's the only way they survive, especially if they don't do drugs. You don't have the right mentality. I'm sorry if you find that insulting."

I smiled. "I don't. It seems more like a backhanded compliment, actually."

"So are you in? It will just be a few weekends mostly. I will give you double what you get on a regular job plus expenses, danger pay and wardrobe."

"Wardrobe?"

"Yes. Tell me your sizes," he handed me a notepad

and pen. I watched his face for any sign that he was kidding. If he wanted to pay me that much and buy me clothes I wasn't about to argue. I'd do a little recon first and find out what Jesse knew about the place, just so I wasn't walking in totally blind.

I wrote down my sizes, including shoes, and handed the pad back to him. I was pleased he hadn't tried to guess; I was not slim and top heavy and had trouble finding clothes that fit nicely. I also didn't like to spend tons of money on clothes so that didn't help either.

"When would I start?" I asked.

"Let me work out the logistics and get back to you. I should know by Thursday. Your cell number is still the same?"

"Yep," I replied, getting up and heading for the door. "What's the club called?"

"Ren. Oh, and Cas?" Chris called as I stepped into the hallway. I poked my head back into his office.

"I trust that you'll keep this discreet. Especially when talking to Ted," it was more of a statement then a question.

"Of course."

Jesse was already waiting in the lobby when I came out of my office. He was all smiles, as I figured he would be once he got cleared by the clinic.

Ramona beamed at us like a proud Mom from behind her desk. Jesse was a likeable guy, even with his flaws, and he had charmed Ramona a long time ago.

Jesse got up as soon as he saw me and grabbed my bags, leaning over to kiss me as he did so.

"Hi honey. How was your day?" he asked as we waved goodbye to Ramona and headed out.

"Long. How was yours?" I said. He put my bags in his backseat as I got in the passenger door.

"Uneventful. I had a weird night last night so I didn't sleep well so I spent most of the day in bed."

"You ok?" I asked as he got in the driver's side and we pulled away. I noticed an envelope sticking out of his visor where it was folded against the ceiling. I assumed that was the results from the clinic and he'd got the written proof I'd wanted.

"Yea, love, I'm good. I am just looking forward to the day I can leave my shithole apartment and we can get a place together."

"Well, Lewis brought me in on a side job so I will be bringing in some extra cash. Hopefully if it goes well he will bring me in more often and I can start saving."

"What sort of side job?"

I examined Jesse's face for any signs that being honest wasn't the best option. He knew how important being taken seriously by Chris Lewis and my Uncle was to me so any complaint he had better be a major one.

"I'll be waitressing at a club called Ren. He needs me to watch a few things and get a handle on what's going on."

"Does he know about your Kinkaid issue?"

"I don't think so. Why?"

"Because last I heard Ren is a Kinkaid operation. Owned and run by."

I couldn't help but smile. "Well, that seems a little like fate, doesn't it?"

"Maybe I should come with you, just in case you...."

"Nope. It's time for me to put my big boy pants on."

"Just don't do anything that would put yourself or your license at stake, ok Cas?"

I saluted him. "Yes sir!"

He smiled now, that stupid smirk that made my insides melt. I thought about asking him why he was at the school but I didn't want to ruin the moment.

"Your test results?" I asked, pointing at the envelope.

"Yes ma'am. Would you like to see?" I could tell by the look in his eyes that he was clean and all was well.

"I trust you to tell me the truth. Or else I'll cut it off."

"What's 'it'?"

I pointed at his crotch. "That's it. Don't believe me? Try me."

"You don't have a better nickname for him then 'it'?"

I lowered my eyebrows. "No. Does he need one?"

"Nah. And to answer your question I'm good to go."

"Good. So my place or yours?"

5.

Jesse's apartment was like a cocoon for me. I could just go in and feel wrapped in warmth and comfort; it was like a safe haven. It was one of the only places I felt free and like I could truly be myself.

I put my bags down beside the couch and sat down. Jesse did his usual circuit, putting his keys and other paraphernalia in a bowl he kept on his kitchen counter while getting us something to drink. He'd cleaned up, which was nice. He knew I'd feel compelled to if I was here so I was happy to see he'd put some thought into it.

He turned on the TV and put on The Food Network. One of my strongest memories of my Mother was watching The Food Network with her when I got home from school. It was my happy place.

"What did you do?" I asked as he sat down.

"Nothing. Why?"

"You seem to be going above and beyond to make me feel comfortable. I just assumed you were softening me up for something."

He chuckled. "Couldn't I just want you to be happy and relax while you're here?"

"Sure. Sorry. Suspicious is my default setting."

He pulled me into his arms and I leaned in, my body relaxing in his embrace.

"It's my fault. I get so caught up, and with the drugs and.....," he started. I cupped his face in my hands and looked into his eyes. The blue of his pupils looked like crystals, I couldn't help but smile.

"We've gone over this. It's done. If you feel yourself sliding back you can tell me and we'll figure it out. You just need to talk to me," I kissed him, and tried to put all the emotions I was feeling into that kiss. The hardness that often ran through his body began to ease, as it usually did when we were alone. It was part of his armour, something he had always done to protect himself in his dealings with the world, whether they were law abiding or not.

His was physical. Mine was verbal. I took great pride that I could talk myself in and out of most situations.

"It's embarrassing. I don't like you seeing me like that, Cas. I don't want you to know that part of me," his tone got sad. He pulled away from me only far enough so he could look in my eyes.

I couldn't help but smile. "If we're going to stay together you need to know that I'm not going to run away if something bad happens."

He ran his fingers through my hair, kissing my cheek on the opposite side. He slowly began kissing along my jaw and down my face to my neck.

"Are you hungry?" he asked.

"Of course. Did you actually buy groceries?"

"Do Doritos count as groceries? I thought we would order some pizza and wings or something."

"Ok. Then we'll get down to business after?"

He laughed. "Business?"

"You know," I said, trying to do my best gangster face. "The 'bidness'."

He laughed even harder. I pretended fake annoyance and pulled him closer to me, hugging him to my body and wrapping my legs around his waist.

"I missed you," he whispered into my hair. "I missed the person I am when I'm with you."

"I missed you too."

We ordered food and randomly removed clothing items once it arrived to get more comfortable. I tried my best to find comfortable work clothes but was not always successful; I took off my work shirt and folded it neatly over one of Jesse's dining room chairs. It wasn't much of a dining room actually, just a small wooden table we had got at Ikea that I mostly used as a desk. But it did the job, and by the time we were done eating we were both sitting in our underwear.

He had got thinner since the last time I had seen him shirtless, but his body was still well muscled. He had always been slim, but his current physique was from the drugs and him not eating at all, let alone properly. He had a small patch of blonde hair on his chest and a line that came up from below his belt line to his belly button that I loved. He had shaved his face clean; his hair was about two inches long all over and sticking out on top.

I knew very well that he was good looking, and that a certain type of woman would throw over their own mother for a chance to be seen in public with him. They would do worse things to *be* with him.

There were these junkie twin sisters in high school that fought over wanting to be with him and one poked the other's eye out. Literally blinded their twin sister for the possibility of being with Jesse, and he didn't even know their names let alone do anything with them.

He smiled at me; I guess I must have looked like I was daydreaming.

"What are you thinking about?" he asked.

I ran my finger along the line of hair down from his belly button. "That."

He kissed me hard, trying to hide his eagerness as he unhooked my bra. His hands on my skin were like heaven, the tips of his fingers exploring my body. It was like being reunited with an old friend.

Before we went any further Jesse scooped me up and carried me into the bedroom, which was no easy feat considering I was not a tiny person.

He lay me down on his bed, kissing my body. I revelled in every second. I wanted to reciprocate but he wouldn't allow it, removing my underwear in one fluid motion.

He started with his fingers, then his mouth, and before I even realized I was writhing in pleasure, my body quaking in orgasm. He dug his fingers into my thighs, trying to contain his own need as I opened up in front of him.

I was breathless when he stopped and started kissing up my body. I grabbed his arms and pulled him upwards, wrapping my limbs around him and kissing him hard on the mouth.

He pulled away from me momentarily and looked deep in my eyes.

"Condom," he said, leaning across the bed towards his bedside table. I kissed his neck and tickled the tip of his earlobe with my tongue as he put it on, his eager noises making me smile.

It seemed like it took him an eternity to get the condom on. Once he did he lifted my rear up slightly before he entered me.

I gasped, he laughed softly as he nuzzled my neck.

"I missed you so much baby," his voice was breathless and heavy as he whispered in my ear. "I'm so sorry. I promise I will never leave you again."

I couldn't form words, I was too far gone. My body was erupting, my senses heightened as the waves of pleasure flew through my body. I moaned in response to his moans, our bodies falling into sync.

He began to speed up and I knew he was getting close. The quicker motion caused my desire to heighten, bringing me to the edge. He thrust harder and deeper and my body thundered in orgasm, he quickly followed suit. He kept thrusting even though he was finished as my orgasm rode out so my pleasure would continue; I thought I would burst at the seams.

When it was done I was spent.

He lay on top of me, still inside me, and we breathed as one. He shifted his weight slightly and I chuckled.

"You're not even heavy. Did you eat anything when we were separated?" I asked.

He laughed. "Nothing good. And the drugs and lack of sleep contributed to it."

"Is that why you didn't sleep last night?"

He rolled off me, taking off the condom and tossing it in the waste basket beside the bed.

"You were at the school this morning," I made it a statement and not a question. "I saw your car in the lot when we dropped off Cuddy."

"Thought one of you might. Rollo's the new custodian. I went to wish him good luck on his first day."

Rollo was Jesse's childhood friend; affectionately nicknamed for the time he tried to shove Rollo chocolates up his nose. He was the only one of Jesse's friends I hadn't wanted to run a background check on.

I nuzzled up beside him and we curled ourselves together, our limbs intertwined.

"That was nice of you. I'm surprised they would hire

him considering how many times he almost levelled the place."

"Believe me he is too," he kissed me softly on the cheek. "I know you're worried and I am sorry. I hate what I have done to you."

Before I could reply there was a loud knocking at his front door.

He nuzzled my neck. "Ignore it."

A high pitched, shrill voice yelled from beyond the wood. "Jesse! Jesse, I know you're in there! I can hear your TV!"

The voice was most definitely female and bloody annoying. But something about it made the hair on the back of my neck stand up, so I put on my panties and one of Jesse's shirts.

He grabbed my wrist. "Cas."

I knew by his facial expression that the girl I had caught him with was on the other side of that door.

"Why is she here?" I asked, my voice was shaky.

"I don't know. I haven't seen or spoke to her since that night, and after you saw....," he started to cry, "I told her I had made a mistake and we were done. I don't know why she is here; I didn't think she knew where I lived!"

I twisted from his grip and headed for the door, he continued to cry. I wanted to tell him to stop but I had to get rid of her first.

I grabbed a frying pan from the kitchen then headed for the door. I checked the peephole to verify it was her; bleached blonde in white denim, she tried to cover her meth scabs with makeup.

I opened the door; her eyes grew wide when she looked at me.

"I don't believe we've been properly introduced," I said and I swung the frying pan. She ducked out of the way, I made it look as if I missed by accident.

"What the fuck? You crazy bitch!" she yelled. "Jesse! Jesse!"

"Bitch, are you fucking retarded? Or would you like me to crack open your skull?" I said angrily. My voice was sharp but not unbalanced. I had played this moment out in my head and it was going how I had thought. I wasn't going to lie and say I hadn't fantasized about crushing the skank's skull with my bare hands.

Any normal, sane person would have had the same thoughts. It's only natural to want to destroy the thing that almost destroyed you.

"He's done with you. If you fuck off now I won't bash your face in," I continued, pointing at her with the frying pan. "Forget you ever met him. If you see him on the street don't look at him. And if I catch you even breathing the same air as him...."

I laughed, twisting the handle of the frying pan in my hand.

"Are you sure this is what he wants?" her frosted pink lips twisted into a snarl. "He came to me! He told me I was everything he ever wanted!"

I grabbed her by the hair; she stumbled in her cheap plastic heels.

"He lied," I said coldly; bringing the flat side of the pan close to her face.

"Alright! Alright!" she shrieked. I shoved her towards the wall, then turned and went back into the apartment. I slammed the door shut, locked the door and put on the chain, returning the frying pan to the kitchen before I noticed Jesse in the bedroom doorway.

His face was red and wet with tears; it looked as if he had cried through the entire incident.

"Exactly how did you think I was going to react?" I snapped. He said nothing, just stared at me.

"Do you want me to leave? I could go get her on the way out," I gestured to the door and he started crying again. I sighed loudly.

I went and found my phone on the coffee table, texting Ted to tell him where I was and that I wouldn't be back tonight, allowing Jesse to stand there and cry.

"I was hoping you would be relieved that I got rid of her with no blood being spilled," I went on, standing beside him in the doorway. "In a way you should be happy it was me and not you. Unless you didn't want her gone?"

He shook his head quickly no and I continued. "Well ok then. I don't know why you're doing that. It's ok. Everything is ok now."

"No, it's not. You attacked a girl with a frying pan. That's not you, that's the person I've turned you into. I'm so....," he blubbered.

"Will you cut that out? *Maybe I need to be that person.*

Maybe I need to show the world that I'm not someone they can fuck around with anymore."

We stood in his bedroom doorway eye to eye; his shirt not quite fitting me in some spots, stretched tight across my breasts and loose other places, the bottom just grazing my thighs. He in his boxers, hunched over in defeat and sadness. I felt like I had put on whatever weight he'd lost.

I suddenly felt self conscious about my appearance and went back to the bed to cover myself. I took off his shirt and wrapped myself in his blanket. Yes, I was less covered but was far more comfortable, the stretching of fabric being the offending culprit.

He stood and watched me for a while. All I could think to do was stare back.

"My years of therapy have helped me control my temper. But that set me off. I'm not going to apologise," I finally said. "You are the one who slept with her, not me."

He slinked across the room and crawled into bed beside me. I pulled him into my arms and put his head on my chest and he began to run lines across my stomach with the tips of his fingers. I lay back and closed my eyes.

He began to wiggle around a bit and started kissing the side of my neck as he played with the waistband of my underwear.

"You confuse me," I said.

"Why?"

"One second you're in tears and the next you're feeling me up? I don't get it."

"Do you want me to stop?"

"No."

He pulled himself farther up so he was lying beside me. He looked deep into my eyes, running the tip of his finger along my jaw.

"It was just a shock. It's been a while since you lost your temper like that."

I smiled. "I don't like to."

"I'm hoping that I won't do anything to piss you off like that again."

"I hope so too."

6.

When I got to my office the next day there were several garment bags hanging on the back of my door, and Ted was sitting by my desk.

"Good morning buttercup," he said, motioning to my coffee mug on my desk. "You have quite the admirer."

"Lewis asked for my help with something. He said I needed some clothes for the job," I replied. I knocked over a few shoe boxes that were piled close to the wall as I put down my bags and slid across by desk.

"What is this 'something'? Or should I not ask?" Ted grumbled.

"You don't trust me?"

"It's not you that concerns me," he sipped his coffee.

"Ted, I'm not a child. I didn't think I needed to report to you."

"Camille...."

"It's nothing to worry about, Ted. You'll have to take my word for it."

He sighed, gesturing to the manila envelope on my desk before walking out.

"Your honest work arrived earlier," he called back to me. I closed my door behind him, unloaded my gear and sat down before I opened the envelope.

I wasn't entirely surprised to read that Thomas Lowry wasn't Jane's father. I felt like running into Ted's office and yelling, because his so called 'honest work' will be putting me face to face with the man who may have killed my parents.

I would need an alias of some sort when I went to this club with Chris Lewis; it's pretty easy to figure out who my parents were and throwing the name Bishop around in a Kinkaid club might not be wise. A simple last name change would work, as not to confuse myself, but I'd have to pick one that I would remember.

I read through the rest of the paternity report as my phone started to buzz, my eyes locking on a specific line in the report that surprised me. The buzz was from reception; I picked up the receiver and clicked the button that put me through to Ramona.

"Jane Lowry is on her way here," Ramona said quietly. I assumed there were people waiting and she didn't want anyone to hear.

"What? Why?" I asked.

"She knew her paternity results would be here so she called to say she was coming, and that she would wait all day for you if she had to."

"Shit. Ok, let me know when she gets here," I quickly hung up and examined the report more closely.

There was some kind of abnormality that the lab thought was worth noting.

I dialled the number on the top of the sheet, citing a reference number and arguing a bit until I got the actual lab tech that ran the test on the phone.

"I need you to explain this abnormality to me please, so I can explain it to my client. It is rather important," I began.

"There is not much to explain. It's something that needs further analysis. Since you were only running a DNA test all we could deduce was that it is an abnormality that is most likely genetic," the lab tech said, her tone sounded annoyed.

"Does your lab do that kind of testing?"

"No. You would have to send it to U of T for further analysis. We only do a certain level of blood work at this lab. And this would require blood," she continued.

"Do you have a name of someone you could recommend at U of T that I could get in contact with?"

"No."

I paused, trying to decide if I wanted us to get black listed from this company. "Why would you recommend U of T? Don't any private companies do similar testing?"

She sighed loudly like she was talking to an idiot. "U of T has the best lab in the country. It's your call what you decide to do but if you don't feel like wasting money you need to speak directly to them."

"Ok, well, thank....," before I could say any more there was a dial tone.

I grabbed the test and quickly headed to Ted's office, peeking down the hall to make sure Jane Lowry wasn't in the waiting area before I went.

I knocked quickly on Ted's open door. "Do we know anyone in the U of T labs?"

"What sort of lab?" he asked.

"One that would test blood for genetic abnormalities."

"Not off the top of my head but give Q a call and see what she can do," he cocked his head to one side then held out his hand. "Let me see the test."

Q, given name Tabitha, was our resident tech geek and went to U of T, the University of Toronto. I handed the test to him, and he asked me if I'd spoke to the lab that tested it as he read it.

"Of course. While I would have liked to cuss off the bitchy lab tech I decided against it. But she said U of T has the best lab in the country, but no referral to an actual person," I continued. "Fun part is that the client is on her way and wants to know what's what. Do I discuss this abnormality or do I keep it aside for now?"

"Tell her. There might be a database related to this that would narrow down her search for potential fathers. You may have caught a lucky break, kid. Paternity cases with no hints to the real father often don't get them."

"Any way to find out if Kinkaid has this abnormality? I know he's locked up pretty tight but the cops must have his DNA on file."

"That would be a question for Kiera. I don't even know if she can tell you," he said. "Before you go poking around about Kinkaid we need to talk, ok? This is not something you can do solo."

I saluted him, his eyes lowered into a scowl as he said, "That's an order as your boss, Camille. Not fun directions from your happy go lucky uncle."

"I get it, boss man. Don't poke the bear unless you hand me the stick. Loud and clear, commander."

"Good," he said, and I turned and left his office before he could say anything else.

I grabbed a small cosmetics bag from my desk and went to the staff bathroom to put on some makeup. I always put on a little for work and I had forgotten to take the bag to Jesse's so it had to wait till I got here.

As I examined my face in the mirror I thought of my Mother. I used to watch her putting on her makeup in the morning and dreamed of the day I would do the same. But I have never been as pretty or confident as she was; Marie Bishop knew she was awesome from a young age, she must have.

When I put on makeup I always thought of her. What she would have taught me, if she would have thought I was pretty. I felt pretty unremarkable.

My dyed black hair hung at my shoulders with a slight wave I got from tying it up while it was still wet. If I hadn't done that it would be super straight and limp.

My face was round, my skin pale. My dark eyes were

large and round and I accentuated them with black liquid liner and mascara. A little tinted lip balm and I felt ready to go.

As ready as I ever felt. I tried to push all self conscious thoughts from my mind, if I didn't I would never leave the house.

I adjusted my t-shirt and blazer and went back to my office.

Q was an interesting girl.

I didn't know where she came from, or where Ted and Chris found her. I thought she did something big, like some kind of hacking crime, and the guys agreed to not bust her if she came to work for them. I would find out eventually but I liked her enough that I didn't pry. I liked the idea of her and me becoming friends but I didn't want to look too needy.

I called the daytime number we had for her. It rang once then went to her machine.

"Q, its Camille. Got a head scratcher for you, was wondering if you knew anyone in the blood lab at the University of Toronto. Apparently U of T is the primo place. Gimme a call when you can, cell after business hours," I hung up. When I put the phone down Ramona paged me from reception.

"Jane Lowry is here to see you," Ramona said.

"Send her in."

"Now?"

"Yep. I'm solid. If Q calls put her through."

"No problem," Ramona disconnected and I prepared for one of the toughest parts of this job.

Jane Lowry was all smiles when she came in my door. Her dirty blonde hair was still wet in its ponytail; she must have rushed over here. I didn't want to disappoint her.

"Good morning," she said happily as she sat down. "Sorry to be so pushy but do you have any news for me?"

"Actually I do. But it's a bit complicated of an answer," I began. "I have your DNA test and it is as you suspected. Thomas Lowry is not your father."

She nodded, her face blank as I continued, "The testing company found some kind of anomaly, and they said that it could be used to find out who your father is because he, most likely, has the same anomaly. They didn't mention if it is something that could have come from your mother but we will certainly explore that, if you give me the go ahead."

"I suspected there was something," her voice grew quiet. "I have these....."

I took out my notepad and started making notes. "Please tell me so I can mention it all when I talk to the blood lab."

I tried to keep my expression level and even. I didn't want her to know that I knew about The Dollhouse, not yet. She clearly had not told me for a reason and I didn't want to fuck this up before it even starts.

"The official diagnosis from the doctor is that I am

allergic to sunlight. Can you even believe that? I guess you really can be allergic to anything in this day and age," she began, grabbing a pen off my desk and holding it like you would hold a cigarette. "I wonder if anyone is allergic to oxygen yet. I get these cravings for super rare meat during certain times of the month even though I'm regularly vegan. Those times I also have to wear sunglasses, even inside. Florescent light is brutal."

She paused, took a breath and continued, "My mother has also mentioned mood swings. She wants me to get medication for it. She thinks I've got a mood disorder or something but I disagree. Because I feel perfectly fine in my mind and frankly if I do have mood swings I don't realise."

"It's good to note anyhow. Is there anything else your Mother has mentioned?"

"No, not really," she said. She ran her hand over her face like she was exhausted.

"Sorry. I guess I'm a bit shocked that he's really not my Dad, even though I knew he wasn't. I guess I didn't really want to believe it," she told me, her voice going quiet.

"To be completely honest I would be more concerned if you weren't a little shocked. It's shocking to get that kind of confirmation. It would be wise not to mention it to either of your parents while I am still investigating. We don't want to stir up trouble without any potential possibilities."

"I suppose that makes sense. You don't think I should

confront my Mother? She's been lying to me my whole life. Did she think I would never find out what happened to her? What that man did to her?"

"No. Don't mention it yet. It will hurt your parent's marriage. I'm assuming Thomas Lowry doesn't know you are not his child either. Do you have any siblings?"

"No. Supposedly my Mother had fertility issues after having me. Maybe this anomaly would explain that. Could it mean I won't be able to have kids?"

"I can't answer that. But it will be a question for the blood lab. Now, I have a call in and I will get back to you when they need to collect a sample."

She smiled, carefully placing my pen back on my desk. "Thank you Miss Bishop."

"Miss Lowry, if you don't mind me saying, Thomas Lowry may not be your blood but he is still your father. Do you understand?"

"Of course. I can't take that for granted."

She stood, a strange smirk on her face when she saw me slide out from behind my desk.

"I will call you as soon as I have something," I said. I walked her to the doorway that leads back into the waiting area.

"Thank you, Miss Bishop," she touched my shoulder softly. I stood in the doorway and watched her go.

"How did it go?" Ted asked as I stood in his doorway.

"Good. I look totally unprofessional sliding out from

behind that desk," I sat down in one of his chairs and folded my feet under me.

"If this case goes well we'll get one custom made for you."

"Good. I'm waiting on a call from Q but other than that I'm free for the day."

"Good for you. Is Jesse coming to get you?"

"Nope. He's doing a construction job today."

Ted got that look on his face. Whenever I talked about Jesse and 'work' Ted got this look on his face like it was some weird joke. Like the idea of fuck up king Jesse Garrow having a real legit job was the greatest joke he had ever heard.

"You don't have to do that. It's my choice to let him try."

"I just worry that you'll keep giving him chances and he will keep breaking your heart."

I couldn't look directly at him. I knew he was right but that didn't mean I had to like it.

"I'm going to go get a sandwich from next door. You want something?" I asked.

"No, kid. I'm good."

The black car with the diplomatic plates was parked out front. Again. I thought about going to get Ted but didn't. If it was there when I got back from the cafe next door I would tell him, but my hunger took higher priority.

We got lucky when The Whistlestop Cafe opened next

door to the office. Before we either had to bring our own lunch or order in, and the rest of the office wasn't so into take-out. And ninety percent of the time I didn't feel like cooking so having the cafe saved me most days.

Millie, the owner, smiled brightly at me from behind the counter when I came in the door. She had long dark hair that was thick and luscious with piercing blue eyes. She often wore darker red lipstick and it made her look so refined that she looked out of place in her own shop.

"Hi there Camille," Millie's slight accent gave her voice warmth. "What can I get you? The usual?"

"Hi Millie. Yep, the usual," I replied. She started making my turkey and Swiss on a pumpernickel bagel, grabbing the container for my pesto potato salad while she worked. Just looking at food made me hungrier. Millie's food reminded me of my Mother. It was good home cooking and I found it comforting.

"How's it going over there?" she asked.

"Nothing exciting," I said. "But that's the business. It's mostly unexciting."

"You keep saying that but I'm not so sure. I think we should trade jobs for a few days so I can see for myself."

I laughed. "If you want but I have to warn you, cooking isn't my strong suit. I'd probably poison people."

"Didn't your Mother teach you anything about cooking?"

"My Mother died when I was a kid so she didn't have time."

She put her hand to her lips. "Oh dear. I am so sorry,

Camille. I didn't mean...."

"Hey! It's ok. You'll just have to teach me about food before we switch jobs. In truth, Ted would probably be happy to be rid of me for a while....and that I could finally cook something other than Kraft Dinner."

"It's a deal," she replied, and she continued getting my meal. I glanced up at the sign behind her, Whistlestop Cafe written in beautiful script with a symbol beside it that sort of looked like a snake coiled around a sword.

I opened my mouth to ask Millie what the symbol meant, something I had always meant to do but seem to have forgotten, when the snake began to move. It looked as if it was slithering around the sword and I had to take a step back.

Millie paused and watched me as I stared. I could see her in my peripheral vision; she looked as if she was waiting for me to do something.

"You ok Camille?" she asked. I shook my head and snapped out of my trance.

"I'm great."

She handed me my food and I paid her, dropping a few bucks in her tip jar.

"Better now that I have this," I continued. "Thank you, as always."

"If you ever want me to teach you how to cook, job swap or no, my door is always open," Millie said. Her warm smile was infectious and I couldn't help but do the same.

"Thanks," I waved as I walked out.

My Mother had been on my mind a lot lately. She always was, but lately much more than before. I always wondered if my Aunt Cindi had been around and I'd had more of a female influence if I wouldn't get these deep and painful aches for my Mother.

Pain that felt like a gaping hole in my stomach that I could not fix or fill.

For some reason, when I missed my Father it wasn't that kind of pain. Losing him was like losing a hero where losing my Mother was like losing a limb. I had to learn how to exist without my Mother as one would have to learn to exist without an arm.

It wasn't like that with my Father. I felt bad about it, but it just wasn't.

Things were hectic in the waiting room when I returned to the office. Clients looked up at me like puppies in a pet store eager to be taken home, but none of them were mine. Most perspective clients wanted to see the boss men first, even though I had substantial field experience my youth made it hard for people to take me seriously. So I got the weird and interesting ones, like Jane Lowry.

Once I got in my office I went to go through the garment bags Chris had left while I ate my lunch.

Everything he picked was fitted and the tops had buttons down the front so I could decide how much or little cleavage I wanted to expose. The colour palette was muted; grey, black and navy blue really emphasised my pale skin. I was supposed to blend in and other then my boobs this wardrobe should do it in a strip club. Chris Lewis had enough sense to know that if Ted saw me leave the house in what he picked he'd never hear the end of it so he erred on the side of modest.

The shoes, on the other hand.

Now, mind you, I hadn't spent that much time in a strip club to know for sure but I didn't think the waitresses wore similar shoes. It seemed like a death trap for someone to walk through a crowded strip club with a tray of drinks, or food, in these shoes.

I giggled to myself. The idea that strip clubs served food amused me.

I examined the six inch stiletto ankle boots. I was pretty confident that I would look like Bambi learning to walk in these things. It's hard to blend in when you're slipping around like an idiot.

I slipped off my flat black boots; they were knock off Frye boots, which held me over while I saved up for the real thing.

It was not that I was opposed to high heels. I had some. I even had some that I wore to work. But six inches was far beyond what I was used to.

I slipped on the boots and stood, they were surprisingly comfortable. I took a few steps; I could pull it off if I really concentrated. It would be interesting with a tray with drinks, but once I got used to it I would be ok.

There was a sharp knock at the door, Chris Lewis

stuck his head in and smiled at me.

I posed in an exaggerated way and did my best duck face. "Am I cute?"

"Always," he said with a chuckle. He handed me a folded up piece of paper.

"This is where you're going," he continued. "I'll already be there when you arrive so come find me. You need a different last name; Bishop's are not well received."

I chuckled. "What did Ted do now?"

"Oh, this one isn't all on Ted. It's a bit Ted, your Dad, your Uncle Don and your cousin Benny."

My cousin Benny and his Dad, Don, were both angry narcotics officers that caused a shit storm wherever they went. After my Dad died his little brother Don went into self destruct mode, and Benny learned by example. I did not want to be associated with them on any level.

"I'll be Camille LeFaye," I said.

"Ok, who's LeFaye?" he asked.

"My Mother's maiden name."

He smirked. "I had forgotten. It has been a while since I've heard that name."

"And it's uncommon enough that it shouldn't raise any red flags. What time should I be there?"

"Between 11 and 11:30. Don't be late," he said, thumping on the door frame as he walked away.

"I won't!"

Ted and I rode home together. I'd heard nothing from

Jesse and I was ok with that. After my little outburst when that girl showed up I figured he would need some time. He wasn't used to me getting angry; I usually hid that from him. But I thought it was time that I started to. He and I had been together long enough that he needed to know exactly how his actions affected me.

At home it was easier for me to lay out what Chris had bought so I could look at the things as complete outfits. He had decent taste....well, I thought it was him. He didn't have a woman that I knew about, other than Ramona, that did things for him and she would have told me if she had had to buy these clothes.

I picked out a dark grey button down shirt and black trousers. They were a bit wider at the bottom and flowed over the boots quite nicely once I had them on. I pulled my hair back off my face in a loose bun and put on more makeup, including a bit of red lipstick. I didn't want to look like I was trying too hard.

Once I was dressed and as presentable as I could be I texted Jesse. I thought I would give him the option to drive me, just to keep him calm. I wouldn't want him showing up at the club and blowing the whole operation.

He responded back rather quickly, the phone must have been in his hand, and said he would drop me off. I agreed and headed down to the living room to wait for him.

Ted was sitting in his favourite armchair watching Grey's Anatomy, of all things, and drinking beer. He must have had a rough day; he wasn't one to drink when we had to work tomorrow.

"Are you really watching that?" I asked him, motioning to the TV.

"Cuddy said it's hysterical on mute," he replied. "We got to find out what is in that kid's weed."

He glanced over at me and did a double take. "You look nice. Off to sell your soul for Lewis's approval?"

"It's not like that. If Jesse comes in don't do that, please. I don't want him trying to be a hero when it is totally unnecessary."

"He's taking you? Good. I am in no state to drive."

"Rough day?"

He chuckled. "I would love for you doing Lewis's dirty work to be my biggest problem."

"You are going to have to trust me, Ted. I'm a big girl."

He took a big swig of his beer and said, "Its Chris Lewis that I don't trust, Cas," before the doorbell rang.

I decided not to get into it with him any further and went to get the door.

I let Jesse in, telling him I was grabbing my purse as I left him in the hallway. I heard thumping on the porch and Poppy came in behind Jesse.

She snorted at Jesse. "You're still around? Shocker!"

"Well hello to you too, Poppy. Long time no see," Jesse said with a smile. Jesse always played fake nice with my cousin, it was easier for him to hover under her radar. Especially since she got a badge.

"Whatever," Poppy grumbled. "Daddy, I need...."

"I'm not in the mood Poppy," Ted called from the

living room.

"But Daddy," she whined, pushing past me and shoving me into the wall.

"Jesus Christ, Poppy. Do you try to be a bitch or is this just your personality?" I snapped.

"No Camille. I've just been trying for so many years to show you that you're not wanted here but you are too stupid to get it," Poppy snapped. "You're a parasite. Why can't you just disappear?"

"Poppy!" Ted roared, getting up out of his chair. "I am so sick of your juvenile bullshit! Leave Camille alone already. This has been going on for too fucking long. Either leave Camille alone or move the fuck out."

We all stood in the hallway in shock. Ted had always said she should go in private but never directly to her.

"Now, I have had a long, hard day. I want to sit and watch Grey's Anatomy in peace. So either shut the fuck up or leave!" he yelled. He thumped back down in his chair and turned the volume up on the TV loud enough that he couldn't hear us.

I grabbed my purse and pulled Jesse out, ignoring Poppy as I did.

Jesse was silent for the first little while as we drove. Once I told him where we were going, a club called Ren, he got quiet. Which made me a bit nervous.

"So," I finally cut through the silence. "Are you going to tell me why you have that look on your face since I mentioned the club's name, or do I have to guess?"

Jesse's expression remained blank. "What do you

want to know? Ren is not a safe place. I don't like the idea of you being there on your own."

"I'm not on my own. Chris Lewis is there. He will be watching over me. He's not going to leave me alone in there."

He snorted. "How can you be so sure?"

"Because it's Chris fucking Lewis, Jesse. He would never risk his name on me screwing up his bidness. You should know that."

"Are you so sure? Can you really be sure he's not going to leave you to the wolves? You'll get eaten alive in a place like Ren."

"Since you spend so much time there you know it so well?"

He paused again, knowing his next move could bury him. There were details of things that he did that I wasn't sure I wanted to know, but I also didn't like the idea that he was doing bad things under my nose.

"Babe, while I appreciate your concern you are going to have to trust that I can take care of myself. And after that shit with Poppy...."

"What did Ted say?"

"My Uncle trusts that I can take care of myself. He has faith in me and my abilities. He also knows that if I got myself into trouble that I couldn't solve I would call for help."

Jesse sighed loudly as he put the car in park; I looked outside to find the glowing neon Ren sign beside me.

"That was awfully quick," I mumbled.

"You text me. Whenever you get a chance, you text me. You call me to let me know you are OK," he began. "If you need anything, you call me. And when you are done I will come get you. That is not up for discussion."

I saluted him. "Yes, sir!"

"Camille, I am not fucking around here...."

"Jesus Christ, will you chill the fuck out already? I've had enough of you and this bullshit."

He leaned over and kissed me roughly, grabbing the scruff of my shirt and pulling me towards him.

"I don't like being worried," he said as he pulled away. I smiled and looked deep in his eyes, we were only a few inches apart.

"That will give you a taste of how I feel when you take off. Only you know where I am, and that I am coming back," I said quietly and his expression flattened. "Now, I have to go. I will call you when I am done."

I got out without looking back.

I stood on the sidewalk and waited for Jesse to pull away and he didn't. It seemed he was waiting for me to go inside. I stared up at the neon sign and tried to ignore the butterflies in my stomach, taking a breath and walking through the heavy doors.

7.

Strippers, in my mind, are kind of like unicorns. They're bizarre mystical creatures that frighten and amaze; women are either obsessed with them or absolutely loathe them.

I had seen some before; walking into Ren wasn't my first rodeo. But that didn't mean I didn't gawk when I first walked in. The lights, the sounds, the noises, the men sitting around the main stage staring like kids in a candy store, it all took a few seconds to sink in.

But as part of my job I couldn't stand around like a dumbass and stare. It didn't exactly scream covert.

I took a deep breath and began my walk through the club towards the back, as Lewis's instructions had stated. Eyes turned as I made my way through, regulars would always look at the new girl, rack or no rack. I was amazed at the range of people, from construction workers to fancy suit businessmen that filled Ren. I hadn't really had an expectation of the type of people but if Chris Lewis was involved they had to be making some serious coin.

On the back wall of the club there was a door well blended in with the decor. I knocked three times, as I was instructed, and waited.

It seemed like I waited forever. The thumping of the music was hypnotic and I lost track of time.

But then the music changed to something I recognized and my eyes turned to the stage. As Amy Winehouse's raspy voice began one of my favourite songs, Valerie, a girl with long dark hair came strutting across the stage. She had her makeup done like Winehouse, and I'm guessing when she wasn't on stage had her hair in something similar to that trademark beehive. It was cool, for what it was. Looking at her face as she began her dance she looked familiar but I couldn't figure out where from.

I could feel my phone vibrating in my purse; when I checked it was a text from Q.

I breathed a sigh of relief that it wasn't Jesse being all paranoid and weird. I wouldn't let him fuck up my chances to impress Chris Lewis.

Because the reality was that I wanted to be the B in L&B when my Uncle Ted decided to pack it in. With or without Jesse.

Q's text, as they often were, was random but brief. It said: Got ur msg. Lookin into it. Tricky 1 but have sumthin tmrw I hope.

I quickly texted her back, told her I was doing 'big tings' for CL and we could talk later. She texted me back a smiley face.

The door finally opened and Chris Lewis appeared. He was clean shaven and groomed to a T, his dark blue suit was so finely tailored it looked like a second skin. He smiled at me; his teeth glowed in the black lights.

"Evening Camille. Good to see you," Chris began, looking me up and down. "Looks like things worked out better than I thought. Good for you. I have some people you need to meet."

When I came in the doorway it was like I was stepping into the office of a strip club in every mob movie. Red velvet and gold everywhere, with cherub statues that almost made me laugh. I wondered if Lewis had the same decorator.

"Camille LeFaye, this is Mr. Oleg Cassini, Mr. Pavlov Stanislav, and Miss. Malah Raynara. This is their club," Chris said, and I smiled happily.

"It's lovely to meet you all, and thank you so much for the opportunity," I extended my hand and shook all of theirs. Seemed like the most professional thing to do.

When I shook Malah Raynara's hand I was enveloped by her powdery scent, most of it seemed to come from her expertly coiffed blonde hair which hung in perfect ringlets down her shoulders.

It must take hours to get her hair like that; her flawless makeup was another story. She could have taught a master class in female grooming.

"If you need anything, please let us know. Chris will bring you up to speed," Malah said, her deep voice and thick Russian accent was almost hypnotic. She was clearly the brains of the operation, she seemed so relaxed and comfortable it was clear that this was her domain. I wondered if her appearance was a cloak and dagger operation to hide how smart she actually was.

"Of course. Thank you," I replied. The three of them left, leaving Chris and I alone.

He took me across the room to a small couch that was upholstered in soft red velvet. He pat my knee, an action that unsettled me a bit.

"Now, I know you're nervous but you don't need to be. I just want you to observe," he began. "Just a heads up, the VIP section is full. That's not where your focus will be but there are names you will recognise if you hear them. Take it however you want but that is not what I have you here for."

Which meant that there was a Kinkaid or someone who worked for the Kinkaid's in the VIP. It was nice of him to give me a heads up.

"Now, there are several low level dealers and thugs here that do their thing. They pay a premium to be here, that's how it works. Problem is they don't like each other. But they have been ordered to behave, and I want you to watch them and make sure they do. Also, there is a strict policy with the girls. No drugs, no sex," he continued. "That is being violated. I want to know who, what, where and when. Why isn't relevant. I have been watching them for a while and they are good enough to hide it from me, so this won't be easy. You good? Got everything?"

"Consider me officially debriefed. I'm waitressing? I should go to the bartender first then?" I asked.

He smiled and nodded. "Yes. You have all the good qualities of your father, Camille. Did I ever tell you that?"

My face grew hot, I knew I was blushing. "No, you haven't. Thank you, I appreciate that."

"Just relax and do your thing. You're a talented kid. This is a breeze," he pat my knee again.

I gestured towards the door and he nodded. He handed me a locker key and directed me towards the door.

"Lockers are through the employee door to the left of the bar," he said, opening the door for me. I nodded and smiled, he quickly shut the door behind me when I stepped out.

"Well, ok then," I mumbled to myself. I headed over to the bar, flagging down the bartender when I got close to the employee door.

She smiled. "New girl Camille?"

"Yep. And you are?"

"Tor. Put your stuff in the back then I will get you started."

I quickly went in the back and put my stuff in my assigned locker, keeping my cell phone in my pocket. I checked myself in the mirror on my way back to the bar; I was as presentable as I could be without professional assistance.

Tor was in her mid thirties, looking more like her mid forties when she smiled. I didn't know what kind of life she'd had but her position at the club made her a good friend to have.

She smiled again when she saw me, her red lipstick absolutely perfect making her teeth glow pearly white. I wondered if she was of the same generation as my Mother, one who had been raised that red lipstick was classy. It suited her. She looked nice.

"You ever waited on tables before?" she asked.

I didn't know what Lewis had told them so I just said, "Not like this."

She chuckled. "Well, this ain't no Denny's. Don't let anything these bloodsuckers say bother you. Alcohol and naked women bring out the worst in people. Just bring them their drink and keep your head down. Don't engage. Don't giggle or bat your eyelashes. Be nice but don't flirt. Got it?"

"Got it."

"Your wardrobe is good. Keep it like that," she said. She started placing drinks on a tray then motioned to me.

"Asian businessmen, close to the stage. You can't miss them."

"But how do I know who had what drink?"

She chuckled again. "Doesn't matter. Just put them on the table and come back. It's an easy first tip."

"Ok, thanks," I picked up the tray with both hands and

started making my way through the club.

I couldn't figure out how people carried these trays on one hand. Balancing with two hands in my Bambi shoes was already funny enough; I didn't want to think about how I looked.

The table of Asian businessmen was easy to find, and they cheered loudly when they saw me. I put the drinks on the table one at a time and they were quickly snatched up, a stack of bills left behind. The smallest bill we had in Canada was five dollars, the idea of a stack of them made me smile. I grabbed the money and headed back for the bar.

Tor handed me a jar with my name on it. In the light I noticed some of the bills were twenties.

"Congrats, you are now officially a waitress," Tor said. "You'll probably have to do that fifty more times tonight but the tips are worth it. Your section is small for now, the businessmen and the five tables left of the stage. I may send you up to VIP at some point but don't worry about that yet."

"Ok. I'll go see if anyone needs anything."

She smiled and nodded. "Good idea."

I stood up as straight as I could and headed back across the club.

The thing that I loved about doing surveillance and undercover work was that I could invent a persona. I showed people what I wanted them to see, there was no preconceived notion about who I was because of my last name or my past. I wasn't the weird girl who had no friends. I wasn't the girl with the dead parents. I wasn't Jesse Garrow's girlfriend. I was just Camille.

A table flagged me over as I headed across the club. They were cloaked in shadows so I didn't get a clear look until I got close.

The first thing I saw was a gorgeous smile. Perfect teeth with a well defined jaw line and big lips. Dark hair was cut short on the sides and long on the top, big blue eyes and dark lashes framed the penetrating gaze.

I could not tell whether this was a man or a woman and it didn't matter. There was a real magnetic attraction that made me smile wide.

"Hi! You're the new girl, right?" she asked. After some examination, no Adams apple meant woman.

"Yeah. I'm Camille," I said, awkwardly holding out my hand from under the tray.

"Well, hi Camille. I'm October. How are you enjoying your first day?"

"It's a little overwhelming, actually. But everyone has been really nice so far," I replied. She hung on to my hand, rubbing her thumb along mine softly.

"I'm glad they're being good to you. If you have any problems please come let me know," she said. "I am more than happy to take care of you."

I smiled and tried to look flirty, something which wasn't my strong suit. It seemed like it would be useful for her to like me by the way others looked at her and her companions; a skinny random looking guy who could have been one of Jesse's buddies, and a girl that had to be a cage fighter in her spare time. They both ignored me completely which suited me just fine.

"Thank you, I appreciate that," I replied. "Now what can I get you?"

"Gin and tonic, and keep them coming every 20 minutes or so," she handed me a neatly folded bill that I took and put in my pocket.

"I'll be right back," I smiled and tried not to stumble as I went back to the bar. Tor already had the drinks ready when I got back, Chris Lewis was sitting at the bar sipping a beer. I ignored him and took the drinks back to October's table.

She smiled again as I set them down.

"Thank you Camille," October said. She leaned over to speak closely into my ear.

"You know, you should consider cutting your hair short. I think you would look dynamite." Her warm breath touched my neck as she spoke the last words and I shivered a little. My face got hot as I blushed.

"That's very sweet. Thank you. I will see you in a bit."

She smiled again as I walked away, this time making sure to show teeth. Her perfect white straight teeth.

The rest of the night went by rather quickly. I was good with my stupidly high heels and a drink tray, and after a while I actually got comfortable and grew more confident. I didn't know if I looked good but I felt better than I had earlier which was progress.

October came over to me as I counted my tips at the bar; Chris Lewis sat at the opposite end still nursing a beer.

"Before I go I wanted to give you my card," October held my hand for a few lingering moments as she handed me the card. Her smell enveloped me, a warm musk with a hint of vanilla that I liked a lot.

"Like I said before, if you need anything you call me," she continued.

"I will. Thank you. I'll see you tomorrow I'm guessing?" I asked.

"You bet. Goodnight Camille," she smiled as she walked away, I saw Chris Lewis watching us out of the corner of my eye.

Before I could do anything else my phone started vibrating in my pocket. I had totally forgotten about Jesse. It was probably him and he was probably angry.

"You got a ride home, kid?" Chris asked as he came over to me. I checked my texts quickly, and the last one from Jesse said 'I'm outside' in all caps and it was from 10 minutes ago.

"Yep. I'll see you tomorrow?" I gathered up all my things and rushed for the door.

"You didn't text me," Jesse said angrily as I got in his car.

"No I didn't," I replied. I couldn't help but sigh, I wasn't in the mood.

"Why?"

"I was busy. I can't exactly stop to text you while

carrying a tray of glasses and walking in these shoes."

"I was worried."

"That's nice. Would you like a cookie?"

He scowled at me and was about to say something when I raised my hand to silence him.

"Don't start with me. I've been gone for what, like five hours? You knew where I was. You could have walked into Ren at any time and seen me. It's not like I disappeared. It's not like you couldn't find me for days," I felt myself snarling. "Just take me home, please. I'm tired."

We said nothing else on the ride back. I should have blown Jesse off and got a ride with Chris Lewis, just so he could debrief me. I was not in the mood to listen to Jesse's insecure bullshit, let alone coddle him. He needed to know how it felt for once.

He watched me for a long time when he parked in front of my house. "Babe, I'm...."

"I'm tired, Jesse," I said quietly. "We'll talk tomorrow, ok?"

I got out without another word, without formally saying goodbye. I didn't look back at him, didn't do what I always do with him because I was weak and foolish.

I breathed deeply as I climbed the stairs and went inside. I heard his tires spin as he peeled out and sped down the street.

8.

Q sat cross legged on my desk with her tablet in her lap, some friend in the chair doing something important on their smart phone. Well, I assumed it was important because of how intently they were staring at it.

"Wud up Q?" I said, dropping my bags by the doorway. I was surprised they were at the office before I was.

She chuckled. "Wud up, Bond. This is Lemme."

"Wud up, Lemme."

Lemme raised her hand. She was small like Q, Asian of some connotation like Q, and dressed like a rap video extra like Q. Her head was half braided in cornrows, it looked like they came here before they could finish.

"Lemme works at the U of T lab you were asking about. Since I don't speak that level of science I thought I should bring her along so you could describe what you need."

"Bitchin. Well, I got a client who had a DNA test done and they figured out that it wasn't a match because of some blood anomaly. My question is could you get a DNA match without blood?"

Lemme chuckled. "One has nothing to do with another so yep."

"Could you tell if a DNA match had the same anomaly without the blood?"

She pondered that for a minute. Q looked up from her tablet temporarily and rolled her eyes.

"Yo, Lemme. You buggin?" Q asked.

"No, dude. To answer your question, Bond, yeah. I could do it."

"Good. Q's standard rate ok with you also? But I will need an actual name to write on the check."

The mention of money perked Lemme up, which didn't surprise me. I don't know if she knew Q's rate but I'm glad it made her happy. I loved it when people were cooperative.

"You bet. Q gave me your info, so when I find something I will contact you. You'll get both samples to me?" she wrote some things down on the notepad on my desk and pulled a few mouth swabs out of her bag and tossed them down beside it.

I hadn't totally thought about how I was going to get Kinkaid DNA but I would figure that out later. My head was full of enough crap today.

"Of course. Thanks for coming by. Now, if the two of you will excuse me I have clients," I said.

"Is Lewis here yet?" Q asked. "He called for tech support last night."

"I just got here so I haven't seen him," I replied. Q got up, Lemme following behind her.

"They got to get you a bigger office, dude. Or a smaller desk," she turned and pointed at my desk, "because that shit is seriously messed up."

"Don't I know it. I'll talk to you two later."

Q smiled as they headed out my door. "If you need me, you call me. I'll make sure Moneypenny has Lemme's info before we leave."

After contacting Jane Lowry to let her know I'd found someone to do more tests and I needed more samples from her, I sat down at my desk in front of my laptop and just stared.

When I'd got home last night I'd went straight to bed so I'd had no time to ponder everything that had happened. I'd done well my first day, even caught the attention of someone important. If Jesse hadn't had his little temper tantrum it would have been perfect.

A buzz on my phone pulled me from my thoughts; Ramona was letting me know I had a client. I would have to get used to having more than one case at a time, dividing my attention, it least for a little while.

I buzzed back to let her know it was ok to send the client in. I straightened out my desk as I waited.

The woman that came in was stunning, with long

perfectly dyed blonde hair and a purse that would have cost my monthly pay check. Her engagement ring looked like an ice cube wrapped in silver.

"Hi," I said, standing up to shake her hand, "I'm Camille Bishop. It's nice to meet you Miss...."

"Mrs. Tanner. I was expecting someone...."

"Older? Male?"

She smiled. "I'm sorry. I guess I watch too much television."

"I get that all the time, don't worry. Now, what can I help you with?"

"I'm concerned that a former flame is stalking me. When I decided to marry Mr. Tanner my former boyfriend took it rather hard and I think he's hired someone to spy on me."

"So you're hiring a P.I to see if you're being followed by another P.I?" I chuckled. "That definitely sounds right out of a television show. Have you asked this person to identify them self?"

"I....I....I didn't know I could."

"If they are an actual P.I they have to show you their license if you ask to see it. That's my free tip."

She laughed. "Well thanks for that. I want you to see if someone has hacked into my email and if someone is tracking my phone."

"Let me find out if technology can allow it before I say we can. I'll need a list of your concerns and I will look into it. I'm hoping Ramona discussed my standard rate?"

"Yes, and money is no object," she said happily. She

seemed overly proud of that fact, which made me think that she hadn't always had money.

"Great. Let's get started."

Chris Lewis appeared shortly after Mrs. Tanner left.

I showed him the list of things she wanted me to look into. "Can I even do half of these things?"

He tilted his head as he read through the list; I was waiting for him to stick his tongue out in concentration.

"Make sure she's not using you to cover up her own affair," he replied as he handed my notepad back to me.

"Son of a bitch! Why didn't I see that?" I exclaimed. "I shouldn't have taken her on."

"Yes you should. There is no guarantee she isn't actually being stalked. If she's trying to hide something you'll know it, trust me. Some of those things you'll need Q for and she'll know pretty fast what's up," he began. "By the way, did you see Q's friend? Where are kids learning how to dress these days?"

I chuckled. "Her name is Lemme and she's my lab geek for my paternity case. Don't fuck that up because you're getting old."

"You're lucky I like you, Bishop," he said with a big smile. "So I noticed October chatting you up last night."

"Should I be worried?"

"No, but your delinquent boyfriend should be. She's been known to charm the pants off even the straightest girl. But she's also one of the house dealers I need you to keep an eye on."

"What about her?"

He paused. "I thought you said 'what part of her' for a minute. I'll be ok. One of her thugs is selling something bad behind her back. I need to know which one and what, if you can find out."

"She doesn't know about it?"

"Apparently not but I don't believe that. She could be playing both sides just to make an extra buck. She's not a stupid person by any means, be very careful of her. You don't want to owe her a favour."

"Right. Anything else? I'll be there tonight."

"Try to get Tor to put you in VIP. I'll say something to her but its better coming from you."

I saluted him. He waved me off and left, Ted crept up behind him.

"We didn't get a chance to talk about how it went last night," Ted said, slowly closing my door behind him.

"I didn't drop a single drink, if that's what you're wondering," I proclaimed.

"Good to hear. Chris was satisfied with your work?"

"I guess so. Jesse had a tantrum because I didn't check in with him every five minutes, but other than that I thought it went ok. How was the fallout from Poppy?"

He rolled his eyes. "She cried. It was great."

"I'm sorry I missed it."

"I'm not. She actually accepted the idea of moving out, snot faced and all. I should have taken photos," he chuckled. "Not sure that would have happened if you were there."

"Probably not. I'm going back again tonight, to the club I mean."

"I figured as much. Have you told Jesse yet?"

"No. I was wondering if you could take me."

"Jesse's tantrum didn't resolve itself?"

I paused. "No it didn't. I'm not going to be the one to fix it anymore. I'm too tired."

He gave me that all knowing parental look; like he knew not to get into it, but I was doing things the way he wanted. I knew how Ted felt about Jesse. He would never actively get involved, unless he thought I was in serious danger. I hadn't been so far.

"Good for you," he stood and started to leave. "I'll take you, but you'll have to get Lewis to bring you back or get a cab home."

"Ok. Thanks Ted," I said. He smiled as he left.

The day went by as most others do. Quiet and uneventful. It was good for humanity, I thought, that we didn't have a line-up out the door but it was bad for business.

That's what happens when you make money off of other people's bullshit.

It gave me a chance to do a little research into Ren and October.

Since I learned how to vet people, I vetted *everyone.* I wanted to know who I was talking to at any given time, how much I should trust them and whether or not I needed to be worried. I am not into surprises in any way so this made me feel better.

Ren was owned free and clear by the three people I had met in that office, and on paper they were three upstanding citizens. Malah Raynara had a very active social media life and was photographed with some very attractive men, including Chris Lewis. She and Lewis looked awfully cosy in a few shots; Lewis and Ms Raynara having an affair would explain why he was so concerned about what was going on at the club.

With a little digging I found some possible links to both Oleg Cassini and Pavlov Stanislav and Russian organized crime. Goodie.

But on a positive note it was organized crime actually in Russia, but not so much here. I didn't really know how that worked but it was something I would have to keep in mind when dealing with them.

October, full name October Daniels, was also active on social media. It looked like she was a model, and cashing in on the popularity of androgyny was doing well for her. She was hot, I couldn't deny that.

Of course her candid photo's had her with a string of beautiful people, both men and women. Perhaps she swung both ways. There were no clear identifiers in any of the pictures of where she was, which was probably done on purpose. Any hack with Photoshop could edit an image to suit them and post it online.

But she understood enough about projecting an image to know what to put out there and what not to. I didn't expect a sign that said 'I'm a drug dealer, ask me how' but some people can't avoid sketchy photo's showing up online, especially when they spend time in shady places.

October Daniels knew exactly what she was doing. There was a good chance she also knew exactly why I was there. I would have to be careful.

I was happy to head home that day. I had still heard nothing from Jesse, which would make it the time that I normally start blowing up his phone.

But I didn't.

I put my phone in my purse and left it while I got ready. I didn't go so far as to turn it off but I did my best to forget about it.

I put my hair up, something I didn't do very often because Jesse always said he preferred it down. Having it up made me feel confident, like a superhero with her awesome ponytail. Like a Barbie doll, which made me chuckle to myself as I put on my makeup.

Ted smiled as I came into the kitchen. "You're in a good mood."

"I am. Let's hope it stays that way."

"Nothing from Jesse?"

I smiled. "I don't know. My phone is in my bag."

"Well okay then. Are you ready to go?"

Poppy stomped her way in, grunting in my direction as she headed for the fridge.

"Did you make anything for dinner, Daddy?" she asked without looking at either of us.

"No, and it will have to wait until I drop Camille off

at her job," he said. Poppy looked at me, scanning me up and down. I was waiting for her comment, for the mudslinging to begin.

"Don't worry Dad, I'll make something and have it ready for when you get back. Do you want some for later Camille?" she asked, turning back to the fridge.

I glanced at Ted in confusion. "Uh, sure. That would be great. Thanks Poppy."

Ted motioned for us to go and we both backed out of the kitchen, calling bye to her as we left.

"What the fuck was that?" I asked once we got in the car.

"I told you we had a talk. Looks like she heard me," Ted's voice got quiet as he stared at something in the rear view mirror.

"We good? What's up?" I asked.

"Do you see that guy? By the streetlight?"

I looked through the rear and side mirrors to try to get a look. Sure enough, that same shadowy figure stood in the same spot that I had previously seen him.

"That's the same dude I told you about," I told him. He didn't reply but continued to watch.

"Should we go have a chat with him? It's fucking weird, right?"

"No. We'll just watch him for now," he took out his phone and took a photo of the rear view mirror and what he saw. We both casually watched the dark figure as we drove off into the night.

9.

Ren was abuzz with activity when I got inside, and I learned as I got closer to the bar it was because there was a big group in the VIP section. I heard the names Rufus, Tobias and Marcus all used by the other waitresses when I went in the back to drop my things.

Could it be? The three Kinkaid boys all in the same place? Maybe I was starting to get lucky. I had to get in the VIP section.

When I got out to the bar and went to talk to Tor, Chris Lewis pulled me aside.

"We have a problem," he held tight onto my elbow and directed my attention to a table about ten feet away from where October and her boys were seated.

Jesse.

Mother Fucker!!

"It's not a problem. I can control him," I reassured Lewis.

He scowled at me. "You better. I expected more from you, Camille. If he screws this up you can kiss not just this job but *your job* goodbye."

"I understand," I said. I got my first drink orders and made my way across the club. I dropped them off then went to Jesse.

"Why are you here?" I grumbled in his ear.

"You don't want to let me know you're okay then I am going to keep an eye on you," he proclaimed, like he was doing something nice.

"If you fuck this up or cause a scene I will lose my job," I snapped. "You're willing to fuck up my life for your foolishness? That's pretty disgusting."

Before he could reply I continued, "Sit here and behave. If you value our relationship at all you will mind your fucking manners, *do you understand me*?"

"Is this really about your job? Or is something going on with you and Chris Lewis?"

"Just do what I say or I will have you thrown out," I growled at him then walked away.

October flagged me over as I headed back to the bar. She smiled happily when she saw me.

"Good to see you, Camille," she said. "Everything alright?"

I had a split second to decide how to play this. "That? Oh, that is just my foolish boyfriend. I'm sorry you had to see that."

"You could do better."

"Thank you. His jealousy is unattractive."

"Let me guess, high school boyfriend?"

"Is it that obvious?"

She chuckled. "Dear, sweet Camille. Not only can you do better, he is not what you think. I hope you remove the wool from your eyes before you get badly hurt."

I paused, taking in all that she had said, then smiled and walked back to the bar.

It bothered me that a total stranger saw things like that about him. I saw things too, but I didn't want to believe them. I did not want to think about who he was becoming. Or already was and I was just too pig headed to accept it.

The night continued on the same as the previous night. The Amy Winehouse girl was working the floor tonight, and once I got a better look at her face I realized I knew her. Her sitting down to talk to Jesse only confirmed it. We'd gone to high school together.

She caught me by the side of the bar.

She smiled. "Hey, Camille? Hi, I don't know if you remember me. I'm Bliss. We went to high school together."

"Right! Bliss Fiori, right? How are you?" I said. I tried my best to smile and be gracious; I didn't want her getting suspicious.

"I'm good! I'm doing this and going to school part time to be a nurse. What are you up to? Is Jesse Garrow here with you?"

"Not exactly," I showed her my drink tray. "He's overprotective so he's hanging out while I work."

Her eyebrows rose. "I must admit this is the last place I expected to run into you."

"Ditto. I caught your act. Love the whole Amy Winehouse thing. It's really original, I respect that, and it works for you."

I'd forgotten how pretty she was. Bliss Fiori's life was almost as complicated as mine; with well known family gang connections, she wasn't expected to ever do more then be a princess. Which, it seemed, wasn't what she wanted.

"Thanks, I appreciate that. We should meet up and have coffee sometime," she said. I scribbled my cell number down on a napkin and handed it to her.

"I'd like that."

She folded the napkin and stuck it in her cleavage, patting me on the shoulder and returning to working the floor.

I glanced over at Jesse, who watched Bliss in a way that made my stomach drop. I could never compete with a girl like Bliss, no matter how hard I tried.

Jesse and Bliss both came from a world I didn't understand. Justice and order were in my blood. Bliss was born into a world that those things sat in a murky grey area.

What was Jesse's excuse?

Chris Lewis sat at the corner of the bar with an impossibly large man, I had to look up even though he was sitting on a bar stool. He wore all black and had one of the darkest complexions I had ever seen. Lewis motioned me over and I put on the best smile I could.

"Camille, there is someone I would like you to meet. This is Mr. Gray. Gray, this is Camille LeFaye," Lewis began. Mr. Gray's ears seemed to perk up when he heard my name.

I smiled as wide as I could and held out my hand. "Hi! It's very nice to meet you."

Mr. Gray opened his mouth; his perfectly shaped white teeth were a little off putting.

"Camille LeFaye, it is lovely to meet you," Mr. Gray said, taking my hand in between his cold palms and squeezing. He had a slight accent that sounded French.

I felt a strange tingle in my palm when our skin touched and I tried not to let my facial expression show how weird it was.

I gave him my best work smile. "It's lovely to meet you too. I'm sorry I can't really chat."

"Of course," Mr. Gray said, and I waved again slightly as I walked away from both men.

Before I had a chance to absorb what had just happened Tor bombarded me with a line up of drinks.

"This is for the VIP section. Mind your P's and Q's, the Kinkaid's are good friends of Ren," Tor said as she loaded my tray with glasses.

"Of course," I replied. I hoped she hadn't noticed me

perk up when she mentioned the Kinkaid's. I couldn't help but wonder if Chris Lewis knew, that's why he wanted me here.

Tor pointed towards the back of the club, to the far left of the main stage. I motioned to her that I understood and headed in that direction.

Four men in dark suits sat in the large velvet booth in the far back corner of Ren. Since I had never seen what the Kinkaid boys actually looked like I would have to try to overhear their conversation to figure out which is which.

The blonde with the slender face smiled at me as I set down the drinks, his eyes flashing bright green for a split second. I smiled back and he placed a neatly folded up bill on my tray.

"Keep 'em coming, new girl," he said with a grin.

"Sir, you need to...," the man next to him began.

The blonde turned quickly and scowled at him. "We're celebrating. Are you going to stop me from celebrating?"

His companion cowered under the threatening gaze. Mr. Blonde here was my best guess for being a Kinkaid.

I decided to take a chance. "My name is Camille, by the way. And thanks for the tip."

"Hi Camille. I'm Tobias Kinkaid," he held out his hand and I shook it.

"Nice to meet you, sir. I'll be back later with more drinks," I smiled a little too wide and walked away.

That was easy.

On more than one occasion I noticed Jesse deep in conversation with two large men, and with their backs turned to me all I could discern was their size. The hair on the back of my neck stood up.

October examined my face as I brought her a drink. "You okay, love?"

"What? Oh, yeah I'm good.. .," my voice wandered as I glanced at Jesse.

"Wondering who his new friends are? Let me just say that not everyone in this club is as nice as me."

"What do you mean?"

She pulled me down so she could whisper in my ear. "Thing One is into the brown. Thing Two likes to break bad. If you catch my drift. Those are the nice things. Pretty girls like you don't need to know what they're really up to, but I'm sure you can imagine."

"Oh," was all I could manage. I prayed that Lewis couldn't see him. I was so upset I couldn't form words. Heroin, a.k.a the brown, wasn't Jesse's drug of choice but he, on occasion, was super cliché and did some meth like that famous television character with the same first name. Cocaine was his thing, and OxyContin. I didn't often tell anyone about the Oxy's because it felt too much like a bad episode of Dr. Phil.

October took my hand, her skin was very smooth. I felt an immediate pull to her when she touched me, like she had some kind of magnet in her chest that drew people closer.

"You deserve better," she told me, her eyes staring deep into mine.

"I....I have to go," I pulled away from her and headed back to the bar. I saw Chris Lewis out of the corner of my eye standing by the bathroom door, he signalled me to come over.

"We'll talk about them later," he gestured towards Jesse. "You've been in the VIP section?"

I smiled, remembering my luck. "Yep. I will be going back regularly."

"Good," he handed me something, shoving it into my palm like someone would secretly hand folded up money. "You might need this."

He padded me on the shoulder and walked away. As I walked back to the bar I checked what he handed me; a neatly folded zip lock bag, confirming what I had suspected.

Being able to work my case would give me just the point of focus I needed to not pay attention to Jesse's nonsense for the rest of the night.

I returned to the VIP section several times, and against the advice of his companions Tobias Kinkaid got shit faced drunk. It was a good thing he was handsome because his obnoxious behaviour wouldn't fly with an average looking person.

Near the end of the night I came back and Tobias was in a heated debate with one of his people. He picked up one of the empty glasses before I could clear it and proceeded to smash it on the table top, cutting open his hand. I ran back to the bar as quick as I could to grab a brush and dustpan and towels.

In what seemed like swift action, his companions bundled his hand and shepherded him out of the club, leaving me with the broken glass and a 200 dollar tip.

With the VIP section empty it was easy for me to collect the shards with blood on them and put them in the bag that Lewis had so kindly provided. Luckily there were some that were clean so I had something to toss in the garbage can, along with the blood stained towels, being careful to avoid any cameras.

When I finally got back to the bar and Tor saw the mess she actually laughed.

"Why does it not surprise me?" she said. "I'll send back a bus boy to do a proper clean up. Thanks for doing what you did; most girls would have not even touched it. Did they at least tip you good?"

I smiled and nodded, motioning to the changing room. She nodded and went back to work, giving me the chance to stash my glass bag in my purse.

I tried to hide my excitement as I finished out the night. October seemed relieved at my sudden mood change, but we didn't get a chance to speak again and she was gone by the time I was finished. It was weird to have her and Jesse both watching me.

Chris Lewis was outside the change room door as I walked out to head home.

"Thanks for the help. I really appreciate it," I said, smiling happily.

He grinned back. "Happy to. But that doesn't mean you are off the hook for your shit head boyfriend."

"I know. We'll chat later? Have a good night," I squeezed his shoulder before turning and heading for the door.

Jesse was parked right outside when I stepped out onto the sidewalk. I was tempted to ignore him and try to find a cab but decided against it.

"Feel better?" I asked when I got in his car. He wouldn't look at me as he pulled out into traffic.

"What's going on between you and Chris Lewis?" he snapped.

"Excuse me? He's my boss. Who were those two random dudes you spent half the night talking to? Since when do you make goo goo eyes at Bliss Fiori? Her brother would kick your ass."

"It seems like you're enjoying this assignment a little too much."

"It's a crime to like my job? I was actually able to retrieve something today that will seriously help my paternity case, something that would have been super fucking hard for me to get in general *and* I only got because of Chris Lewis. So, yeah, I am happy. It was a good night other than your bullshit. I also made a butt load of money in tips."

He sighed loudly. "Okay, I get it. I'm just the dumb civilian. I'm sorry."

"You're not dumb. You're just paranoid and you don't need to be."

"Do you blame me? I spend a lot of time waiting for you to figure out you're too good for me. I'm shocked by every day that goes by that you don't."

I took his hand and held it tight in mine. I would not let him ruin this for me, so I squashed the fight while I still could. We rode the rest of the way back to my place in silence.

He leaned across the seat and kissed me, cupping my face with his hand. I eased in to the kiss, the anger inside me melted as I felt enveloped by his warmth.

"I'll talk to you tomorrow?" I said when I finally pulled away.

He stroked my cheek with his thumb. "Of course. I love you, Camille."

"I love you too."

10.

I was so excited in the morning I could barely find the right words to text Lemme.

I finally settled with 'got something better then a damn swab for you'. I could not believe how good my luck was, which meant something bad was going to happen. It was just a matter of time.

The first bad thing was in the kitchen when I came downstairs.

My Aunt Cindi drank coffee with her pinkie out; her two inch red fingernails looked like talons. It was never a good sign when she got past the doorway.

"Good morning, Aunt Cindi," I said as cheerfully as I could, pouring myself some coffee.

"Good morning Camille," her voice was like nails on a chalkboard. "Don't worry; I'm not here to discuss how you almost got my daughter kicked out of her home. I'm here to talk to your Uncle about Christian's schooling."

"Cuddy's a smart kid. He'll get as far away as he can on a free ride. He may be the only Bishop that ends up being a doctor or, God forbid, a lawyer," I replied, fixing myself a bagel and cream cheese. I sat down at the opposite end of the breakfast table, her perfume burning my nostrils.

She was about to say something when Poppy and Cuddy came in. Cuddy actually looked happy to see her for once. Cindi had left when Cuddy was quite young and he always resented her for it. I didn't blame him, she was a Grade A piece of work.

"Did you want to give me a ride to school today Mom?" Cuddy asked her. Ted came in before Cindi could answer and she watched him to gauge his reaction. If she could plant a knife in someone's back she would do her best to turn that shit at the same time.

"If your Dad says its okay," Cindi began. "By the way Christian, have you given any thoughts as to what you want to do after high school?"

Ted handed Cuddy a plate of food and a cup of coffee.

"I want to do the vampire tour of Europe," Cuddy said. "You know, take the Orient Express into Eastern Europe like Jonathon Harker did...."

"She means college, Cuddy," Poppy interrupted.

"Right! I'm going to U of T," he said with complete confidence. "I am torn between law and medicine. Law would drive Grandpa insane, but medicine would make Grandma super proud, and I love my Grandma."

Grandpa Bishop, veteran police officer of Toronto

Police Services with a near 45 year perfect record, and one of the highest solved case rates *ever*, had a very low opinion of lawyers.

And Grandma Bishop, God love her, just wanted *one* of us to become a doctor. She was also the closest thing Cuddy had to a real mother so he was very interested in pleasing her.

"Would you like your Mother's opinion?" Cindi asked with a smile, her lip gloss streaked her teeth.

"Nope," he replied, and I had to fake choking to hide my laughter. I, of course, wanted to know why she thought she would get an opinion at all. Not like she was paying for it.

"We can discuss it on our way," Cindi scowled at me from across the table.

"If you're only being nice as a way to manipulate me I would rather walk. What I do with my life is my decision, not yours. You already fucked up your life you don't get to fuck mine up too," Cuddy said and I wanted to high five him. Instead I locked eyes with Ted, and he gave me his 'time to go' look and I hurried to get my stuff together.

"It was nice to see you Aunt Cindi!" I called back as I rushed for the door; Ted was close at my heels.

"You trust her in the house?" I asked him when we finally got in the car.

"I trust my son to get rid of her promptly and without sympathy. Chip off the old block, isn't he?" Ted replied.

"So that's why Grandma calls him 'The Great White Hope'?"

Ted started laughing hysterically, waiting until he calmed down before driving away.

"Hey, I have news!" I exclaimed. "Oh my God, the coolest thing happened yesterday! I got actual Kinkaid blood! I don't know if Lewis set that up...."

"How did you get Kinkaid blood?" he asked.

"Tobias Kinkaid came into Ren last night, got super wasted and smashed a glass and cut up his hand. Luckily I was working the VIP and got to clean the glass, and bagged me some blood."

"And Lewis knows?"

"He gave me a damn baggie, like, 10 minutes before it happened! That was the fucked up part! It was like he knew it was going to happen."

"He may have. This is his stomping ground. Don't tell him I said this but he's a smart man and good at his job," Ted chuckled. "You were careful? Messing around with the Kinkaid's is a bad idea."

"I was, but in all seriousness Tobias Kinkaid was super duper loaded. He probably won't even remember being at Ren in the first place. Lewis is also the only person in the club that knows I'm a Bishop, other than this stripper I knew in high school but she probably doesn't remember my last name and wouldn't say it anyhow. She's a Fiori."

His eyebrows rose. "The Fiori girl from your class is a stripper? Her family must love that!"

"She said she's doing it to pay her way through nursing school. I'm going to try to have coffee with her or something."

"Sounds good," he said, pulling in to his parking spot at L&B. "Jesse behaved himself I'm guessing?"

"Other than showing up and mingling with the riff raff? Sure. But I'm too excited to concern myself with him. I can't wait to talk to Q!"

It seemed like forever before I heard from Lemme.

I finally got a random 'and???' text about midday so I just told her to get her ass to the office. I texted Q after and told her the same thing. Q texted me back quickly to let me know she would wrangle up Lemme and get here before I left for the day.

It was shortly after noon when Ramona buzzed me.

All I got was Ramona saying, "That girl has no manners....," before Q and Lemme burst into my office.

"You know, pissing off Ramona is not a good idea," I told them as they sat down.

Q waved it off. "Bah! She's a pussycat. Now, what's good?"

I smiled, probably a little too happily, and pulled the bag of broken glass out of my purse and put it on my desk. And, yes, I had the bag in my purse. Any good lady P.I has a purse that can literally carry anything.

"What the fuck is that?" Lemme gestured at the bag.

"It is broken glass with blood on it. The blood that I need for that case I called you guys in about."

"Bitchin! How did you score that?" Lemme asked.

"Long story, but I got it without having to do anything fucked up. Now, as soon as I hear from my client...," before I could finished my phone buzzed.

"Jane Lowry is here," Ramona said. I covered the receiver and asked Lemme if she could take a blood sample here. She smiled and pulled out a little plastic kit from her messenger bag.

"Send her in," I told Ramona and hung up, continuing, "My client is here. Let's do this. I am so pumped! Shit never works out like this."

They both looked at me, then at each other and laughed.

"I know I'm a nerd, but please don't laugh at me in front of my client," I said, standing up when there was a knock at my door and motioning for Q to open it. "Jane. Hi! These are my colleagues; they're here to take your blood sample."

Jane's expression immediately brightened. Q studied her face for a few minutes then a look of recognition flashed in her eyes; a hacker would know about websites like The Dollhouse.

"Great! You were able to get a sample from the Kinkaid's?" Jane asked.

I couldn't hide my smile. "Don't you worry. I told you I'm good at my job."

Lemme took out her kit and began to lay out her tools on my desk. I half expected Jane to get squeamish at the idea of drawing blood in such a fashion, but the girl who secretly was a 'vampire' didn't even blink. She watched

Lemme like she was laying out pencil crayons instead of a syringe.

"So how long will this all take?" Jane asked as Lemme sat her down. Q sat on my desk. Lemme swabbed down Jane's arm with alcohol then I had to turn away.

"Normal labs would take six weeks. But because you're dealing with top tear science bitches it'll take me a week, maybe ten days," Lemme said proudly. "That's just how I roll."

I wanted to ask if top tear science bitch was a technical term but I kept my mouth shut. We needed to look as professional as possible.

"Great! The waiting is the worst part," Jane replied as she applied pressure to where the blood was drawn with a cotton swab. Lemme put a band aid over it then started to sterilize her tools. All I could think of was that she sure had a lot of stuff in that bag. Maybe more than my bag.

Why does she carry around a kit for taking blood samples?

"Well, I will get back to you as soon as I know anything," I shook Jane's hand before she left.

Q immediately grabbed my arm. "You know what your client is into, don't you?"

"What are you, new? Of course I do. I vet everyone. Literally *everyone*," I told her. "Except you two. Haven't got to you two yet."

"Lewis never told you how we met?" Q asked.

"Nope and I didn't ask."

"Good. You need to be careful of your client. Girls like that have the tendency to shoot themselves in the foot."

I hadn't really thought too much about what Jane would do if she found out she really was a Kinkaid. Or what the Kinkaid's would do if there was a confirmed daughter on the loose.

"You can handle it, dude," Q pat me on the shoulder. "But we're out. Gotta take care of some other bidness. I know you have another consult for me; we'll talk about it later. Call me if you need anything."

I did a bit of digging on Mrs. Tanner and made a list of questions for Q for later. I'd have to do some surveillance on her house and look for this other P.I she thinks she is seeing. My hope was that she would ask the guy for his ID, get his name and report back to me so I could talk to the guy and nip this in the bud. I wasn't foolish enough to believe that I could get any information from another private investigator but perhaps professional courtesy would allow me to figure out if this was, in fact, a stalker or her husband.

It was a really slow day. I had no clients, and it sounded like no one came in at all. I was surprised and a little relieved.

My phone beeped a few times. It was texts; I ignored it at first because I assumed it was Jesse. He knew I wouldn't answer if I was busy and I would tell him I was if he asked.

Just before I was about to leave I checked my texts and there was two from a number I didn't know.

One asking if I wanted to meet for coffee, and another letting me know it was Bliss.

I couldn't help but smile. It would be nice to have someone new in my world.

I texted her back and said I was just leaving work and I would text her when I got home. Ted came to my door and gave me the 'we out' wave, so I packed my things and headed home.

When I got home I made plans to meet Bliss for coffee. Luckily she still lived close by so we met at the local Starbucks, which was about half way between us.

She smiled brightly when she found me in the line-up. "I haven't been here since high school."

"I've only been here a few random times, there is a much better place by my day job," I replied.

"How is the P.I biz anyhow?" she asked, continuing before I could come up with a lie. "Don't worry, I won't tell anyone. I think it's cool actually."

I tried not to blush. "Thanks. It's actually kind of turned into the family business."

"We've had a few Bishop's pass through Ren. But they are just regular cops, aren't they?"

"Which is why, according to Ren, my last name is LeFaye."

She chuckled. "I don't blame you. I don't exactly publicise the name Fiori."

"How do they feel about you working at Ren?" I asked.

We grabbed our coffees and headed over to a table.

"It was like I was telling Jesse when I saw him with Bucky, it's only temporary and for a good reason."

I felt my eyebrow rise. "Jesse was with Bucky?"

She paused, unclear if she had done something wrong. Bucky was Bliss's older brother and he had been all in to the Fiori's criminal lifestyle since we were teenagers. He ran the drug trade at our high school even after he graduated, he may still run it now. I would have to ask Cuddy.

"It's ok, Bliss. I have no illusions as to who, or what, Jesse is," I began. "I don't know all the details but I know he has his toes dipped in some unsavoury things."

"You can do better, Camille."

"You'd be surprised how often I hear that!"

"Clearly not enough if you are still with him, especially after all these years and all the rotten shit he has done!" She clearly knew more about him then she was letting on, but I didn't want this to end up as the bitch about Jesse hour.

"So why nursing?" I asked.

"I genuinely want to help people. Because of all the bad shit my family has done I feel like I need to do some good in this world."

"That's really noble of you."

"It would be hard for someone like you to understand."

I tilted my head. "Like me?"

"You come from the law, Camille. It would be hard for you to understand feeling like you have to atone when your family doesn't do bad things."

"Everyone does bad things," I checked my phone, nothing from Jesse. I was starting to get a little confused.

"Is that Jesse?"

"No, I actually haven't heard from him since he dropped me off after working last night."

"Oh," she paused for a long moment. "Is that weird for him?"

"Is something wrong? Do you know something that I don't?"

She sighed. "Look, I don't want to upset you. I am sorry if I sound like a geek when I say this but I was kind of liking the idea that we could be friends and I'm worried that if I say something about Jesse that you don't like you'll hate me."

I couldn't help but smile. I'd never had anyone say they actually wanted to be my friend before.

"It's like I said earlier, I have no illusions about Jesse anymore. I like to think I'm not the same naive little twat I was in high school when it comes to him," I began. "For what it's worth, I like the idea of us being friends too."

"Ok, cool. I think he is into it pretty deep with Bucky. Not in terms of owing him money but they are doing something together or Jesse works for him. Something along that line. Bad enough that if he got arrested they may try to take your license just for associating with him."

The only thing I could think to say was, "Oh." She didn't have any concrete proof but, really, she didn't need it. I knew in the back of my mind something was up, and it had been scratching at my brain since that girl showed up at his apartment when he said he'd told her to beat it.

"I'm sorry," Bliss said.

"Don't be. You're not the one doing anything wrong."

"Is there any way you can find out what he is doing? Like could you do surveillance on him or some other P.I magic?"

I pondered that thought for a minute. Following him seemed excessive and childish; besides, I had taught him how to spot a tail years ago.

"I'll have to think about that. I would have to find something he wouldn't expect, especially from me."

"Well, I got your back. I'll find out what I can and quiz Bucky the next time I see him."

"Thanks Bliss. I really appreciate it."

"Always happy to help a friend."

We talked for a few hours and through one more coffee. It was nice to chat with someone different, and I didn't feel so alone when we parted ways.

Bliss's comment about 'P.I magic' really sat with me and I couldn't help but wonder what I could do in this situation.

I texted Q and reminded her that I needed a consult about a case, and asked her if she knew of any surveillance tricks that I hadn't thought of.

She texted me back a bit later and asked about a cell phone GPS chip. I had too many questions to ask in a text so I called her.

"Yo," she picked up after three rings.

"You can track a phone if the GPS is off?" I asked, not bothering to question why it took her so long to answer if she was just texting me.

She laughed. "I can. And I can show you if you ask real nice. This is about the case?"

I paused, I guessed for too long, because she continued, "Dude, if you want to track your delinquent boyfriend I have no problem with that."

"Am I that obvious?"

"We've all done it. Just don't abuse it or it upgrades you to lunatic really fast."

"Ok, so how does this work?"

"I will come by L&B tomorrow and install the software and we can talk about it then. It can wait until tomorrow can't it?"

"Of course. Thanks Q."

"Anytime Bond."

11.

Q handed me back my list of things for Mrs. Tanner's case. "I did what I could. You get an email when any of the things are triggered."

"Cool. Thanks," I replied.

"I also installed the GPS tracker," she said with a smile. "So give me the digits and let's do this!"

I could not help but laugh. I gave her the number, and sat in my chair and waited. I actually prayed silently in hopes she would find nothing.

Q tilted her head slightly. "He's at a halfway house?"

"How do you know it's a halfway house?"

"Google. Duh."

I paused, lost deep in thought.

"What the hell would he be doing at a halfway house?" I said out loud.

"Wanna go see?"

I did a double take. "Excuse me?"

"I got a ride. Let's go creep on this bitch," Q said with an abnormal amount of enthusiasm.

"And you're down? Just like that?" It was the end of the day. No reason not to go.

"Just like that. Ride or die. I know you would do the same for me," she replied, jumping up and heading for the door. "You coming?"

Q drove a Jetta that changed colour, transitioning from dark blue to purple in certain lights. She drove like a maniac, way too fast and whipping in and out of lanes like a video game. I hung on to my seat and the door handle for dear life as she sped downtown.

We sped past downtown proper and into the more seedy part of town. Q turned up a small street and parked in front of a row of red brick buildings.

She flipped open her laptop, queued up the GPS tracker program and typed in Jesse's number.

"He's in there," she pointed at the large, run down old Victorian mansion across the street. I grabbed my phone and used the zoom on my camera to take a closer look at the perimeter.

I heard the keys on Q's laptop clicking, and then she said, "The cops have come by several times, mostly for noise complaints. There is a note that the reporting officers were suspicious of...."

"Suspicious of what?" I asked as I continued to

examine the surrounding area.

"Prostitution. They think it's a brothel but couldn't find any concrete evidence."

I sighed loudly. "You've got to be fucking kidding me. He could not possibly be that stupid."

"Then we need to get some proof," Q said confidently. She continued to type quickly while I watched the house.

"I doubt we could get in there unnoticed. I might be able to peek in a window, but...."

"Camille, please. This is the digital age! Why peek through a window when you can peek through a webcam?"

"Without you I would be peeking through a window. I thought that hacking into webcam thing was only in the movies."

"Nope! I just have to see if they have any."

"Can they tell they're being hacked?"

"Not unless they're good and, really, does that place look like it has any high tech computer pros in it? Hackers don't get sent to half way houses in the ghetto when they get out of prison."

I wanted to ask how she knew about hackers and prison but decided to wait until later. I didn't want to piss her off. I really needed her help.

"So it looks like they have a few webcam's and what I think is an Xbox Kinect. I haven't got in to one of those yet but I'm willing to try."

"Ok. Can we go through each of them until we find him?"

She continued to type furiously. "That was the plan. Just give me a few minutes. Keep watching the door in case he leaves and we have to follow him."

I continued to monitor the front of the house, snapping a few photos of the people who came in and out. A few scantily clad women and a familiar face pulled up in a black SUV.

I hadn't seen Bucky Fiori since we graduated high school. He hadn't changed much. A few more tattoos and a larger silver chain, but everything else was the same. It may have been different up close but from this distance he could have been transported through time and no one would have noticed.

I took some shots of him so if I decided to discuss this with Bliss I had something concrete to show her. I didn't know how well 'I saw your brother at a whorehouse' would go over.

Q turned her laptop screen towards me; it was divided into four squares of feed from different cameras.

And there, in the bottom left hand corner was Jesse.

Rolling up a dollar bill and doing a line of cocaine off a coffee table.

In the top right hand corner was the blonde who came to his door, getting screwed doggy style in a rumpled bedroom by a dude old enough to be her father.

I had to hold back my revulsion.

"You alright, Bond?" Q asked. I covered my mouth and shook my head no.

"Don't worry. I'm recording everything. If you can't

talk now we can do it later," she said and I tried to smile.

Thank God for Q.

I watched him. Watched this man that I love do all the things he had told me he had stopped doing. Watched him destroy himself. Watched him suck what was left of our relationship, what feelings I had left for him, up his nose.

The old man handed the blonde a wad of cash, and she crossed cameras completely naked as she walked through the house to hand Jesse the money.

"Cops are stupid," Q proclaimed.

"They can't legally do this," I managed to say. "That's why I can't take it to them."

"I know. That's why they're retarded. But don't you have a hook up with the cops that you could show it to?"

I chuckled. "I would be the laughing stock of my family, since they all know him. We'll sit on it for a bit then decide how to get it to them."

"You ok, dude?"

"I'm glad you're here. And no, no I'm not."

"He's a sleazebag."

"Funny thing is he cheated on me with her. I almost cracked open her skull with a frying pan a little while back."

Q laughed. "I knew there was a reason I liked you. Tell me you got tested. And got him tested. And made him double bag it."

"Yes, yes, and double bagging doesn't actually help."

She laughed again. "You seen enough?"

"Wait," I said, watching as Bucky came on to Jesse's screen. We watched as Jesse pulled out more money from in his pants, a tightly rolled wad of probably ten thousand dollars, and gave it to Bucky.

"Ok, I'm done," I told her. She shut her laptop and turned on the ignition.

"Let's go get a Frappuccino!" she exclaimed as we drove off.

Bliss messaged me before I had a chance to text her the next day. It was the simple 'I have something to tell you, but you're not going to like it'. I assumed when I called her back that she had found out about Bucky and was preparing what I was going to tell her.

"Hey Camille," she picked up after three rings. "How are you?"

"Ok, how are you? You working tonight?"

"I'm actually at Ren right now, but I had a little time. You got a minute? I have to tell you something but it's not going to be easy."

"What's up?"

"Jesse came in a while ago. He asked me if I wanted to do something, propositioned me actually. I'm surprised, considering his involvement with Bucky."

"What did he want you to do?"

She paused. "I'm just going to say it. He asked if I was interested in porn. Apparently he had a few...."

"Did he ask you not to tell me?"

"What?"

"Bliss, did Jesse ask you not to tell me?"

"That's the fucked up part. No. He didn't."

I immediately burst into tears. Of course it was worse than I thought. With Jesse it was always worse than I thought.

"Holy shit! I'm so sorry! I shouldn't have….."

"No! It's not that. I caught him at a brothel yesterday. Not screwing hoes, but running it," I sobbed. "Bucky was there. I'm sorry Bee."

"Are you sure it was him?"

"I have photos. And illegally obtained video, but still video."

She was silent for a few minutes, then said, "You ok, Cas?"

"Am I ok? I just told you you're…."

"He's a criminal. This isn't surprising. Jesse has been hiding this from you."

I sobbed even harder. I felt awful for crying on the phone to her but I couldn't stop myself.

I tried to blubber out some words and they didn't come.

I had devoted so much of my life to this clown.

I was so stupid.

I took a deep breath and managed to say, "This is the end. I am done with him for good this time. I have forgiven his bullshit too many times, and this is too big. If anyone found out I could lose my license. My Uncle would disown me and kill him."

"No one will find out. You're done with him; if anyone comes at you you can tell them that. How many people witnessed his behaviour at Ren? They could testify to it. I will if you need it, I'm sure October would too."

There was a sharp knock at my bedroom door and Ted came storming in.

"What did he do now?" Ted yelled.

"I have to call you back," I told Bliss. She said ok and we disconnected.

"It's complicated," if I told Ted the truth he would go on the warpath, but if I didn't he would go looking.

"Are you in danger?" he asked.

"No! Not at all. But if he calls the house make up an excuse. I'm not interested in talking to Jesse in any format right now."

He paused, studying my face. "Do you want to talk about it?"

I chuckled. "Eventually. But not now."

"Ok. Well, if you need me you know where to find me," he said, turning and leaving rather easily. I figured it would be more of a fight but, hey, I'm not complaining. No fight meant he was going to find out for himself.

I grabbed by teddy bear from my nightstand and curled into a foetal position. This was what I did when I was sad. The bear had been a gift for my tenth birthday from my parents and had got me through some rough times.

I didn't know what to do, so I thought it best to do nothing. I wouldn't speak to Jesse but I wasn't prepared to turn him in.

Yet.

I had to have substantial evidence that could be used in court before I could move against him.

The idea of moving against him made my stomach ache. It didn't mean I wouldn't, it just hurt.

I heard something sliding, and I jumped up to see a book fall off my desk on to the floor. I brushed it off and ignored it.

I fell asleep curled up in the centre of my bed. With everything that was going on in my head I was surprised I slept at all.

12.

I lay low for a few days after that, quietly going to work and keeping to myself.

Ted must have told everyone to piss off because no one bothered me unless it was necessary.

It was nice to have some time to myself before I had to go back to Ren. I needed the time to prepare to face Bliss.

I needed to come to terms with the fact that I would have to learn to live without Jesse.

For years I had prepared myself for the fact that he could die. He was an addict. Addicts overdose. I had even prepared myself for the idea of leaving him, trying to figure out within myself exactly how much I would take.

I didn't know what pissed me off more, the fact that he was pimping or the fact that blondie in white denim was the hoe.

I got a text from Lemme as Ted and I were driving home. She said we needed to talk in person, so I told her to come by the office tomorrow at lunch.

"Is that him?" Ted asked as we drove.

"No. It's Q's girl about my paternity case. By the way, did I mention how much I like Q?"

"Have you spoken to him yet?"

"No. Why?"

"I was just curious. Usually you'd gone back by now."

I turned away so he couldn't see my face in the mirror. "This is too big. I can't go back. Even if I wanted to. And I don't."

I felt his eyes on me. I knew he was watching my reaction.

"Ok then," he said and I quickly turned back to him.

"What do you know?"

"I tracked his phone. If you didn't get anything, I...."

"Q got some hacked video feed. Nothing really usable unless I give it to Kiera."

"Well, I have a few things if you want them. But it's on you. They're waiting when you're ready."

I smiled and squeezed his forearm affectionately. "Thanks Ted."

"Everyone has been filled in that you are unavailable to Jesse regardless of the circumstances so don't worry. Just focus on work and you'll get passed it, I promise."

"It's going to take some time. Especially since I have to turn him in."

He paused; I could tell he was trying to hide a smile.

"When you're feeling better. But I have to tell you that your cousin Poppy would *love* to bust him so if you really want to fuck with his head...."

"I will keep that in mind," I replied. The idea of getting to sic Poppy on Jesse amused me. That would be the ultimate fuck you.

I would have to consider it.

Ted dropped me at Ren that night. I was happy to be there, keeping busy would distract me.

I prayed when I walked in the door that Jesse wasn't there. I wasn't ready to face him. But he hadn't called or texted recently so I couldn't help but wonder if he had decided to drop off the face of the planet again.

Maybe he would leave me and I wouldn't have to be the one to break it off. Didn't bother me one bit; although I did like the idea of being the one to tell him it was over for good.

October smiled happily when she saw me, a little brighter than previous times. I couldn't help but wonder if she had some kind of radar that could spot a newly unattached girl.

Because that's what I was. The words may not have been said yet, but Jesse and I were completely over.

After I dropped off their drinks I noticed one of October's goons look uncomfortably at his phone then excuse himself from the table. I was able to watch him as he crossed the club and had a quick word with someone by the door that was cloaked in shadows. October seemed to not be bothered but he took great care to make sure she wasn't watching.

She was, in fact, watching me. It made me uncomfortable at first but after a while I started to enjoy it.

October handed me a business card when I came over to her along with a twenty dollar bill. "Tell them I sent you. They'll take care of you."

"What is it?" I asked as I examined the card with a smile. I couldn't read the writing on the card clearly in the darkness of the club.

"The best salon and spa in this end of the city," she replied. "You look like you could use some pampering."

I smiled; tears began to well up in my eyes. "You have no idea."

"My phone number is on the back. Just in case you need someone to talk to."

"Thanks. I appreciate that," I put my hand on her shoulder as I spoke. Her penetrating gaze made me wonder if she knew exactly why I was upset.

I put the card in my pocket and headed back to the bar. Regardless of what October knew she was right. I could use a spa day.

Amy Winehouse came thundering on a short time later, and I stopped to watch Bliss do her routine. I hadn't caught it before that her stage name was 'Amy'. Her beehive held up surprisingly well as she climbed that poll and spun around, her acrobatics were impressive. I'd have to ask if she would teach me, it looked like a good workout.

The night passed on relatively quickly and I felt good. Keeping busy was a good thing.

Bliss was waiting for me by the employees change room after I had grabbed my things.

"Hey! You need a ride?" she asked.

"Actually I do. Most of my tip money would have gone to a cab. Thanks," I said. I followed her out through a side door where an enormous security guard escorted us to Bliss's car.

"You seem in good spirits," she said once we got moving.

"I am. Keeping busy was a good thing. October gave me a number for a spa, said she would take care of it," I replied.

"Cool! Do you think there are strings attached?"

"I don't know if I care or not. It's nice to be pampered. I've never been pampered before."

Bliss smiled. "And October wouldn't be such a bad rebound."

"I hadn't really thought about it. I'm not really in to women in that way."

"October Daniels is a different story. I'm not into women either but something about her."

"I learn something about you every day."

"So are you ready to be fixed up yet?"

"Not yet. But do you have someone in mind?"

"Actually I do. Someone from high school that had a thing for you but was too scared of Jesse to say anything. Well, in high school he was. Now I highly doubt it. You should see him too. Wow!"

"Who is it?"

She laughed. "Oh, I'm not telling until you're ready. I just wanted you to know that other guys have looked, so don't get the idea in your head that you're undesirable because that jackass is a knob."

"Thanks Bliss."

"No sweat. That's what friends are for. Now, in terms of this October funded makeover, what are you going to let them do to your hair?"

The house was dark when I came inside. It was late; often someone was up watching TV but not tonight. I was actually happy about it; I didn't feel much like talking.

Tomorrow was going to be a busy day.

13.

I'd liked Lemme from the first time I met her, but I liked her even more because she was prompt.

Not just prompt but on time. To the fucking minute.

I was amazed when there was a knock at my door as the clock turned to noon, exactly when she said she would be there.

"Come in!" I called, and she and Q entered.

"On time to the second. I love it!" I said as they sat down.

"Well, we got something crazy for you. It deserved to be prompt," Lemme began. "Let me start by saying that these two are, without a doubt, related. Your girl and whoever's blood was on that glass. They have this weird anomaly, it's hard to explain but it has to do with their blood. Porphyria is an explanation that some scientists and historians believe explains the situation, but I don't...."

"Porphyria? What's that?" I asked.

"They believe it explains the stories of vampires in folklore."

"Exsqueeze me? Run that by me again?"

"Your girl and her new family could be considered, clinically, a type of vampires. They are also deficient in a lot of major enzymes and vitamins. My colleague believes you could only get them by ingesting raw meat, which is kind of like drinking blood."

I sighed loudly and leaned back in my chair. "Crap. I can't mention vampire shit to this girl, she's a...."

"Oh, we know what she is," Q interrupted before I could stop myself. "That's why we removed certain words from the report so she wouldn't twist it into some weirdness. And, by the way, that shit that she does is fucking weird!"

"Oh, I know! I didn't find out until a different client came in asking me to go after The Dollhouse for overcharging his credit card."

"As long as you know," Lemme reached in her bag and handed me a folder. "Here are the reports. Yours is on the bluish paper, it's got all the info."

"Awesome! So what do I owe you?"

"Moneypenny already took care of it," Q said. "Are you good, Bond? I've been meaning to call you."

"Yep. Fan-fucking-tastic. Ted's got some stuff too, for when I decide to turn him in."

She smiled and nodded. "Ted's good shit, isn't he?"

"The best," I smiled back. "Thanks for this, guys. I'm

sure this is the beginning of a beautiful friendship."

I did my best Godfather impression; Q rolled her eyes at me.

"If she's Q, who am I in the Bond analogy?" Lemme asked.

"Smithers," Q and I replied in unison.

"Who?"

"Watch For Your Eyes Only and Octopussy," I said.

"Alright," Q jumped up and gathered up her things. "We out. This isn't the only stop we gotta make. C'mon Lemme. Let's roll."

Once I was alone again I called the spa October had given me the card for. I told the receptionist that a friend had recommended them and gave them October's name.

"Wonderful. Are you Camille?" the receptionist asked.

I was speechless for a minute, shocked that she knew my name. "Yes, I am."

"Great! October mentioned that you would be calling; we'll take great care of you. Are you available tomorrow?"

"Yes, I am. Can you give me an idea of how much it might cost?"

"Oh, don't worry about that. October is taking care of it. She just wants you to enjoy yourself."

I chuckled. "It sounds a little too good to be true."

"Well it's not!" she exclaimed. "Please don't worry. Just come and enjoy. What time will we see you tomorrow?"

After making that appointment I was floating on a

cloud for the rest of the day. I texted Ted to tell him I had a spa appointment the next day, a treat from a friend, and he was ecstatic I was doing something for myself.

I was so happy that I had to make a conscious effort of keep my voice calm and level when I called Jane Lowry.

I got her machine, and I let her know I would be out of the office tomorrow but I could see her the day after if she was available. My cell phone vibrated while I was talking, I was hoping it was Bliss so I could tell her about my appointment.

It was Jesse.

I watched my phone for a long time as it sat in my hand, dark because it wasn't being used. It had been several days since I had heard from him and I didn't know how to respond to whatever bullshit he had to say without giving away what I knew.

I didn't want him to know that I knew, or how much I knew. I was going to turn him in eventually; it was a matter of when not if. And his wrath when he found out it was me was going to be unpleasant.

The question was did I let it slip that October was treating me to a spa day?

I texted him back and said I was busy working on a case and I would get at him later. I got the obligatory 'is everything alright' message, which I responded with my standard five by five. We exchanged I love you's and that was the end of it, he didn't try to call or anything. Part of me was disappointed that he didn't push, for some foolish reason.

The next day couldn't have come any faster and I practically skipped to the spa.

It was beautiful, all dark wood and marble with this amazing warm floral smell that I wanted to ask if they bottled and sold. I was greeted when I walked in by a small girl with beautifully dyed dark pink and purpley red hair cut in an amazing asymmetrical bob that's longest part just dusted her shoulders.

"Your hair is amazing!" I exclaimed when she got close to me.

She giggled. "Well thank you so much! You must be Camille?"

"Yep! And if you can't tell I am super happy to be here!" I sounded like a dork even to myself but I was just so excited.

"That's amazing! Now, let's get started. My name is Nina by the way," she said, linking her arm in mine and guiding me into the spa.

After the massage I was comfortable. But after the mani pedi, something I had never had before, I was relaxed. The pedicure was the most amazing thing in the world, and my matching cherry red fingers and toes made me feel so glamorous.

When I sat down in the hairdresser's chair I really looked at myself in the mirror. My hair hung limp and flat, the black dye made me look really pale in this light. It wasn't doing me any favours and had become a bit of a security blanket.

"So what are we thinking?" the hairdresser asked.

He was a thin man dressed in black with a silvery grey pompadour.

"What about something like Nina's?" I asked. I bit back the nervousness that was beginning to bubble up in my stomach. It was just hair; if it was so terrible I could change it.

He smiled brightly. "That will be dynamite on you! Are you attached to the black?"

"No, not at all."

"Good. I'm thinking where Nina has purple yours should be more plum but for sure the pink. Let's get started! Are you excited?"

I wanted to close my eyes while he worked his magic but I didn't want to look silly. I was so excited but nervous at the same time that it was hard for me to sit still and relax.

"When was the last time you really changed your hair?" the hairdresser asked while he was applying the colour.

"Never. It's been this way forever. I didn't want to rock the boat with my....," it took me a few minutes to finally say, "My ex."

"Ooh, a breakup makeover! Don't worry, sweetheart. Paul will take good care of you!" he exclaimed, seeming to get pep in his step.

He turned me around while he was drying my hair and Nina was doing my makeup. I was pleased; I had to work at Ren tonight and I wanted October to see that her money didn't go to waste.

When Paul finally spun me around and I got to look at myself I gasped a little. He and Nina grinned back at me in the mirror like two happy hyenas and it brought tears to my eyes.

"What's wrong, hunny?" Paul asked.

"It's more wonderful than I could have imagined," I said with a smile. I touched my hair, still in shock that it was mine.

They both clapped lightly, and began cleaning up.

Walking out of the spa I felt like a completely new person. It was amazing. I hadn't known that completely changing my hair would make me feel so good. I strutted my way down the street to the subway and headed for home, smiling all the way.

Ted smiled brightly when I walked into the kitchen.

"Well hello there!" he exclaimed, Cuddy looked up from his food and smiled.

"Wow! Cas, you look amazing!" Cuddy said with his mouth full.

I stroked my hair affectionately. "You like?"

"Yes! Very much," Ted replied happily. "I don't even mind that you skipped work to go get your hair done knowing it looks that good."

"Thanks! Are you ok to drive me to Ren tonight Ted?"

"Can I come?" Cuddy chimed in.

"No," Ted and I said in unison, than Ted continued, "Yes, I will take you."

"Great!" I said, and I headed for the stairs to go get changed, bumping into Poppy on the way.

She looked at me for a few minutes, squinting a bit, and said, "Cute hair."

"Thanks Poppy."

It was officially the best day. Ever.

Heads actually turned when I walked into Ren.

Heads turned. For me. That had never happened in my entire life.

October was already at her table when I got out of the change room, she smiled so big when she saw me I was sure I could see all of her teeth.

"I owe you a big thank you," I leaned over to speak closer into her ear after I dropped off her drinks. "That spa you recommended was incredible! They work miracles, as you can see."

"You look absolutely beautiful, Camille," she said, touching my cheek lightly with her finger.

"Is it going to cost me an arm and a leg to go back on my own?"

She laughed. "No, sweetheart."

One of October's goons, the same one who was shifty with his phone previously, glanced at me out of the corner of his eye then checked his phone under the table. If he was trying to hide something he wasn't very good at it.

"How would you like to have dinner with me one night

you are off?" October asked. I paused, remembering what Bliss had said.

"I would love to," I replied. I wrote my number on a napkin and handed it to her. I saw Bliss out of the corner of my eye motioning me over, so I politely excused myself and went over to her.

"Your hair looks amazing!" she exclaimed. "Holy shit! I can't believe you went for it."

"It was spur of the moment but I'm glad I went for it. And thanks!" I replied.

"Hey, so I got tickets and backstage passes to see Obsidian Butterfly this weekend. You want to come with me? I know its short notice but I thought I would ask."

"Fuck yeah! They're my favourite band!" I replied. Obsidian Butterfly was a local hard core rock band that had recently signed a huge record deal. I loved them, but Jesse didn't like them so I didn't think I would ever see them live.

She smiled. She seemed surprised I was so excited.

"Great! I don't have much time to chat right now, but we'll talk later, ok?" she kissed my cheek before heading out onto the floor.

I couldn't hide my smile.

It astonished me that all these cool things happened all at once after I made the decision to end my relationship. Maybe it was the world's way of telling me that Jesse needed to be out of my life for good.

October's questionable goon, who I aptly nicknamed Shifty, continued with his weird erratic behaviour through most of the night. So one of the times he left her table I followed him.

He slid into the VIP section and headed to the very back. He nudged his way into the darkest corner he could find and pulled something out of his sock.

It was too dark for me to see what was going on so I took out my phone and took some photos. I could adjust them in Photoshop later to get a clear idea of what he was doing but I had my guesses. I'd have to tell Lewis later that I suspected it was a different type of drug problem.

I took a short video, just in case the photos didn't work out. I quickly tucked away my phone and left, I didn't want him to see my face at any point other then when I was talking to October.

I lay low for the rest of the night, trying not to attract too much attention. I was still happy, still floating on cloud nine, but knew better then to have people looking at me for too long when I had taken photos without someone's knowledge.

I was going to see my favourite band with a friend and I had a date, how could I not be in a great mood?

Bliss found me later and said she would drive me home, so I texted Ted and told him not to come. I practically bounced out to the car; the security guard who walked us out was looking at me like I had lost my mind.

"How did you score tickets, and back stage passes, to

Obsidian Butterfly? They must have cost an arm and five legs," I began when we got in the car. "I have to tell you, I am so excited. I didn't get to listen to them much before because Jesse doesn't like that kind of music, and now I get to see them live! I've never seen a live band before!"

"Well, you are in for a treat. I've seen them live a few times and they're awesome," Bliss replied.

"Killer! I am so excited! I can't believe all the cool stuff that has happened once I decided my relationship is over."

"What cool stuff?"

"October asked me out to dinner."

She smacked my shoulder. "Shut up! Are you serious? Did you say yes?"

"Of course I did. I think it will be fun. And she's hot."

Bliss's smile was so big it made me laugh. She seemed happier then I was.

"I am so proud of you I don't even know where to begin," Bliss said with what looked like a tear in her eye.

"What? Why?"

"You are bouncing back. It's admirable. Not a lot of people can do that."

"Well, it helps to have some friends around and an awesome job. I'm hoping to wrap up my first big case tomorrow, it depends on if I have to talk to the Kinkaid's."

"The vampires?"

My breath caught in my throat and I started to cough.

"What? You mean you didn't know?" No reflections, they only come out at night, they drink blood. I'm telling you. Fucking vampires."

"You've seen them do all this?" I asked.

"Yeah. I'm their favourite. I have seen them, and been asked to do, some seriously fucked up shit by the three knuckleheads."

"I had no idea. Do you know Tobias? He was in the VIP section recently."

"Tobias is a nutcase. Gorgeous, but nuts. Have you seen the sister? Lucia? Jesus," she shook her head. "Bitch is fucking insane."

"Thanks for the heads up."

"If you need help with something in regards to them just say the word."

"Depending on how all this plays out I might just take you up on that," I said. I couldn't help but think of Jane Lowry and what tomorrow was going to mean for her.

Bliss and I chatted the rest of the way home about nothing in particular. It was nice to have a girl to talk to.

I wondered who Jane had to talk to, if she had friends. If she had a person she could vent all of this to who might be able to help her work through it.

I couldn't be that person. It wasn't in my job description. I would have to be very careful with how I approached this situation, especially with this vampire weirdness.

The next morning I was still in a good mood, flying

high on my new found happiness. I was able to style my new hair myself and it still looked awesome. I even put on a little more makeup than I normally would to complete the look.

Jane Lowry was my first appointment of the day; she wasn't there when I arrived so I had some time to prepare.

I separated the files Lemme gave me and put the ones specific for Jane in an envelope, scanning them quickly before sliding them in. I put my version of the papers in a file in my desk drawer.

I had not had a chance to talk to Ted but once I told Jane I would. I hoped with this information and the weirdness of it he would give me my Dad's files on the Kinkaid's.

Jane was a bit late. She was heavily made up, her dirty blonde hair slicked back in a tight bun, I assumed to hide it under her wig. My guess was that she was shooting for The Dollhouse before she came.

She sat and fidgeted nervously. I was going to say something but she went first.

"I'm sorry. I'm super nervous," she said sheepishly. "But if I'm not a Kinkaid we just have to keep looking, right?"

I smiled. "Right. I'm glad you have such a positive outlook on this. But where did you hear the name Kinkaid?"

"I'm sorry, Miss Bishop. I should have mentioned. After the Thomas Lowry paternity results I did some digging on my Mother and found the coverage on the rape cases, which is how you found the name Kinkaid, I'm guessing."

I should have known she'd get on the internet. "That's fine. I should have mentioned it and I would have once we figured out if you were, in fact, a Kinkaid."

"Oh my God, does that mean I'm not? Oh crap, where would we even start looking?!"

"Just relax and let me tell you what's going on," I began. "So according to the blood test you are a Kinkaid. If it came up for debate you have an anomaly in your blood that exactly matches the person we tested, which is genetic."

She paused, sighing. "Wow."

I handed her the envelope of information from Lemme.

"The info my girl gave me is in there. You should take it to your doctor and discuss it. Porphyria is nothing to sneeze at."

Her eyes sparkled when I said that.

Fuck.

Of course she knew what porphyria was.

She took the envelope and stuffed it into her tote bag.

"So, now that we have this info what would you like to do?" I asked.

"What do you mean?" her eyes were glazing over a bit.

"What steps would you like to take next? I can recommend a lawyer who could approach the Kinkaid's...."

"I don't know if I am ready for that," she said quickly, shaking her head.

"Ok, I totally understand. You should take some time to process it. Give me a call if you want me involved in the next steps. If you involve a lawyer I will have to be involved, just a heads up."

She sighed again and stood. "Thank you for everything. I paid up when I came in, if you were wondering."

"I wasn't, but thank you," I crawled out from behind my desk to walk her out.

She appeared visibly shaken and walked like she was in a daze. I was concerned so I walked her out to her car.

"If you need anything, please give me a call," I said. I held open her driver's side door for her and she got in. She didn't look at me as she mumbled a thank you and closed the door. I watched as she pulled out of the lot and drove away.

The black car sat parked across the street. I hadn't noticed it recently, and I started to wonder if it had something to do with Jesse's new business venture. The feds would want to keep an eye on his associates as well, which made it an ideal time for me to distance myself from him.

I flipped the car off and went back inside to find my Uncle.

Ted was sitting at his computer when I knocked at his door. He waved me in and I sat in the client chair.

"So I just told my client she is a Kinkaid," I began.

"She ended up being one, huh?"

"Yep, matching weird ass blood disorders and all. She took it harder than I expected, considering she had a pretty clear idea that the man she calls Dad is not her actual Dad."

"That is not a surprise. No one is ever prepared for news like that, no matter what they say."

I smiled, showing as much teeth as I could. "So, can I see those files now?"

"What files?"

I rolled my eyes. "C'mon Ted."

"Not yet. Let's make sure the Kinkaid's aren't going to come after us first."

"Shouldn't I see the files to prepare for that possibility?"

"Give it a break, Cas. You'll get the files in due time. You need to have a clear head. You can't go into this situation like a bull in a china shop."

"I know, I know. I'll be distracted for the weekend. I'm going to see Obsidian Butterfly with Bliss."

He smiled brightly. "Cool. Glad you're going out and being social. Should I ask about you know who?"

"No need. I brushed him off, hopefully I can keep doing that for the next little while and I can make a clean break."

"Let's hope. But don't worry. We have enough to take him down."

I paused. "What did you do?"

"Close my door," he started. I got up and shut it, quickly sitting back down.

"I was worried, so I GPS tracked him again. Considering how long you guys dated for you'd think he would be smarter about how he went about things."

"He would think we trusted him enough not to do that," I replied, my voice growing quiet. "Doing that is dangerous Ted. It's not worth it."

"Give me some credit, Cas. I am actually okay at this job, he would never catch me unless he knew what to look for," he continued. "He doesn't get to do this to you. Now that you are done with him I am going to make sure you have enough to take him down. What kind of parental figure would I be if I didn't bring you dirt to get your shithead boyfriend arrested?"

I couldn't help but laugh. "Ex boyfriend."

"Whatever. Your Dad, God rest his soul, would come back from whatever layer of Hell he is in and rip me to shreds if I didn't. Unless you're Mom got to me first."

The mention of my parents made my breath catch in my throat. Whoever created this notion that grief lessens or eases with time is full of horseshit.

"I'm going to go work on my stalker case," I said. He waved me off and went back to his computer.

I spent the afternoon cleaning up and fixing the pictures and videos I took of October's goon last night. It was as I suspected.

I'd never seen anyone shoot a needle in between their fingers, but he did it. I think he thought he was being clever; the needle between his toes would have been clever, between his fingers had so many things that could backfire it wasn't worth it

I hadn't seen Chris at all so I emailed him what I had when it looked decent. The only way this guy was poaching October's business was if he was getting so high off his own supply it was making a significant dent. I didn't know a lot about the drug business but that seemed highly unlikely.

I didn't say that in the email. Chris would come to his own conclusions. I wondered if Chris already knew this guy was a junkie. I sent them anyway just to be cautious.

Ted and I left early and picked up Cuddy from school. Jesse's car was in the parking lot again. I couldn't help but wonder what Rollo had to do with Jesse's current enterprise.

"Jesse stopped me in the hall today, Cas," Cuddy said when we got moving. "He wanted some info on one of the girl's in my class. I told him to stop being a douche; he said it was for Rollo but whatever."

Cuddy was the first person to call me Cas. He randomly started calling me that when he was about two and learning to talk. It stuck, and that became my official nickname with the Bishops, then everyone else who heard it. I never knew why he didn't call me Cam and I didn't ask. I wasn't fond of Cam or Cami.

"Don't worry about him, Cuddy. Just brush him off and ignore him," I replied. "Last time I checked Rollo can get his own girls. They shouldn't be scamming on high school girls, that's just skeezy."

I saw the muscles in Ted's hands tense around the

steering wheel, his knuckles turning white. I didn't like the idea that he could get to Cuddy so easy either. We would have to do something about that.

I was happy to get home and to be able to dig through my closet to find something to wear to the concert. My clothes looked different with my new hair; it was almost like I was a different person going through the things of a dead girl.

I found a low cut red top with small black dots that tied in a decorative knot in between my cleavage buried in the back of my closet. I remembered buying it; I had found some cute things on a website that sold pin up style clothing and bought two tops. They weren't entirely appropriate for work and I didn't think Jesse would like them so I had put them in my closet and forgot. I was thankful now, with dark jeans and my black leather jacket it was perfect. I smiled to myself, pleased that I also had something I could wear when I went out with October.

As I was getting ready for bed my phone rang, I wasn't surprised it was Jesse. I debated not answering, but the Cuddy issue was too important.

"Hello?" I said, trying to keep my voice level.

"Hey love," his voice was a low purr, a sign to me that he was high. "How was your day?"

"Okay. How was yours?"

"Good. Did Cuddy tell you I saw him?"

"Yep. Is that why you're calling? You worried I think you're hitting on teenage girls with your buddy?"

He chuckled. "Should I be?"

"That's your call, dude. But don't bug The Great White Hope at school. He is the future of the Bishop family, you know."

He laughed loudly. "You're funny."

"I wish I was kidding. Grandma Bishop would tear out your throat with her teeth if she thought you were fucking with the kid. Just smile and wave when you see him. But don't tarnish his rep at school. You're bad news, remember?"

"Oh right, I forgot. So what's going on this weekend?"

"Plans with Bliss and a stake out. Two separate things."

"You're spending time with Bliss? Really?"

"I am. I think we're going to be friends. Is that a problem?"

"No! No! Not at all," he stuttered out. "I am just surprised that you would want to hang out with someone like Bliss Fiori."

"And who exactly is Bliss Fiori?"

"She's been involved in some bad shit, Cas. And she's a stripper."

I couldn't help but laugh. "You out of all people shouldn't be judging someone who is trying to improve their life."

He stayed silent; the drugs clouding his mind enough that it took some actual thought to lie. "You're right, you're right. Just be careful. I wouldn't want you getting mixed up in something you can't get out of."

I chuckled. Coming from him that was hilarious. But the whore house was probably his idea, I was being naive.

"Honey, I'm a P.I. It's kind of my job to get mixed up in things I might have trouble getting out of."

"So, when am I going to see you? I could come by now....or when are you at Ren again?"

"Do not come back to Ren," I snapped. "That did not go over well the first time, and I am positive I cannot talk Lewis down a second time. Unless you want to watch me sleep there is no point in coming here tonight. I have had a long day and I am exhausted."

"Okay well I won't keep you. I just wanted to remind you that I love you and when you get some free time it should be for me, okay?"

I smiled to myself.

If I had it my way he wouldn't see me again.

"I will. Don't worry. Have a good rest of the night and be safe," I replied, quickly saying bye and hanging up. I had to get used to not telling him I love him and find ways out of it in conversation. I wouldn't allow myself to be duped by him again.

I fell asleep that night thinking of my Mom. I couldn't help but wonder what she would advise me to do. What she would say about this messed up situation I was in.

As I closed my eyes I thought I could see her, sitting on the edge of my bed, stroking my hair like she did when I was a kid and I couldn't sleep. The tears started to flow; the ache began to radiate from my stomach outwards.

Just before I dozed off I swore I felt her hand on my head.

14.

Bliss showed up about an hour before the show was about to start.

I practically ran out the door when the bell rang, calling back to Ted who was parked in front of the television as I flew by. Everything was falling into place today; my new hair styled easily and my outfit was actually working, my makeup looked decent enough that I might even allow someone to take my picture.

Bliss looked startled when I answered the door all jumpy and smiling.

"You got something you want to share with me, Cas?" Bliss asked with a smile. "Because I am all for a little recreational drug use if you are."

"Nope, just excited! And drugs aren't really my thing but I could be talked into a drink or two," I replied. We headed out to the car and she put on Obsidian Butterfly's album as we drove to the concert.

They were playing at Lee's Palace which was an iconic downtown Toronto venue. I hadn't been before, I had always wanted to go and I couldn't hide my excitement.

Bliss laughed as we walked out of the parking lot. "You look like a little kid on Christmas morning. You have to relax!"

"I'm sorry. This is just....oh, I sound pathetic saying this, but it's like a dream come true! I never thought I would actually get to go, and to Lee's Palace!" I exclaimed.

"Well I am glad you are so happy. You deserve to be yourself and not how someone thinks you should be."

"Thank you. Which reminds me, just a heads up, I did tell Jesse we were hanging out this weekend as well as having to go on a stakeout. Not related of course but two separate things. So if he asks I thought you should know."

"A stakeout? Now that sounds exciting. Can I come with?"

I laughed. "I don't have a vehicle so I might take you up on that."

We breezed by the front door and went right into the main part of the venue; I stopped by a poster of the band.

The lead singer, Fray, was actually smiling.

"What's with the look?" Bliss asked with a big stupid grin. I could feel myself blushing.

"He is so good looking I don't know what to do with myself," I said.

She laughed. "Well then you are in for a treat! You know I have backstage passes, right?"

My gaze turned quickly to her. "If you told me I totally forgot! I'll probably pass out in his presence."

She grabbed my arm and pulled me into the main room as the lights started to go down.

Obsidian Butterfly took the stage, each of the members wearing black leather pants and black shirts, tattoo's peaking through. Fray walked out once the others were set up, his stride graceful but masculine at the same time.

Fray was tall and thin, his white skin peaked out from a mesh shirt and his black leather vest that had a devil face and the word *prophet* painted in white on the back. His black hair was shaved on the sides and long on top, his skin and hair causing his blue eyes to pop.

He started singing and I fell into a trance.

About three songs in he spoke into the microphone, "This next song was the favourite of a girl I once knew."

He started into Our Lady Peace's Somewhere Out There, one of my all time favourite songs. It felt like he poured his heart out on the stage, he must have loved the girl who loved that song.

"Have you figured it out yet?" Bliss asked.

"Figured what out?"

"Figured out who that is?"

I cocked my head to one side. "Run that by me again? I don't get it."

She sighed and I knew rolled her eyes without having to look. "You are looking at the Nirvana cover band from our high school, and your former lab partner Noah Fray."

My mouth gaped open as I watched Fray turn his head and saw the boy I once knew. The gawky kid that was my lab partner almost all the way through high school, who was the only guy brave enough to talk to me when Jesse was around.

"The boy who would date you in a heartbeat once Jesse is gone for good. He sings Somewhere Out There for you at almost every concert hoping one day you'll hear it."

"Wow," was all I could manage. I had a flash of the band formerly known as Heart Shaped Box performing at our tenth grade talent show and getting booed off the stage.

I wondered if I was the last person to know about this.

The longer part of Noah's hair fell just around his ear and when he smoothed it back, a very Elvis like move if I had ever seen one; girls screamed.

I had to cover my mouth to hide my smile. I couldn't believe that this gorgeous rock god was nerdy Noah Fray from high school. That the whole band was guys that I knew from high school.

"I can't wait to take you back stage!" Bliss exclaimed.

I stumbled like I had been kicked. I had forgotten we were going back stage.

"I....I can't! I don't look....I mean, do I look okay? Crap! I'm going to meet Fray?!" I said.

"No, sweet pea. You're going to chill with Noah and the boys. It's no big. Really I promise," she examined at the look on my face. "What is freaking you out?"

"I've not really done much chilling. It's always been me and....I don't know how to act in this situation. And yes they are Noah and the boys but they are also my favourite band. Real life rock stars."

She kept watching my face, I wondered if it was to see if I was joking. "Hey, Cas, you'll be okay. Just be yourself. And I'm sorry."

"Why are you sorry?" I asked, turning away to hide the tears in my eyes.

"It's not your fault. People liked you, people wanted to be your friend in school but he blocked all of that. I promise you, now that he is gone that will change," she smiled and squeezed my shoulder. Just then Obsidian Butterfly's big hit song came on, and we stopped talking so we could dance.

Bliss was wearing her dark hair down and loose so it swung when she moved; it probably needed a break from her Amy Winehouse beehive. She could dance and I cannot, so we must have made quite the pair to onlookers. The beautiful dark haired dancer and her awkward friend who looked like she was doing some messed up version of river dance.

When the concert was over the anxiety began to bubble up and tap dance in my stomach. Before we could speak I dragged Bliss to the bathroom so I could wipe the sweat from my face and it least try not to look like crap.

"What's wrong?" she asked when we got in front of

the mirror. I grabbed some paper towel and began to pat the sweat off my brow.

"I am not walking in there looking like a sweaty sea monkey," I began, and I started grabbing my makeup out of my purse. "Just let me freshen up and we can go. This is the first time these people have seen me since high school. I don't want to look like crap."

She chuckled at me, leaning up against the sink counter while I fussed with my makeup. Girls actually manoeuvred around us even though we were blocking a sink. I imagined that was what it was like to be one of the cool girls. People just let you do your thing with no consequence.

I did the best I could with my makeup. I was decent. My hair had got a little wave around my face where it had got sweaty and it actually didn't look bad. After one last swipe of tinted lip balm I was ready to go.

Bliss pulled two lanyards out of her purse with the passes attached and put one over my head like I had won a medal. I couldn't stop smiling as we headed through Lee's Palace to the backstage area.

The open door was at the end of the hallway and my anxiety began to bubble up again. I let her lead me down the hall; she motioned for me to wait as she poked her head in the doorway.

"Wud up rock bitches!" she exclaimed, and the room called out her name in response. Sounded like she did this often.

"An old friend wanted to come by and say hi," she

grabbed my arm and pulled me in the doorway, I felt my face go beat red.

The room was quiet; it took everyone a minute to recognize me. I heard someone say my name like it was a question and I smiled and waved.

Fray turned from where he was perched on a stool talking to a platinum blonde with big boobs in a black leather bra top, glancing at first then falling off his stool when he realized it was me.

"Camille?" he stuttered. "Wow, it's been a long time. You...."

"I am such a huge fan! I am embarrassed to admit that I didn't know it was you until Bliss pointed it out but now....I remember you guys getting booed off the stage at the high school talent show and look where you are now!" I blurted out.

Eamon, the guitar player, smiled from behind long dark hair. "It's good to see you Camille. I'm happy that someone is finally around to remind us where we came from and keep us humble."

"How did you too....?" Fray began, finally beginning to not look so dumbfounded.

"It's a long story," Bliss said with a smile.

"How's Breaking Bad, Camille?" Toby, the drummer, asked. He sat next to me in English freshman year. He was quiet and didn't really talk to anyone. I remember he almost talked to me once, but Jesse intervened. I guessed that had a lasting impact.

"Gone," I said proudly. "I am a free agent and ready to

start enjoying myself."

Fray smiled and my heart skipped a beat. I didn't remember him looking like that in high school. His face was perfectly smooth, his skin like porcelain. His blue eyes glowed with happiness and when his lips parted to show white teeth I saw the Noah I knew. I remembered thinking he had gorgeous eyes and teeth; if I hadn't only had eyes for Jesse maybe we wouldn't be standing here.

"Well, that sounds like a reason to celebrate if I ever heard one," Fray said, his raspy voice had gotten deeper but I wondered if that was from the strain of performing tonight. He grabbed a bottle of Jack Daniels from the counter and started pouring shots.

The random groupies got excited, the leather bra girl moved towards Fray and he shooed her off like a disobedient animal. It bothered me a bit that he could be so callus but after I thought about it I understood.

If I had a bunch of vapid morons hanging off me because I'd made it I would treat them like crap too.

Fray dusted off a love seat for Bliss and me to sit and handed us our shots. I took mine and cringed after I drank it.

"Sorry, not much of a drinker," I said as I handed him back the glass. He smiled at me, brushing his cold fingers on my hand as he took it from me.

"So I guess he didn't rub off on you too much," Fray replied.

"Thankfully, no. But he is no longer an issue and never will be again," I told him. If he wanted me to elaborate some other time I would, but not now.

"Can I geek out for a minute?" I continued with a big stupid grin. "I can't believe I am backstage at Lee's Palace having drinks with Obsidian Butterfly!"

Everyone started laughing and I almost puked I was blushing so hard.

Eamon pulled out his phone and took a picture of my face. "That was the cutest thing I have ever seen. I just need a picture of the look on your face."

"I know, right?" Fray said. "Why aren't we geeking out about Lee's Palace? This is pretty epic!"

Fray turned and I got a look at the inside of the tattoo sleeve that covered his right arm. He had a white chess piece close to the inside of his wrist that I had to squint at to identify. I hoped he didn't notice I was staring, if he did I would just pass it off as shock.

I was pretty confident that he had a white bishop chess piece tattooed on his arm. I didn't know if I should be flattered or frightened. Jesse had tattoos but the only connection they had to me was the fact that I was present when he got them. And bankrolled one or two.

We chatted and drank and I got the full low down on how they changed their whole style since high school, and how after doing their 50th battle of the bands at the El Mocombo nightclub downtown an executive from Virgin Records approached them about a deal. Fray chocked it up to dumb luck but Eamon and Toby were confident that someone had finally recognized their talent.

"There are a lot of talented people that don't get

deals," Fray said flatly. It sounded like he was trying to force himself to sound casual because he was worried he sounded arrogant.

"So a bit of both then" Toby said with a laugh.

I took a sip of my drink and I smiled to myself as the warmth of the alcohol spread through my body. It wasn't that I didn't drink; it was that I liked to drink and I knew if I did it often it would become a problem.

When I first moved in with Ted after my parents died I used to steal booze from his liquor cabinet. I couldn't sleep and with visions dancing through my head drinking till I passed out was the only thing that made sense. Then I started drinking with Jesse for fun and I enjoyed the feeling a little too much. So I stopped and I decided to wait until I legally could drink before I started again, and even then it was only something I would do socially. With an addict as my social circle up until now it was the farthest thing from my mind.

Watching someone I loved do what they can to escape their problems only made me want to face mine head on with a clear head.

My parents would have expected me to be brave.

After a little while I glanced around the room and I noticed most of the groupies were gone, except the girl Fray had been talking to when we walked in. She seemed to be hovering around the edges of the room on purpose as if she was waiting for Fray to get bored. I wanted to grab his arm and show her the tattoo, then show her my ID so she knew I was the Bishop in question.

But after really looking at her I realized my time would be wasted. She wouldn't know what a chess piece was. She looked very young with really heavy makeup, which is probably how she got in the door. I would like to think Fray knew how old she actually was but I doubt it. If hooking up with an underage girl didn't tank any other rock star's career why would it tank his?

"So what are you doing with yourself Camille?" Fray asked. I paused for a minute and I felt Bliss nudge me in the ribs.

"You can tell them the truth," she said. "They might need you one day."

I shrugged my shoulders. I hadn't planned on lying anyhow.

"I'm a private investigator. I work for my Uncle Ted, he has a firm," I replied.

"No shit? That must be cool," Eamon said.

I chuckled. "Not really. Mostly a lot of paranoid people or harsh reminders that no one really trusts anyone anymore. And, of course, cheating spouses."

"Sounds okay to me," Fray added.

"Well if this rock star thing doesn't work out for you give me a call, I will show you the ropes," I continued. "You'll change your mind an hour into your first stakeout."

"Why do you do it then? If it's so boring?"

"I enjoy it. I enjoy solving problems, and helping people. I enjoy helping people get some small amount of justice in a way they might not get otherwise."

He smiled and something stirred inside me. I wondered if he would still like me once he got to know me now, and he figured out that I am not that big of a deal. I never have been.

"Have dinner with me," Fray said as we stared in each other's eyes.

"Right now?" I asked. He laughed which showed off his perfect white teeth.

"No! You're cute. I mean another day, like this week or something."

I smiled back and tried to look flirty. I wondered if I could capitalize on the adorable dork thing even though I am in my early 20's. What's the term? Adorkable?

"I would love to," I replied. I grabbed one of my business cards from my purse and wrote my cell number on the back. The napkin with October's number fell out and I snatched it up before anyone could see it.

I now had two alarmingly hot people who wanted to go out with me. I must have fallen into some alternate reality of some sort.

I handed him the card and his cold fingers brushed mine again. A tingle radiated through my body and I was suddenly hit with a pang of guilt.

I needed to end it with Jesse. And I needed to do it sooner rather than later. But how to go about it was a whole other story.

We drank a little more, and then Bliss decided we should head out. As I went to the door, Fray took my hand and pulled me into his embrace, hugging me close to his chest. He smelt like cinnamon and cloves. His mesh shirt felt weird on my cheek.

"It was good to see you, Camille," he said into my hair. I could see the rest of the band grinning ear to ear behind him.

"It was good to see you too," I replied when he finally let me go. Bliss had to grab my arm and pull me away.

Apparently someone up there was listening to me because when we got back to my place Jesse's car was parked out front and he was passed out in the driver's seat.

Bliss and I stood outside his car and watched him. I knew he was high. There was even drug paraphernalia in the passenger's seat.

"What the actual fuck," was all I could manage.

"What do you want to do?" Bliss asked. I took out my phone and started taking pictures, circling the car to make sure I got everything, even taking a screenshot of myself taking a picture so it had the time and date on it.

"You can go home. I am going inside," I said.

"You're not going to do anything about it?" she gestured wildly at the car, clearly ready to blow a gasket. She was hopping around like a boxer ready to pounce.

"Nope. I'm not ruining a great night with this bullshit," I replied. I pulled her into a hug, putting my chin on her shoulder.

"Thank you for an awesome evening," I said.

"Happy to. Let me know if you need me."

"Don't worry," I told her, tapping my forehead as I went up my walkway. "I got a plan."

15.

The next morning I texted Q. I would need her help if I was going to pull off my plan.

'Need to catch Captain Douche in some shit so I can dump him now. I got dates. You in?' was as much detail as I got into. I didn't expect to hear back that early but within five minutes I heard back with 'I got you boo. Me and Lemme coming by your crib later'. So I got myself and the house ready; my family was not home so it was perfect timing.

Most people would have flipped their lid last night when they found him passed out outside. Nope. That wasn't going to cut it. I was too angry.

It was time to really make my point.

Shortly after lunch Lemme and Q arrived, laptops in hand. They handed me a ginormous Frappuccino, they each had one in their free hand.

"Morning Bond. Thought we'd bring you some brain food," Q said happily. "Now, before we get started, you got dates? As in multiple?"

"Yep. Two," I pulled out my phone and brought up October's Facebook page and showed it to her. Her eyes widened a bit and Lemme scoped a look, then I showed them Fray.

"You have a date with Fray?!" they said in unison.

"Yep. I went to high school with the band. Didn't even know till I went to the concert last night. Weird, right?" I replied.

"Look at my girl racking up two hotties in no time," Q chuckled, nudging Lemme with her elbow. "We're proud of you boo boo!"

"Thank you," I answered as I showed them into the living room. "Now I need to get rid of the dead weight. I know he's using again but I want to catch him with that whore if I can."

Q opened her laptop and started typing. "Shouldn't be too hard. We just have to follow him and wait. We're down if you are."

"Cool. Let me grab my bag and we'll roll," I started running around the house grabbing my gear. Q kept typing on her computer; I assumed tracking his cell phone.

Some might say that going about breaking up with my long term boyfriend this way was devious.

But I preferred genius. Or inspired.

I was fucking proud of it.

"Got him," Q said and we rounded up our stuff. I grabbed some snacks out of the pantry and we headed out.

Jesse was at a bar downtown within walking distance of his whorehouse. I sat in the back seat in case he spotted the car I could hide easier. He didn't know Q so I wasn't too worried.

"He's in a bar during the day. That's commitment," Lemme said, typing furiously on her laptop. "Let me see if they have a security camera."

I sipped my Frappuccino. "Did I mention you guys are awesome?"

Before anyone could reply Jesse stumbled out of the doors of the bar to his car. We followed at a safe distance as he pulled away.

"Let's hope he doesn't get arrested before we can catch him," Q grumbled. I'd had the same thought but I didn't want to say it out loud.

"Quick sidebar, have you looked in on your little vampire girl lately?" Lemme asked. "Cuz she has a bunch of insanity posted on The Dollhouse that you need to see."

"Later. Later," I replied, watching Jesse's car ahead of us. I was already running scenarios of how I would just randomly run into him somewhere in my mind. He was intoxicated, I didn't know how heavily, so I didn't have to make it too complicated. I was so pumped on sugar and adrenaline I didn't even care. I just wanted it done so I could move on with my life.

We drove around after him while he picked up money and what I assumed was drugs. Anyone with half a brain could follow him and see what he was doing. I was shocked he could be so stupid, it made me wonder how far he had fallen down the rabbit hole. And how I could be so blind.

Finally he stopped and parked, walking a bit down the street to what I thought was a strip club.

"Isn't that blondie from....?" Q began. I looked up and it was the girl from the whore house. The same one he had cheated on me with.

"Day shift at a strip club?" Lemme chuckled.

"Watch my back, will you?" I said as I got out of the back of Q's car. I started down the street in their direction, pretending to read something on my phone while I put myself on a collision course with them. I ignored the anxiety that was dancing a jig in my stomach.

I banged head first into the girl; I looked up quickly and tried to look embarrassed.

"Oh my God, I am such a knob! I'm so....wait," I looked from her to him to her again. "You've got to be kidding me!"

"Camille!" Jesse exclaimed in total shock. "It's not what it looks like! What are you even doing here? And what did you do to your hair?"

I raised my hands in defeat. "You know what? I don't even care anymore. Jesse, we're done. For good. Goodbye."

"Wait! Cas, please!" Jesse began.

I smiled at the blonde. "You can have him, sweetheart. Good luck, by the way."

Jesse reached for me and I saw a flash of silver at his waist as his open button down shirt moved. I backed away, watching his face before I turned and ran back to Q's car.

"Go! Go! Go!" I exclaimed as I fell into Q's back seat, thumping on the back of Q's chair. She didn't say anything, pulled out and sped off.

It took a few minutes before I realized I was hyperventilating.

He had a gun.

A goddamn gun.

"I did it," I said out loud, smiling to myself. "The son of a bitch had a freaking gun!"

Lemme did the full turn but Q only glanced in the rear view.

"A gat? You pulled that off on a dude with a gat?" Lemme exclaimed, turning back to Q and poking her arm. "Yo, your girl's got some seriously big lady nuts. I probably would have pee peed my pants."

"Bond does not fuck around, bro. 007 type shit," Q replied. "Every time someone does something badass now I'm going to call it 007 type shit."

She and Lemme fist bumped, and then they did the same to me. I felt like I was part of their little clique and it made me really happy.

"I can't believe it worked! I wasn't sure it would all

line up and I was worried we were on a wild goose chase but, fuck me. It actually worked," I said with a laugh. "I feel like a champ. Taking control of my life for once."

Q smiled. "Glad we could help. That was fun! Got any more stalker shit we can help with?"

"Actually yeah. But we'll talk....," I began. Before I could continue Lemme handed me her laptop.

"You need to see this insanity, Bond," Lemme said. "Q, find a Starbucks. We're going to need more coffee."

Jane Lowry had been a busy girl.

She had revamped her Dollhouse page and persona, now claiming to be a 'real' vampire. She had the test results I had given her posted, my information blurred thankfully, and a post calling out Elliot Kinkaid. The entire Kinkaid family, for that matter, and calling them an 'elite network of supernatural creatures who operate like the mafia that are hiding in plain sight'. She even used the word 'cabal'. I would have to look that up later.

Q had gone in and got us more Frappuccino's. I handed her a 10 dollar bill when she came back but she brushed me off.

"This isn't good," I mumbled, taking pictures of each post with my phone. "Can you screenshot this stuff and email it to me?"

Lemme motioned to me and I handed her back her lap top. "No problemo. What are you going to do?"

"I don't know. I'll have to talk to Ted, and maybe my

cousin Kiera. She's a cop. Detective actually," I continued. "What the fuck is this girl thinking? She knows how dangerous the Kinkaid's are."

"Does she?" Lemme asked.

I cocked my head to the side. "Do you?"

"Yo, I watch the news. Maybe she doesn't give a shit."

"Maybe. It plays in to her whole gimmick really well. Either way I have to be careful or this will bite me in the ass."

"Should I be worried?" Lemme asked. As the lab tech that did the report it was a good question.

"Nope," Q answered before I could. "Lewis is good shit. Our asses are covered."

"We should head back. I have to talk to Ted," I said, taking a sip of my second giant Frappuccino.

"Word," Q replied, turning the car around and heading for home.

"Have you lost your freaking minds?" Ted yelled. He'd sat the three of us down on the living room couch like disobedient children and was pacing in front of us. It was like something out of a bad family sitcom.

"You know what Jesse is into now and who he is involved with! He could have hurt you! All of you!" Ted continued. He was yelling and his face was red.

I raised my hand. "In my defence I didn't see the gun until much later."

"The GUN?!? You forgot to mention the goddamn

gun, Camille!" he threw his hands in the air. "While I am happy to see the three of you bonding you will *not* be running any more dangerous missions, do you understand?"

"Yes sir," we said in unison.

I continued. "I also have a problem with my new client. Apparently she has taken her connection to the Kinkaid's public and, well...."

I motioned to Lemme to pull out her laptop. She brought up Jane's Dollhouse page and handed the laptop to Ted.

He sat and stared at the screen, I saw his fingers clicking through things. His expression stayed blank.

"Call Kiera. She should know about this," he said flatly.

"Why? All it is is the ranting of an unstable girl," I replied.

He chuckled. "About the family who killed your parents and countless others for a lot less."

I paused, a loss for words. That was the first time he had ever said so bluntly that the Kinkaid's had killed my parents. I had no idea how to respond.

"You girls want some dinner? I'm making spaghetti and meatballs," Ted handed Lemme back her laptop and went into the kitchen.

"Ok, what just happened?" Q asked.

I shrugged. "Don't ask. Ted makes a mean spaghetti dinner if you guys want to stick around."

"Awesome. I'm down. I love pasta," Lemme said, getting up and heading for the kitchen.

"Yo, I know it was dangerous and all but dude, you were awesome today," Q continued as she stood up, fist bumping me as she did. "You took control like a badass. Now you can do what *you* want. Go get some new clothes for your date with Fray!"

I smiled to myself. "Wow. I've not really done that before. Where should I go?"

16.

I woke the next day and I felt different. I checked my body several times to make sure I wasn't missing any body parts.

He was gone for good. I would have to learn how to live without him, and he was such a major part of my life for so long it would take time. But I could do it.

I texted Bliss on my way to work and told her I had news but I would call her when I was done for the day. It was too big, we had to discuss it. I also texted Kiera and told her I needed to chat about something important and asked if she had time for me to stop in today. When she said to come by for lunch I put together a file on Jane Lowry at the office, complete with the screenshots of her Dollhouse profile, and headed out on public transit.

Kiera's office was at police headquarters downtown, which was a good half an hour on the subway and gave me plenty of time to think.

One would think that I would be pondering the demise of my fifteen plus year relationship and Jesse's descent, but instead I was debating whether I should go look around for something to wear on my dates. I had October's number but I had given Fray mine....what if he didn't call?

I had not been to police headquarters since Kiera's detective announcement. They'd had a little ceremony and the whole Bishop family came; she was the youngest female detective in the Toronto Police Service's history.

At the time we had all stopped and paid our respects to my father's name on the fallen officer memorial. This time they had his photo up, he was in his uniform. I hadn't seen the picture in years.

I had pictures of my parents around the house but I didn't look at them often. They were in frames on a wall or a shelf, like many others. They blended into the background now. Not because I didn't care, more because it hurt too much to look.

My heart felt like it was sinking into my feet as I looked into his eyes. Learning to live without Jesse was small fish compared to having had to learn to live without my parents.

Who was I kidding? I was still learning. I would probably spend the rest of my life learning to be without them. I ached for them, for those eyes to look at me again.

I had to do a double take on the picture when the eyes seemed to move. I opened and closed my eyes, shook my head and walked closer to the photo.

Did it just blink?

"I thought I might find you here," Kiera's voice pulled me back to reality. She had takeout containers in her hand and I smelt bacon.

"Grilled cheese with bacon and fries, just like you like it," she said with a smile. She linked arms with me and we headed for the elevators.

"So I have a few things. You want to hear the drama or the case stuff?" I asked as I sat across from her. She sat at her desk and handed me one of the takeout containers.

"Always the drama," she replied.

"Jesse and I broke up."

"For good this time? That explains your hair, which is awesome by the way."

"The hair happened before but was part of it. Anyhoo, he is involved in some majorly bad shit."

She blushed. "Duh."

"I have some evidence but the good stuff is illegally obtained. I will hand it over eventually; it should give you enough to start looking into him. Ted has some too, not sure how clean his is."

"I don't need to see it particularly. If you give me addresses and general details I can figure it out. What's the case stuff?"

I handed her the file. "Remember that paternity case I told you about? Turns out girlie is a Kinkaid. And she's been writing some rotten shit online that Ted said you should see."

She opened the file and began flipping through as I ate my food. She munched on fries as she read.

"Awww, this is your first case too, isn't it? I'm so sorry, Cas."

"Don't be. I have to be able to handle stuff like this. It's necessary."

"I know. But it would be nice if they were all easy peasy, you know?" she said. She smoothed a few fallen light brown strands from her forehead, her ponytail was coming loose. She didn't dye her hair and I wondered if that was my natural colour too. It had been a while since I had seen it.

"I am happy you brought this to my attention, Camille," Kiera continued. "This girl knows about the Kinkaid's, doesn't she? I guess she wanted to get their attention."

"That's how it seems. She never mentioned any of her 'theories' to me directly," I said, making air quotes when I said theories. "If I hadn't already known about her Dollhouse persona I might never have found out."

"You better give your gear head a gold star."

"Around the office we call her Q."

"Yes, the mysterious Q! I have heard the legends. Did she also help with that illegal evidence against Jesse?"

"The video, yes. I'm hoping she will teach me how to hack into a webcam one day."

She laughed. "I wouldn't mind learning that myself."

Her phone started ringing and I took it as an opportunity to eat my food. My Dad used to bring home food from the diner by the station when I was a kid; it was my absolute comfort food.

"Detective Bishop," she answered on the third ring. I wondered if it would ever stop reminding me of my Dad.

She scrunched her eyebrows as she listened, I could hear some distortion that made me think the person was on a cell phone. She opened the file I gave her back up and flipped through till she found a specific page, examined it, then signed off from her phone call.

"You got plans this afternoon kid?" she asked as she gathered her stuff, slipping my file into her bag. "Well you do now. Let's go."

"Can you just bring me? Just like that?" I asked as I followed her out, bringing our takeout containers. She had barely touched her food; I assumed she would eat in the car.

"Generally no but this is an exception."

This may make me super weird, but I love an older model Crown Victoria. Yes, it was a tired stereotype that all detectives drove one but it was a great classic car and there wasn't a good argument against that.

Kiera had clearly asked for an older model to drive while on the job, she was new enough that she probably had access to the brand new ones but she was smart and had good taste so we got to go wherever she was taking me in my preferred mode of transport.

I finished my food, and after about fifteen minutes of driving I asked, "What's this about, Kiera?"

She sighed, looking at me in the mirror then actually turning to glance at me before saying, "There is a body."

"Come again?" I said, my voice a crackly squeak. She wouldn't take me to see Jesse's body.　　Would she?

No.

That's cruel.

"A woman's body was found in the Humber River by the Old Mill Bridge. Apparently a wedding party spotted it while taking pictures outside. What a shitty story that would be."

"What does this have to do with me?"

"She matches your client's description. It could be nothing, but if it is take it as a professional courtesy that you get the heads up before someone contacts the office."

I couldn't speak. I tried, my mouth moved but there was no voice. All I could think was that the Kinkaid's sure were efficient. What she posted could not have been up for more than twenty four hours.

"You ok, Cas?" Kiera asked. I shook my head no, my voice still gone.

"You couldn't have known," she continued. "You're a smart girl, and good at what you do. I know you. If you'd had even an inkling that she was going to do something like this you would have approached her differently. Diffused the situation."

I managed to croak out, "We don't even know that it's her."

"Honey, I'm good at my job too. In this situation I would be genuinely shocked if it wasn't her. You don't talk like that about the Kinkaid's and have no repercussions."

"Fuck," I replied. "Fuck. I have to call Ted. Like right now."

"Wait till we have a confirmation before you call in the cavalry," she reached over and put her hand on my arm. "It will be alright, Cas. Even if it is her. This isn't your fault. You did your job. You couldn't have known she would react this way."

"I figured she would go the lawyer way."

The front of the Old Mill group of buildings was swarming with police and one news van. We parked behind one of the cruisers and followed the officers down a long flight of stairs to the river bank.

Dorien Reid was the first to see us, the sour expression on his face made me angry. Now was probably an inappropriate time to tell him to go fuck himself.

"What is this, bring a Bishop to work day?" he snapped.

"It's relevant Detective Reid," Kiera told him. "Do we have an ID on the body?"

"No. Her face is bashed in pretty good. We haven't found a purse or a wallet and she has no tattoos."

I tried to rack my brain for things that would identify Jane Lowry, but all I could see was the white sheet about 20 feet behind Reid. There had to be something other than the blood anomaly.

"Other than the blood thing can you think of anything

that would identify your client, Cas?" Kiera asked. One of the tech guys stood up from beside the body, holding something between a pair of long tweezers. He waved Reid over and Kiera followed him, motioning for me to stay where I was.

The tech put whatever it was in a baggie and handed it to Kiera, who took one look at it and headed back over to me.

Fuck.

Kiera flashed the baggie so I got a vague idea of what it was. "Your business card."

"There's a bracelet. A Pandora style charm bracelet. Every time I saw her she was wearing it," I told her, the first time I met Jane flashing in my mind.

Kiera handed me another baggie I hadn't seen her grab. All I could do was look down at it and the brightly coloured beads of Jane Lowry's bracelet.

"Oh God," was all I could manage before I turned to the side and threw up.

Kiera sat me down out of sight from the body and brought me a bottle of water. I was pleased that I hadn't had to look directly at the body, I didn't know if I could take that. One of the many reasons why I didn't become a cop.

Ted appeared. I hadn't seen Kiera call him. I wasn't sure how much time had passed since we arrived. My thoughts were swimming so much I wasn't sure I knew how to walk.

"Hey kid," Ted said as he sat down beside me.

"Are we going to get sued?" I asked, staring off at the river.

"Camille...."

"Everything was going so well. I was reclaiming my life, and my first case had gone smoothly. I really felt like I had helped her in some way. I thought she was smart enough to go the lawyer route. I thought that I would be walking up to Elliot Kinkaid and introducing myself while I served him papers. But now I'm the name on a business card in the pocket of his latest victim."

Ted sighed and ran his fingers through his hair. "I wish I had all the answers for you. I wish I could wave a magic wand and make all this disappear."

"I puked. Is that terrible?"

"No. If you were an actual cop you would get tormented but you're not so don't worry."

"Dorien Reid makes my skin crawl. I think he's dirty. I have for years."

"Don't quote me but I do too."

I turned and looked at him. "You are just full of revelations lately."

"Let's go home, kid. We'll get some froyo on the way," he stood and held out his hand to help me up. When I was finally on my feet he hugged me tightly.

"I miss my parents," I said into his chest.

"I do too, Cas. I do too."

We didn't talk much in the car. He was true to his

word and we got frozen yoghurt on the way home. I assumed he knew that froyo doesn't solve any problems but it did keep me calm for a while and made me think about something else other then the fact that my first client was dead.

"I have to fight the urge not to call Jesse," I told Ted as we drove.

"No one would blame you if you did, Cas," he replied.

"No. I have come too far. This is the perfect test to prove I can go on without him," I said. We finally got to the house and I held his arm as we walked inside.

"Any chance you got a Valium?" I asked. "I don't know how the hell I am going to sleep tonight."

He patted my shoulder as I sat down to take off my shoes. I left my stuff in a pile in the hallway, grabbed my phone and signalled to Ted that I was heading upstairs.

I flopped down on my bed and smushed my head into my pillow. I grabbed my bear and pulled my knees up to my chest so I was in the foetal position.

I should text Q and Lemme, let them know what happened before they saw the news. The cops might want to talk to Lemme since she was the tech who did the blood work, but I would find a way around that. I'm sure the lab techs were running the blood already and Kiera had a copy of both results, the one we gave Jane and my copy, so they would figure it out. But I could not bring myself to type the words. I wasn't even sure if I had processed the whole thing myself.

I shut my eyes and tried to clear my head. When I

opened them again it was dark outside.

My cell phone was flashing that I had missed a call. I must have slept through it ringing. I wondered if Ted had drugged my froyo.

I didn't recognize the number and when I dialled into my answering machine I was surprised by the voice I heard.

"Hey Camille, its Fray. I mean Noah," he began, his voice a low purr, "Or Fray. You can call me either. I was thinking about you and thought I would give you a call. And so now you have my number, in case you needed it or something. I'm sorry....I'm usually much cooler than this. Give me a call."

I deleted the message and hung up the phone. I debated calling him. I wanted to talk to someone, someone who could be comforting. Now that I was totally free there was no reason I couldn't give him a chance to try, not just as a rebound. I mean, I knew Noah. Unless his personality had fundamentally changed since high school he was a good guy. If I hadn't been tethered to Jesse things could have been different. Maybe I would figure out I had real feelings for him all along.

I rolled on to my back and dialled his number, saving it in my phone before I hit dial.

Fray picked up on the second ring. "Hello?"

"Hey Fray, it's Camille," I said, and then it dawned on me that he probably had my number programmed into his phone.

"Hey! It's good to hear from you. How are you?"

"You got a few hours? It's been a long couple of days."

"Come meet me and we can talk in person. Coffee, a drink, whatever."

I pondered the idea for a minute then said, "Sure. Where do you want me to meet you?"

"I'll come get you. You still live in the same place? Text me the address."

My brain was so disconnected from my body that I almost didn't look in the mirror before I went out with Fray. I ran a quick brush through my hair and cleaned up my makeup but stayed in the same outfit. I was presentable, which was important, but I also didn't look like I was trying too hard.

I tapped Ted on the shoulder as he dozed in his chair in the living room. "I'm going out."

"Jesse?" he asked, opening one eye.

I smiled. "No. Noah Fray from high school."

"Your old lab partner?"

"Yep. He's a rock star now. Like has a record deal and everything. I thought it might clear my head before we have to talk to Lewis."

He smiled and shut his eye. "Sounds good. Be careful."

"I will," I said, kissing him on the cheek as I headed for the door.

Fray drove an old black Jaguar, suped up and gorgeous. I seemed to remember that the car belonged to his parents when we were in high school. He must have ended up with it and got it done up when he got the record money.

He got out of the car and glided towards me, like he was floating or something. He smiled and my heart melted. He was wearing a long sleeve black t-shirt and blue jeans, his hair slicked back in the perfect Elvis style hairdo.

"Hey. Thanks for coming to get me," I said, wrapping my arms around his waist and pulling him to me. His smell wrapped around me like a warm blanket. It reminded me of apple pie.

He chuckled. "Well hello to you too. Not that I am complaining about hugs but is everything ok?"

"Not by a fucking long shot," I said as I pulled away from him. He opened the passenger door for me and I got in.

"Good news though, Jesse Garrow is gone for good!" I told him with probably too big of a smile. He glanced at me quickly, clearly not sure how to reply. He focused on driving; I didn't ask where we were going.

"That's not the problem though! So don't worry," I continued. "Have you ever thought that you did something good for someone only to have it turn into something really bad? And that someone got hurt?"

I leaned forward in my seat and put my head in my hands. "My first solo client. After years of paying my dues to prove myself, busting my ass and doing all the crap work, I get a client on my own. And you know what happens? She takes the damn info I give her and uses it to piss off the mother fucking mob and gets herself killed. Killed! As in dead. As in face bashed in and dropped by the goddamn Humber River."

Fray glanced at me again and said nothing.

"Oh and the Jesse thing is like a drop in the bucket. The fact that I caught him with the hooker he is currently pimping and a gun in his waistband has just flown past me. It's just more proof that I'm a goddamn moron and in over my head. What the fuck am I supposed to do? I'm sorry; you must think I am a lunatic. I just unloaded my whole bullshit life on you."

"No! Not at all. Sorry if I freak you out but I'm just happy to be able to talk to you. We spent so much time together in high school it was weird when we just stopped talking when it was done. Sorry if that's creepy."

I touched his arm softly. "It's so not. I didn't know you thought that much of me. I honestly didn't."

He laughed loudly at that. I wasn't going to tell him what Bliss said, I didn't want to embarrass him.

Or myself for that matter. Bliss could have told me that just to boost my confidence. It could be a ploy they both invented so I would sleep with Fray.

"So do you want to know where we are going?" he asked.

"As long as it's not an opium den or a brothel I'm cool," I hit his arm playfully, "Did I tell you Jesse runs a fucking brothel? Sorry, I'm going to stop talking about him now."

"Speaking of high school," I continued, trying to gloss over my continuing to mention my ex. "How did you end up connecting with Bliss?"

"We actually never lost touch. I helped her get into nursing school; she helped us with our look."

"Well you guys look good so you should thank her."

He blushed. "I appreciate that. It hasn't been easy finding our place but the fans have been really responding so I guess its working."

"That's amazing," I turned in my seat so I could really look at him. "I am so unbelievably happy for you. I feel like such a shmuck that I didn't know it was you guys."

"Really? You're happy for me?"

"Fuck yeah! Of course. How could I not be? I like to think we were friends at one point and how could I not be happy that my friend is living his dream."

He smiled at me, his face was scary perfect. The twinkle in his eyes made my heart race. It felt good when he smiled at me.

"I appreciate that. It can be kind of overwhelming at times but for the most part it's awesome. I'm lucky that we all have different strengths, me and the guys I mean, so if one of us is awesome at something that person takes the reigns and the others trust they will do what's best for all of us. Like the business part isn't my strong suit but its Toby's so he takes the lead and we all come along."

"It's amazing that you have your friends with you during this amazing adventure."

He smiled again. "Yeah, I got lucky. What about your friends?"

"You mean Bliss?"

"No. Your friends from high school."

"Oh," I paused, I could feel myself blushing. "I don't really have any of those. That's why reconnecting with Bliss has been so great because...."

He reached over and took my hand. "You must get lonely."

I turned away as my eyes welled up with tears. "You have no idea."

"Well you don't need to be lonely anymore," he squeezed my hand. I managed to push back the tears as we pulled up to a warehouse that had been converted into lofts.

"My place," he said before I could speak. "I'm not presuming anything. I just have an awesome terrace and make a mean cappuccino."

"It's actually a good idea. I can't really say my client is dead in public without turning some heads."

He got out and came around to open the door for me. "Or talk about whatshisface."

"Let's not talk about him, if we can avoid it. I can't believe I stayed for as long as I did," I said as he took my hand and helped me out of the car. I stumbled and fell into his arms; I could feel myself blushing again.

"Sorry. Still a klutzy dork," I tried not to sound like an asshole. I felt like a jackass for talking about myself so much.

"You're alright, Cas," he told me.

His converted loft was bloody amazing. Huge open

concept kitchen and living space, the kitchen done in black, white and grey and shone like it never got touched. His living room was sunk down a little bit, with a sprawling black leather sectional and a gorgeous dark wood coffee table with a large TV on a stand.

"Holy shit. This place is incredible," I blurted out, trying to take in how amazing this place was. Immediately to the left when you walked in was two doors, I assumed the bathroom and bedroom, but every other wall other than that was enormous windows.

"Thanks. Do you want a coffee?" he asked.

"Sure," I replied. I wandered farther in, looking around like a kid seeing a toy store for the first time. He left me to wander as he went to the kitchen.

"So I guess the question of if you guys are doing ok is a dumb one," I said.

"Oh, this is not from the record deal. Well, not just from the record deal. I have a degree in finance from U of T and I've made some money investing that paid for most of this. Music wasn't always my main focus. My parents insisted I get a degree in something useful so I had a backup plan. I'm glad I did."

"I should have had a backup plan. I suppose I could waitress at Ren full time."

"You think you'll get fired over this?"

"I don't know. It depends on what Ted and his partner thinks. But I will probably get demoted. It will be hard to get clients if they find out my previous experience ended up dead."

He paused. "Waitressing at a strip club is not a decent plan, Cas."

"What about what Bliss does?"

"Bliss is only doing that to make money to pay for school. She doesn't have to break her neck making money, she can pay off her loans fast, and by the time she is done school she will be almost debt free. And she won't be indebted to her family in any way, which is what she was most worried about. If she is comfortable doing it, why the fuck not?"

"Oh, I'm not knocking it. More power to her that she can pull it off. I didn't know if you were against it because of what you said about waitressing."

"I said that because being a waitress fucking sucks. I waited tables in university and it wasn't even at a strip club and it sucked balls," he brought over two shiny black mugs of coffee and we sat on the couch. "Bliss makes more money if she sneezes in Ren than you probably do in a week."

"I know it's not a viable plan. I feel like a moron that I had no other plan for my life."

He took a sip of his drink. "Don't feel bad. Not many other people do. What is your cousin up to? The one that was in the same grade as us. The, uh...."

"The bitchy one? You can say it. She's quite proud of it. Her name is Poppy, by the way. And she's a cop. Most of my cousins are."

I took a sip of my coffee. He was right; he did do an awesome job. I stared out the window at the night sky,

I was so zoned out I didn't notice him move closer to me.

"Before things progress any further can I say something?" I began, putting my coffee down beside his.

He shifted uncomfortably. "Sure. What's up?"

"Well, on top of being a huge dork in general I have never been with anyone other than....him. Like never even been hit on or anything like that. I have no experience with this. Never even been kissed...."

He leaned over and kissed me, his lips were smooth but surprisingly cold. I tried to ease in to the kiss as I pulled him closer to me. When I put my hand on his chest he felt cold through his shirt.

He wrapped his arms around me, his tongue passing my lips and gently caressing mine. Kissing Fray was what I had imagined; passionate and exciting in ways I hadn't ever felt.

But I could not forget that this was Noah. My lab partner for however many years in high school. The guy that I had never given more than a passing thought as an acquaintance, mainly because I assumed he never thought of me at all.

Would it have changed anything if I had registered that men thought of me?

Probably not.

It may have been a confidence boost in the times that Jesse took off and I had no one. But I doubt I would have left him.

He pulled away from me, cradling me with one arm as he stroked my cheek with his fingers.

"I'm sorry if I was really bad at that," I said, my voice breathy as I tried to dial back my excitement.

He laughed louder than I expected, burying his face in my neck.

"You are so cute I don't have the words."

"Oh God," I blurted out and he started laughing even harder.

"That's amazing! You're so excited already and I haven't really done anything," he said happily.

"I don't think we can have sex yet."

He pulled away from me so he could look me in the eyes. "Ok, where did that come from?"

"Well, things lead to *things* and I didn't want to piss you off if I didn't. I don't think it's a good idea because I don't want you to think you're just a rebound."

He smiled, shrugged his shoulders, and kissed me again. "Ok. Don't worry. I get it. I would have said the same thing but that I don't want you to think you're just a conquest."

"Saying that would make me think it more."

He sighed loudly and pulled away from me, sitting close to me so we were eye to eye.

"I know you will need time. And I know you are worth the time," he said, running his finger along my cheek. "I'm willing to put in the time, if you are."

I smiled and kissed him again. I couldn't help myself, his touch was addictive. He was cold, the tips of his fingers oddly cold, but it wasn't weird. The situation, on the other hand, was a little weird. It seemed a bit too perfect that this incredible man would fall in my lap as soon as I ousted the shitty one.

Jesse's smile flashed through my mind and it made my heart ache. I was tired of caring about someone who didn't give a flying rat's ass about me.

"I should go before I get myself into a position I don't want to get out of," I said as I pulled away from him, my voice all breathy. I knew if we kept going like this I would get to a point where I would let my arousal override my better judgement.

"Have dinner with me," he asked, running his fingers through my hair. I closed my eyes as he touched me, enjoying the softness of his touch.

"Right now?"

He laughed. "No, silly. Tomorrow. Or the day after. Whenever you want."

"Sure," I said with a smile. "I will probably need to relax after tomorrow. Hopefully I still have a job."

"You will. I'm sure your Uncle and his partner knows you were only doing what you thought was best," he kissed me on the forehead. "Now let's go before I don't want to let you leave."

I held Fray's free hand as we drove. It just felt right. I kissed him goodbye and tried to push everything I was feeling into that kiss. I wanted him to know how much this whole thing meant to me. How much him putting himself out there to show me he really genuinely cared meant to me.

"Call me," I said when I finally pulled away. He smiled at me; his clear blue eyes sparkled like a calm ocean. My breath caught as his lips curled upwards, I could not believe the way my body reacted when he smiled at me.

"Right now?" he replied, running the tip of his finger along my jaw line. I smiled again and got out before I could change my mind.

It was late but I texted Q and Lemme anyway. Just a simple heads up that they had found that poor girl's body and if they were needed I would let them know, but I would do what I can to keep them out of it. They both sent me a quick note back that said if they were needed to let them know, and they were sorry and hoped I was ok. Q even added that I just needed to remember how bad ass I was.

I certainly didn't feel like a bad ass. I felt like a scared little girl that needed her Mommy and Daddy. It least I had a few friends now, for the first time in my life.

And Fray. Now I had Fray.

17.

Someone, I was assuming Ramona, had cleaned up the L&B conference room. It was not often used, but she had dusted and laid out a spread of doughnuts and other baked goods along with the coffee.

Chris and Ted sat on one side of the massive oak table, I sat on the other. I did my best to hide my fear by stuffing my face.

"Thank you for meeting with us Camille," Chris began.

My eyebrow rose. "I didn't think it was optional?"

"Not now, Camille," Ted cut in.

I raised both my hands in defeat. "Sorry, sarcasm is apparently my default setting."

"We are sorry about what happened to Miss Lowry," Chris continued. "After reviewing your file and notes and talking to Q we know that you only did your job. We didn't need to dig through your stuff because we both know this isn't your fault but we thought it was best to be fully aware of the situation before the police came to our door. Now, Ted told me that Kiera is in the loop?"

"She is. I took her a file after what was posted online," I said. "Dorien Reid was also at the scene where the body was found."

"He's homicide. He should be present at a....homicide."

"I know. I just figured it was worth mentioning."

"Thank you," Chris said. "Now, Ted also informed me of the situation with your delinquent former boyfriend."

I scowled at Ted. "And that is relevant how?"

"If dummy comes to the door with a gun it's relevant, Camille," Ted replied.

"He wouldn't do that," I told him.

"Can you guarantee that? He showed up at Ren, I wouldn't put it past him," Chris said. "But in light of this we think you should not take on any more clients, for now. Because of the nature of Mrs. Tanner's case I will be finishing that out for you. You will get any money that she pays out, of course."

"Are you firing me?" I asked. I had to fight back tears.

"No! We just think you should take some time. A lot has happened and we wouldn't want you to have to tap out because of stress," Chris said, and I burst into tears. I put my head down on the table and sobbed.

Both men shifted uncomfortably in their chairs, the creaking of leather had a weird echo. I understood how female crying would make a guy like Chris Lewis uncomfortable but Ted should be used to it.

I felt a big warm hand on my shoulder; Ted had gotten up and was beside me now. I stayed where I was while he lovingly rubbed my back.

"It will be alright, kid," Chris began. "Stuff like this proves your stones as an investigator. You will bounce back. We won't allow you to do anything else."

I nodded my head but kept it flat on the table. Everything moved a lot slower from the table. It would probably move even slower from the floor but I didn't want to be *that* girl.

I heard Chris leave the room but Ted stayed. I wasn't a big crier, and it wasn't something I did in public except in extreme situations.

Somehow Ted was always the one by my side when I cried.

I turned my head so I could see him and said, "I hope I am lucky enough to find a guy like you someday."

"I am not that great, sweetheart. You'll figure that out when you have more experience with men," he replied. "Let me take you home."

I texted Bliss when I got home and filled her in about my work situation. I didn't mention Fray, I didn't feel much like talking and I said that in the message. She said okay, and to get in touch with her when I was up and about.

I decided to do something mindless and watch TV. After about twenty minutes I was surprised when my phone rang.

"Hello?" I answered without looking at the call display, immediately regretting it.

"Hi," Lisa's singsong voice was a bit of a shock.

"Hey, how are you?"

"I'm ok. How are you? How's Jesse?"

"We broke up. But that's not important. What's up with you?"

"You broke up? You can't just brush that off. It's pretty serious. What happened?"

"It's a long story and I don't want to talk about it right now. What I will say is that if you see him try to avoid him. If you can't, just smile and play dumb."

"Men are terrible, aren't they? This new guy I'm dating is totally off the rails. Which reminds me, do you think you could do me a favour?"

"What kind of a favour?"

"Well, this guy has not answered the phone since noon and I was wondering if you could GPS track his phone number for me?"

I checked the time on the TV. "It's two o'clock, Lisa."

"I know but I really need to know where he is."

"I'm sorry Lisa. I can't do that."

Her tone turned angry. "Why not?"

"We've talked about this before. I can't just do that on a whim. It's an invasion of someone's privacy and I could get in a lot of trouble if he decides to be a dick and report me. I could lose my job, and I am not willing to risk that for him not answering the phone for two hours."

Silence, then, "Oh. Ok."

More silence. She finally said she had to go and talk to you later so fast I couldn't get a word in and hung up.

I reprogrammed her number in my phone to say do not answer instead of her name and put my phone out of reach. Luckily she wasn't my only friend anymore.

My phone rang again and I didn't answer. Ted would call the house if he needed me and whoever was calling my cell could wait.

Mindless TV watching was helpful. I could never understand why some people hated on television. Sometimes turning your brain off and doing something completely mindless could be therapeutic.

But I certainly wasn't going to sit around and watch TV all the time until I was deemed fit to go back to work.

I grabbed my phone and quickly texted Chris Lewis, asking him if it was still ok for me to waitress at Ren while I was off. I put it back out of reach and went back to the TV. He would probably need time to think about it.

Ted came back with Cuddy close to dinnertime. Everyone was all smiles and sunshine today, Cuddy was in fine form babbling away through dinner like a two year old enamoured with his own voice. Poppy came in as Ted was putting food on the table and I waited for the jabs to begin. She had to know by now what happened and I couldn't imagine she would let it slide without a comment.

"So, Camille, how does it feel to completely fail at life?" Poppy asked. "I mean, a dead client and a gun toting asshole boyfriend? Your judgement is fantastic!"

"Poppy, I swear to God," Ted began and I raised my hand to silence him.

"No, no, it's ok. Let her go. I need this right now," I said. "I need someone to point out my errors. And while the situation with Jesse is a huge fuck up on my part, I admit that, he's gone for good this time. *I got rid of him and it's done.* If taking charge of my life makes me a fuck up, then I am more than happy to be a goddamn fuck up."

Everyone went to speak and I yelled, "I'm not finished!" I slammed my fist on the table hard enough it almost knocked over our glasses.

"In terms of my client, well, if you are such a cold hearted asshole that you could mock me over something so horrible as that poor girl's murder than you are an even bigger grade A c-word than I had originally thought. You're an officer of the law, for Christ's sake Poppy. If I recorded your behaviour and played it for your C.O you would be riding a desk till you shoot yourself in the head and frankly I am starting to think I should because *that is exactly what you deserve you disgusting bitch*," I growled, my clenched fist still on the table where I slammed it.

They all stared at me with their mouths gaping open. I felt like going on, like really tearing into Poppy like I had rarely done before but I stopped myself. I had made my point, continuing would only water it down.

"Well, Jesus, Camille. It was just a joke," Poppy replied.

Her face turned bright red and she lowered her eyes. She stared so intently at her food I thought she would burn a hole through the plate and the table. I thought about getting up and walking out, but the idea of making my cousin as uncomfortable as possible was too good to pass up.

We went through the rest of dinner without much talk. Cuddy babbled on about some randomness and Ted seemed engaged but I knew he was also watching me. I wanted to ask him how I was supposed to react but stayed silent.

When I got back to my phone there was a random text from Bliss.

'Don't forget who loves me' was all it said. I wasn't entirely sure who she was referring to so I texted her back a huh?

There was a message on my answering machine from a number I didn't recognise. I left it alone; I assumed it was Jesse calling from a random number thinking I wouldn't answer if he called from his. The fact that he did not know I would think of that was almost insulting.

My phone sat on my bed as I decided to dig around in my closet. If I was going to continue to see Fray I would need stuff to wear and I wasn't sure I had anything adequate.

Ted came in a little later and began piling file boxes beside my desk.

He sighed when he finally had them all in, closing the door behind him.

"So, yeah. Here."

I looked at the boxes, at him, and then repeated the action. "I don't get it."

"The files. Your Dad's," he began, gesturing at the boxes. "They're yours. If you have any questions please ask. Don't know if I can answer them, but I will try."

"Why now?" I asked. He sat down on my bed and rubbed his chin stubble with his hand.

"You seem like you need a distraction."

"And you think this is an okay distraction, considering they probably killed her?"

"I thought about that. I trust you. And I also know you won't do anything half cocked. I think this will keep you focused on something other than what happened to Jane Lowry. Maybe even help you feel closer to Will."

I smiled at the thought of my Dad. I missed him a lot. The anniversary of their murder was coming up.

"I can't believe it's been ten years," he said as if he had read my mind.

I sighed, sitting beside him. "Me either. It feels like yesterday but a million years ago at the same time."

"I know. I want you to know that I can't possibly miss them as much as you but I do miss them. Both of them."

I leaned my head on his shoulder and closed my eyes, listening to his breathing for a few minutes before I opened them again.

"I don't know if I ever told you that I thought of your Mom as a friend. Marie was one of a kind."

"I hope I can be like her when I grow up."

"You already are, kid. More then you know."

18.

When I woke up the next day there were texts from Q and Lemme. Something about Lemme needing to drop some science on me, and rather than dissecting it in text message I told them to come by when they had a chance.

No one was home when I went into the kitchen. There was a note from Ted on the kitchen table, telling me to enjoy my vacation and call if I needed anything. Since I'd had no luck with my clothes I'd decided to go shopping. Perhaps it would help me enjoy the forced time off.

I was fed and showered and sitting down to watch television when Q texted me back, saying they would be by in an hour if that was cool with me. I agreed and went to check the fridge to see what we had for drinks and snacks.

"Wup up Bond," Q was all smiles when I answered the door.

"Good morning ladies," I replied, motioning them into the living room.

"Are we alone?" Lemme asked once they got settled. I offered them something to drink and they both said no, so I sat across from them in Ted's chair and got ready to listen.

"Yep, we're alone. I have to warn you that I don't really speak science so you will have to break it down for me," I told her.

"Alright, well, since I ran that test for you it got me thinking. Now, don't get mad at me but I kept a little of the samples you gave me because I wanted to run tests on this blood weirdness that they both had," Lemme began. "Because, for real, this shit was just weird. I had never read or heard of anything like it. And if a scientist was going to discover vampires you bet your ass it was going to be me!"

"But anyhoo," she continued before we could interrupt her. "This blood was like nothing I had ever seen, so I started just doing random shit to it. We had these rats in the lab who had cancer that we were testing their blood for treatments and cures and shit like that, and well, I put some of your girl's blood with the rat cancer blood and it fucking cleaned it, dude."

I stared blankly at her. Q had a similar look on her face.

"Are you two deaf or something? The girl's blood

cleaned the cancer from the rat blood. So I injected the rat with the blood and it's shrunk the cancer and cleared it from its blood. It's better than chemo," Lemme said.

"I don't understand. Are you saying that Jane Lowry's blood is treating the rat's cancer?" I asked.

"I'm saying it fucking cured the damn cancer, dude. Whatever this anomaly is, it cures cancer," Lemme replied.

"Holy shit," Q's mouth fell open. I leaned back in Ted's chair, completely speechless.

"Holy shit is an understatement. This is huge. Beyond huge, actually. This could make my goddamn career. If this is legit we would be set for life," Lemme proclaimed with lots of hand gestures. I still had no words.

"Have you told anyone else?" I finally asked.

"No way, dude! This is Kinkaid blood. I don't want to die unless it's bloody important," she frowned when she saw the look on my face. "Sorry. I didn't mean it like that. We need to talk to a lawyer before I tell anyone."

"How is this even possible? How can blood fix blood? Or cure a disease that attacks the blood?" I asked.

"Beats the fuck out of me. And I'm the damn science," Lemme replied. "But something about this anomaly, I'm wondering if this is another reason that people think they are vampires. If they're blood fights off crazy diseases as well as cures them, it may do something with their aging process also."

"That would explain why they have never been photographed," I said. They both turned to me with crazy expressions on their faces.

"The only member of the Kinkaid family that has been photographed is the wife and she is not a blood Kinkaid," I continued. "But Elliot Kinkaid and his kids, nothing."

"Maybe you weren't looking in the right place," Q mumbled, pulling out her laptop.

"I hope you can prove me wrong," I replied. "I had to do some covert shit to get that sample I gave you, so if anyone asks lie about it. If they find out I got his blood they will probably kill us both."

I sighed loudly, running my fingers through my hair. "I'm sorry for getting you guys involved in this."

They both paused, staring angrily at me.

"Shut up, are you for real?" Q started. "Why would you say that?"

"Yeah, seriously. This is the greatest damn job ever, and we love you dude. We're your squad. Don't ever worry about that," Lemme finished.

I could feel myself blushing. "Thanks, guys. I should call my cousin Kiera, the homicide cop, and see if we can find a way to get more samples from Jane's body."

"Can you do that kind of shit? It sounds hella weird," Lemme asked.

I shrugged. "I can ask. Her blood could be the key to snagging Kinkaid; it would be useful for the case."

I grabbed my phone and dialled Kiera. It rang for a bit and she finally answered.

"Detective Bishop," she said quickly. She hadn't looked at her call display or she would have said my name.

"Hi Kiera, its Cas," I began. "I have a weird thing I wanted to mention to you that might help with the Lowry case."

"Sorry kid, I don't have a ton of time so make it quick or I will have to call you back."

"Alright. Have you guys taken any of Jane Lowry's blood by any chance? Cuz this anomaly that my tech found could be the key to solving this thing."

"Actually we have. Was that it?"

"Any chance you want to send some to my tech? Since she was the first person to spot the anomaly with a bit more to work with she may be able to pinpoint exactly what it is."

"We have techs of our own for that, Cas."

"I know. I just thought I would put it out there. And just cuz you have techs maybe they aren't as good as mine."

Kiera chuckled. "Let me see what I can do. It's not a bad idea, will just take some manoeuvring on my part. And you'll owe me."

"Of course. Thanks Kiera."

"Alright, kid. I will call you later," I couldn't stop smiling when I hung up the phone.

"Is she going to hook it up?" Lemme asked, her eyes so wide she looked like a kid in a candy store.

"Maybe. Is she normally this excited by the science?" I asked Q with a big smile.

"You have no idea," Q replied. Her eyes did not move from her computer screen. She was beginning to look angry. Her perfectly drawn eyebrows were almost a straight line from her scowl.

"You good, Q?" I asked.

"No! How the fuck can there be no goddamn pictures? *Of any of them?!* They're relatively high profile; Big Poppa Kinkaid was crazy high profile in the late 90's, early 2000's. This is fucked up, yo."

"That's exactly what I said, and I can't dig nearly as deep as you can," I began. "Ted gave me my Dad's old files on Kinkaid so I will look for one in there."

"Your Dad was looking into Kinkaid?" Q asked.

"Yeppers. And Ted thinks he killed both my parents when I was 13 years old."

They both stopped and stared at me. I assumed they knew a little about my background but that was a bit of a bomb to drop.

"That's pretty heavy. Do we need to clear this with the boss man? Is he worried about you getting into it with the Kinkaid's?"

"He knows I'm careful."

Q studied my face for a moment then went back to her computer. Lemme pulled out her phone and began scrolling.

"Have you figured out what you're going to tell the other people in your lab when they ask why the cops are sending you samples Lemme?" I asked.

She smiled. "Nope. But my T.A is cool, she'll totally help."

"Who?" Q asked.

"Rory Woo," Lemme replied.

Q snickered. I wanted to ask what that was about but I didn't.

"Anyhoo, it'll be alright," Lemme continued. "It's not like I'm making meth or doing some crazy ass bullshit that could get me arrested. They're more worried about people acting out Breaking Bad these days."

"Well, there is no guarantee that it will show but my cousin is pretty awesome," I said.

The front door opened and Poppy appeared, as if she had heard me say cousin and wanted to show my friends that Kiera was an exception.

Q didn't look up from her computer. She had worked for L&B long enough I assumed she'd had some dealing with Poppy at some point; by her lack of interest either Q and Poppy had crossed paths in a negative way or she'd heard enough about Ted's daughter to know not to bother.

"Do these girls know everything you touch turns to shit, Camille?" Poppy said as she passed by the doorway. "You might want to warn them before they decide to be your friend."

"Who the fuck is this bitch?" Lemme asked, her face contorting in anger. Q held up her hand as a signal for both of us to wait.

Poppy did whatever she came to do and left without another word. She had probably forgotten something.

"That is one of my other cousins. Ted's daughter, Poppy," I replied.

"I suggest ignoring her. She's stuck in angry she-bitch mode. Not sure how the boss man created her," Q said.

"Her mother is pretty vile," I told her

"How can there be no goddamn pictures anywhere of these people?" Q shut her laptop in frustration. "To pull something like that off is pretty hard core. I'm talking like secret military tech type shit. Scrambling a recording device like a video camera is one thing but a photograph? I didn't even know that existed."

"Or Jane Lowry was right and they are vampires. If they don't have reflections it would make sense that they couldn't be photographed," I said casually.

"But she could be photographed," Q quipped.

"She was only half of whatever this is. Her mother was allegedly raped by Elliot Kinkaid."

"Vampires raping human women create dhampirs but if you go by the legend they are supposed to be male."

I smiled. "I didn't know you were into vampires."

"I love the movie Blade, and I read a bit about day walkers."

"Could this just be a different strain of day walker? This anomaly somehow makes them immune to the daylight issue?"

We both turned to Lemme, who seemed to be pondering the idea.

Before she could answer someone started pounding on my front door.

I paused for a few minutes, trying to figure out who wouldn't just ring the doorbell.

"You expecting visitors?" Lemme asked.

"No. And who doesn't ring the doorbell?" I said as I got up and headed towards the noise. I ran through the possibilities of who it could be, and there were too many reasons for it to not be certain people that I was confusing myself.

I looked through the peephole to find Rollo pacing on my porch.

I put the chain on then opened the door. "Rollo? Jesse's not here....we're not...."

"Dude, are you sure he's not here? You haven't seen him? Shit shit shit."

"What are you talking about?"

"Jesse is missing."

"And? He goes missing all the time. Find out where the slut in white denim is, he's probably behind her somewhere."

"This is different, Camille. How much does it cost to hire you?"

I unlatched the chain and opened the door. I could hear Lemme and Q creeping up behind me but hiding in the hallway.

"You want to hire me to find my dirt bag ex boyfriend? Is that a joke?"

"Fuck no. You've got some serious MacGyver stees. I need you. When he goes off on a bender I can find him, but I have been looking for four days. He's not a ghost, he's gone. His phone was at a bar downtown; they found it in a trash can. A fucking trash can, Camille."

I sighed. "Look Rollo, your boy is a junkie. This is what he does. He is a selfish prick who doesn't care about anyone except himself. He would toss you over in a heartbeat if it would get him ahead, or save his skin. You're a fool for still putting up with him after all these years."

Rollo stared blankly at me. "He would never do that to me. You're a girl. You're different."

"Did you forget who you are talking to?" I said through gritted teeth. "If he would do that to me he would do it to anyone, even you! Get a fucking grip Rollo."

"You're just mad that you got played. And for so many years, too."

"Fuck off," I slammed the door in his face and put the chain back on.

"What was that about?" Q asked as we went back into the living room.

"Apparently Cracky McGotta Gun has disappeared," I replied, flopping into Ted's chair.

"We need to run another phone trace? I could go for a Frappuccino," Lemme said.

"No, I know where his phone is. He's a junkie; he probably went off on another bender. But I do need some rock star dating clothes for if I see Fray again. We could grab coffee then if you guys want to come with?" I asked with a smile.

"I'm down," Lemme said. "Q?"

"Sounds good. Let's roll."

Shopping with the girls was an awesome distraction, but four days thumped on my brain like a person thumping their fingers on a table. A thrum of impatience, and an unwelcome pain in the ass.

Where the hell had this moron gone?

Q dropped me off and I happily went inside, bags of new clothes in hand. I was determined to impress Fray with the person I was now, not the dweeb he knew in high school.

Four days was haunting me, but I was determined to ignore it.

The whole thing was probably a ploy just to suck me back in.

I made his life easier; he would fight to keep me.

I think.

Jesse probably sent Rollo to the house to get me all wound up and get me in the mind set of wanting to save him. That's how I always ended up going back.

I just kept repeating to myself that I could not help him.

I was better off.

I went to my room and started to put away my clothes, and decided to reorganize my closet.

While I was pulling things out I found a random shoe box in the back that had my Mom's name written on it in permanent marker. I'd never seen it before, and put it aside for later.

With my closet all perfect I felt much better. I could access my new outfits easily and without much thought. Which was good because I was not exactly the best at fashion. I heard Ted come in and went downstairs to greet him.

"Hi!" I said, sitting on the couch as he slumped into his chair.

"Hey. You're in a good mood," Ted replied.

"Q and Lemme and I went shopping. I have clothes for dates now. And Rollo showed up here. But that didn't ruin my mood."

"Oh yeah? Apparently he cornered Cuddy at school. Do I have to scare him?"

I chuckled. "No. I told him to hit the bricks. He won't come back."

"What did he want?"

"Oh nothing. Jesse is MIA."

"Again? Why did Rollo come here? Doesn't he know about the split?"

"He wanted to hire me to find Jesse. Apparently Jesse's phone was in a garbage can in a bar downtown."

Ted paused, watching my face. "Are we looking for him?"

"Lord no."

"Rollo was worried enough to bother Cuddy. Doesn't that concern you?"

"Is Cuddy upset?"

"No. He referred to Rollo as 'Jesse's dumbass friend'."

"Then no, I am not worried at all. Rollo tried to tell me I'm just mad because I kept getting played. He's a moron. Even if I did care I would have told him no just on principle."

He got out of his chair and came and sat next to me, putting a hand on my knee.

"Ruh roh," I said, staring at his hand. "You only do that when you want to talk about something serious."

"I just want you to be prepared."

"Prepared for what?"

"That one of these times, when he disappears, he's not coming back."

"Like poof? That would be ideal."

"No, Cas. I want you to be prepared that one of these times he is going to be dead."

"Oh," I replied, pausing for a few minutes before saying. "I came to terms with that a long time ago. No worries."

"There is a big difference between coming to terms with it and it actually happening. He is getting far enough down that road he won't be able to come back anymore."

I shrugged. "That's his road, not mine. I will find a way when it comes. If it comes."

He pat my knee softly. "I know."

That thumping of four days turned into a burn as

Ted's words really sunk in. As I lay in my bed that night every time I closed my eyes all I saw was his corpse face down in a river.

In my anxious state I sat up and almost called him. I held my phone in my hand and stared at it for a long time.

I dialled into my answering machine, finally remembering that I had messages.

I was surprised at the first message.

"Hey Cas, its October," her voice was oddly hypnotic. I had forgotten all about her. "I haven't seen you in a while. Just wanted to call and check in, give you my number in case you were done with Ren. Which I kind of hope you are, since you are too good for it."

She left her number and told me to call her. I saved it in the contacts in my phone. She would probably be able to find Jesse. So would Bliss for that matter.

What the actual fuck? *No*. He was not going to penetrate my mind. I was not going to get sucked back in.

I had a cute outfit to wear out with October now. And I would not bring Bliss into this. She was trying to be different than her family, I wasn't about to corrupt that with this bullshit.

There were two other messages, both heavy breathing for a few seconds then disconnected. Both blocked numbers, both Jesse if I had to take a guess.

I checked the time and even though it was late I decided to text Fray. It was just a quick 'thinking of you, let's hang out soon'.

I finally drifted off to sleep with thoughts of Fray. Of his smile, his hair, his smell, of being the girl in his arm who every other girl on the planet envied.

19.

It was four more days before I heard Jesse's name again.

I got a text from Bliss saying, 'Looks like asshat is moving on to porno. Am I that trampy that he really believed I would do it?'. Which meant she must have seen him recently, which meant he wasn't in a river somewhere. I felt like a fool for even thinking about him for that long.

I went about my vacation as any normal person would have. I asked Bliss to observe the Kinkaid kids at a safe distance and listen for anything about Jane Lowry. A lead of any kind could be useful.

I started taking walks in the morning after my coffee; it did a lot of easing my anxieties and clearing my head. I was going to find a way to do right by Jane, no matter how long it took.

I also started baking muffins so Ted and Cuddy had

something amazing for the mornings. Poppy didn't bother trying any; I assumed that she thought I might poison her in my fragile state.

The call from Kiera came four days after that.

"Hey!" I said, happy to hear her voice. "Any leads on Jane Lowry's killer?"

"Cas, we need to talk about something serious. Are you home alone?"

"Yeah, why? What's going on?"

She paused. "I should really tell you in person. That way you can get Ted and come in with me."

"Am I being arrested?"

She paused again. "No, kid. Something bad has happened."

I sat down on the kitchen floor and breathed in and out loudly. "Oh. To who?"

"I'm so sorry Cas. I asked to be the one to call you, you were listed as his next of kin and we haven't been able to locate his parents."

"Just say it, Kiera. Like ripping off a band aid. I can't wait for you to come and tell me Jesse is dead to my face."

"I'm so sorry Cas. We found Jesse this morning. We need you to come in as his next of kin to identify the body. But you have to get Ted."

I gulped in some air. "Why do I need Ted?"

"Like ripping off a band aid? You sure you can take this?"

"Lay it on me."

"Because he has been dead for a week. And it's unpleasant."

I paused, then sighed heavily. "Oh. Well, alright then."

Kiera was silent for a few minutes, probably trying to figure out what to say. They prepared you for a lot of different scenarios when you became a cop but I figured this wasn't one of them.

"We had split up, you know," I began. "A few weeks ago. I found out he's pimping girls out of a house downtown and ended it. I didn't want to be a doormat anymore. He was terrible to me, and I felt stupid for putting up with it for so long."

"You couldn't have known...."

"Yes I did. He is a junkie and junkies die, Kiera. You're a homicide cop, you know that. The life he was leading he was lucky someone didn't kill him years ago. Which reminds me, is foul play suspected?"

"We don't know yet."

"Why not?"

She paused. "Like a band aid?"

"Yep."

"Because the body is in such a bad state we have to wait for an autopsy."

Ted came in the door at that moment, I handed him the phone without another word to Kiera and lay down on the living room floor.

Everything moved a lot slower from the floor. A pain started to spread through my chest and it hurt to breathe.

I didn't hear what Ted said to Kiera, all sound seemed to disappear and was replaced by a ringing in my ears. I would have to inform people as his next of kin.

How the fuck am I going to tell Rollo he's dead?

It's a trick. It has to be. I wanted to ask how Kiera knew it was him, but it was stupid to question her. She was a Bishop, and she cared for me. She wouldn't do this unless it was absolutely true.

At first I didn't feel the hot tears on my cheeks but once I did they wouldn't stop.

Someone else came in; spoke briefly to Ted, than spooned their body around mine on the floor. The scent of pot smoke and Hugo Boss cologne identified Cuddy, and Poppy would never get that close to me.

I couldn't believe it.

How could he be gone, just like that?

"I wanted him out of my life. I didn't want him to die. How could I want him to die? He was all I knew. My love. My life. My only friend for so long," I said to no one in particular.

Cuddy pet my hair. "I know, Cas. We all know. You don't have to explain to anyone."

I tried to breathe, slowly and carefully.

"I am so sorry. You don't deserve this. Any of this. I'm so sorry Camille."

I had to gasp for air between sobs. I didn't know what to do.

I hadn't had to face anything serious without him since I was in my early teens. Everything had been done around him and with him in mind.

"I d-d-don't know if I c-c-can do this C-c-cuddy," I blubbered.

"You aren't alone. Dad and I are here," he began.

"I am sure Q and Lemme and Bliss will be here too if you call," I heard Ted but could not see him. "Kiera is on her way. You have people. We will get through this."

"He was a junkie. Junkie's die," was all I could say. I kept repeating it like it was somehow going to solve all my problems. Like it somehow made it better, more palatable, that he had done this to himself.

I continued on with my mantra as activity went on around me. Cuddy stayed with me, sitting vigil as I began to further unravel. Suddenly I was hit with the idea that he could not have possibly done this to himself.

Maybe the Kinkaid's found out about me after they killed Jane, my business card was in her pocket. Maybe they thought if they killed Jesse I would get off their trail, considering they may or may not have killed my parents.

Clearly they don't know me very well.

Kiera came in my view; she spoke to Ted for a minute then sat down in front of me.

"Someone killed him," I said to her, blinking back my tears.

She cocked her head to one side. "Why would you

say that?"

"He has pissed people off over the years. And if the Kinkaid's found out who I am they may have killed him to send a message."

Kiera looked up, I assumed at Ted, and said something I couldn't understand. She probably asked what I knew about the Kinkaid's, beyond their connection to Jane.

"Send Lemme that blood," I said to her, grabbing her hand.

"Who?"

"My tech. Send the blood to my tech, Kiera."

"I already did. What's that got to do with anything?"

"Is the autopsy done yet?"

"No. His decomp was pretty bad. I don't know how this played out, but either he didn't want to be found or whoever put him there wanted him unrecognizable."

A knot formed in my throat and it hurt to swallow.

"You don't have to ID him until the autopsy is done and they clean him up, Cas," she began. "I got them to put it off until after to save you the trauma."

"How do you know it was him?"

"He had his wallet and we have his DNA on file from his arrests. The tattoos match our photo records."

"Did you see him?"

She paused, staring at my face. "Yeah. I did."

"And you have no doubt that it is him?"

"I don't. I am so sorry Camille."

"He was a junkie. Junkie's die. He was also a pimp and a criminal and involved with some shitty ass people," I stopped mid sentence as Bucky's face flashed into my mind. He could have done it, or be dead himself.

I should get in touch with Bliss.

I started to pull myself up and Cuddy helped me. He took my hand and sat with me on the floor like we had done so many times when we were kids.

But he was grown now. We were big people with real world problems.

"I don't like this adult thing. I think I am done adulting now. Can I go back to being a kid? Because this sucks balls," I said.

"What you have had to deal with lately is fucked up Cas. It has nothing to do with being an adult. Most adults go through life with nothing this bad ever happening to them. You have just had a run of bad luck," Kiera replied.

"Or everything I touch turns to shit."

"Who said that?" Kiera asked, then raised her hand to stop me from answering. "Never mind. I will personally punch Poppy in the mouth for you, if you'd like. She is so wrong it's hilarious."

I nodded my head; the knot in my throat had eased.

"I don't want to be the one to tell Rollo," I began. "Fuck, do I have to find his parents? I really don't want to be the one to tell people. I can't do it."

"We'll find his parents," Kiera said.

"Dad and I will find Rollo at school tomorrow and tell him. Don't worry about him," Cuddy added.

I sighed. "Thank you. What do I do now?"

"How about we start with some tea?" Ted said, smiling

as he went into the kitchen.

Kiera stayed for dinner. They kept the conversation light for the rest of the evening and I felt like a normal person again for a while.

But after she left, and Cuddy went to do his homework, Ted and I sat in the living room and put on the television.

I held my cell phone in one hand, staring at it.

"I suppose I should call people," I said.

"Like who?" he asked. He left the room briefly and came back with two glasses of wine and a bag of my favourite chips.

"Bliss comes to mind. He was involved with her brother. It could be a really bad thing. Bucky could have killed him."

"Could isn't really the question. It's would."

"If we're playing the would game you can add the Kinkaid's on their as well."

He paused. "Why would you say that?"

"They killed Jane for being a big mouth. My business card was in her pocket. They know my name; they killed my parents. They figured if they killed him it would send a message. Scare me away because...."

"I get why you feel like Kinkaid is the boogieman. I get why you would come to that conclusion. But you cannot say that to anyone other than me, do you understand? Not Kiera. Not anyone."

I moved my eyes to him and stared, a hard blink

bringing my mind back into focus.

"Okay. That is not an issue."

"Good. And I think you should call Bliss," he said. "Because whoever went after Jesse, if he was in fact murdered, could go after Bucky too."

I called Bliss once I got to my room. She was happy and cheerful. Fray had told her that we had hung out and she seemed super excited about it.

"But something bad has happened," I said, and I burst into tears.

"Fuck me. What now?" she asked.

"Jesse's dead," I blurted out and I heard her phone hit the floor.

There was some shuffling as she picked it up, then she said, "Are you for real? When? How?"

"More than a week. Don't know how they just found his body."

Silence, then, "Fuck."

More silence. I tried not to sob but the tears flowed down my face.

"I'm so sorry, Cas. This is fucked up," she finally said and I could hear her crying.

"Yeah. Just a smidge. I hate to ask, but when was the last time you saw Bucky?"

"My brother is a piece of shit but he wouldn't do this."

"I wasn't asking because I thought he did it, Bee, but thanks for the clarification."

"Fuck. A while. But he leaves for a bit, that's what he does. I will have to talk to my Mom."

"I don't want to scare her but it would be worthwhile, just in case."

Silence.

"Fuck. If I give you his number can you trace his phone?" she asked.

"Yes. But try other options first."

"Ok. Thanks. Fuck. Are you sure it's him? I mean, are they sure it's him?"

"Considering it's my cousin who told me, and she saw the body, I'd say yeah. They're sure. I have to go ID the body as his next of kin."

"Are you for real? Do you want me to come?"

"Thanks for the offer but I will be okay with Ted, I think."

"Well let me know if you change your mind," she began. "Hey, my Mom just walked in. I'll call you back after I ask her about Bucky."

She hung up without another word.

She texted me a few hours later to tell me that her Mom didn't know where Bucky was and that they were looking for him, and if they needed my assistance they would let me know. I felt bad for upsetting them but if Bucky was caught up in this somehow I would have felt worse for not saying anything.

I texted Q and told her. She didn't call, but texted

back a simple 'let me know if you need me'. It was what I needed at the moment. I wasn't really in the mood for company.

In truth, what I really needed was my Mom. When bad stuff happened, and I mean really bad stuff not just your random everyday crappy shit, I ached for her so badly I almost couldn't breathe. In this situation one might think I would ache for the newly departed, but because of how done I had been with him previously I did not long for him in that way. I felt guilty about it but that was the truth. I was sad he was dead but I did not miss his company.

I needed my Mother to comfort me.

I was lying on my bed when my phone rang.

"Hello?" I answered on the first ring.

"Are you at home?" Bliss asked.

"Yep. Why?"

"Because I am outside. We can't find Bucky and I need your help."

I gathered up my things and headed for the door, telling Ted where I was going on the way out.

I had Q on the phone when I got in the car. I told her the deal, and Bliss gave me Bucky's number so we could trace it. Q gave me an address that was on the other side of town and we headed out. Q promised to call back if it moved.

"So what do you think happened?" Bliss asked after

some time in silence.

"I have a few scenarios that make sense. Bucky might be able to clear them up for me."

"He didn't...."

"I know that. But he might know who did."

We drove the rest of the way in silence. It didn't bother me, I didn't have much to say and I could tell she was on edge. She was probably terrified and I couldn't blame her.

As we got into the neighbourhood I got nervous. We were now in ghetto suburbia; where they shipped all the people from the projects to when they tore down their downtown apartment complex's to build condos. Some of the small bungalows were well kept; others looked as if they would fall down if you blew on it too hard.

We stopped in front of a white house with a brown roof that had a rickety looking metal wire fence and a lawn that hadn't been cut in a year. Without talking to me or even batting an eyelash Bliss got out of the car and headed for the front door. I had to jog to catch her before she knocked.

A tiny pale girl answered the door, a series of increasingly more angry looking meth scabs covered her cheeks and around her mouth.

"Where's Bucky?" Bliss snapped.

Meth Scabs looked confused. "Who?"

"Bitch did I stutter? I said where the fuck is Bucky Fiori?" Bliss gripped the door frame tight as she angrily got in the girl's face.

"I don't know who you're talking about," Meth Scabs replied.

"Fuck this," Bliss pushed the girl out of the way and stormed into the house. I tried to follow as closely as I could, she probably didn't care about getting arrested but I did.

Bliss took out her phone and called Bucky, we followed the ringing down the hall to a bedroom. We found his phone on a table in a room with a bunch of other meth heads lying about.

"Alright, who the fuck had this phone?" Bliss started yelling, and all I could do was stare at an object I saw next to an ashtray. One of the meth heads leaned over to grab it and I smacked her hand and took it from her.

"What are you doing with a dead man's bracelet?" I asked her, and she slinked back into a corner. Her eyes grew as big as dinner plates.

"Jesse's dead?" she asked. I grabbed her by her hair and pulled her towards me.

"What do you know about him?" I said as calmly as I could. Bliss clutched Bucky's phone in her hand so tightly I thought it might snap.

"He was here with his friend a few days ago. He traded the bracelet for a lighter, and his buddy was super drunk and lost his phone," she told me as she squirmed in my grip. "He comes by to smoke up sometimes. That's all."

Of course he traded the bracelet I gave him for a lighter. The silver ID bracelet had his initials on the outside and my name on the inside.

She looked up at me and that was when I noticed the design on her face. It was like someone rubbed blue and pink pastel on her face in the shape of a moth, part of the wings covering her eyes like she was a small child with a butterfly painted on her face.

"What's this about?" I asked, gesturing at her face with one finger.

"We went to a club, and we tried this new shit that was amazing. The greatest high I have ever felt, and Jesse and I made love for hours," she said with a dopey smile. "You can't take that bracelet; it's all I have of him."

I showed her my name engraved on the inside. "Considering *that is my name*, I don't fucking think so."

I took out my cell phone and snapped a photo of her face, she cringed at the flash.

"What the fuck?" she snapped.

"In case the cops want to talk to you," I told her, letting go of her hair. Bliss grabbed Bucky's phone off the table.

"If Jesse's buddy comes back tell him to call his sister," Bliss bent over the girl and yelled. "If it turns out he's dead too you bet your ass we'll be back."

"Something is wrong," Bliss began once we got back in the car. "Bucky would never leave his phone. He's never lost a phone in his entire life. This makes no sense."

"Have you called his people?" I asked. "And moth face's timing is off."

"They're looking now too. No one has seen him."

"You want me to tell my cousin? She's a cop."

"Do you mean the one we went to high school with? Fuck no."

I laughed; I hadn't thought much about Poppy. "No, this is a different cousin. Homicide detective. She's good people."

"While the rest of the family would say no, I'm saying yes. We need all the help we can get."

"Okay," I called Kiera as we started driving.

"I need a drink. You in?" she asked.

"Sure. Let's go."

I filled Kiera in as we drove to wherever Bliss thought it was appropriate for us to drink.

Kiera was good stuff, she told me she would look into it and call me back. She also said that she would make a note on Jesse's file about his known associate being missing. I told her that his family probably wouldn't report it and she didn't seem shocked, she knew who Bucky Fiori was and I didn't have to elaborate.

When I got off the phone I watched the city go by, and as Bliss slowed down I figured out where I was.

"You could have warned me that we were going to Fray's, so I could have made myself look less like a sea monkey," I said as she parked in the lot across the street.

"Sorry. He has the best booze and we don't have to pay," she replied. "And you look fine. To be totally honest you could show up in a paper bag and a tube sock and he would still get a boner."

I shrugged and followed her up to Fray's loft. At the moment I didn't really care, but I knew I would probably stress about it later. It's not like I wasn't presentable; I was wearing a black tank top, rolled up boyfriend jeans, and my Birkenstock flip flops that I'd had forever with a rose pattern on them. My hair was a mess but it was clean and I had on no makeup, I had taken it off earlier before Bliss picked me up because it was all over my face from crying.

If it did put Fray off he was not really worth being with. That was the truth of the matter.

Eamon answered the door; he looked a little stunned to see us.

"Ladies....?" he said quizzically.

"We need booze. Lots of booze," Bliss replied, pushing past him.

I tried to smile. "Hey Eamon, how are you?"

"Hey Camille," he said, confused. "Want to fill me in on what's going on?"

"Jesse's dead and Bucky is missing. Where's the booze at?" his eyes grew wider after I said the word 'dead'. I pat his shoulder and followed after Bliss.

Fray and the other guys were on his couch with a group of, well, groupies. Fray stood when he saw me, Eamon must have signalled something behind my back because he said nothing as I went over to Bliss and his liquor cabinet.

She poured us two shots of Jack Daniels; we drank

them back then sat on the floor with our glasses and the bottle.

Eamon said something quietly to the guys, they all asked him something quietly and he nodded, then they all turned back to us.

"Hey, we're good now. Don't mind us. Just go back to whatever you're doing," I called out to them. They continued to stare as we took another shot.

"Well, isn't this crazy! I went from being the stupid loner who only hung out with her druggie boyfriend to the girl who is drinking with her friends because her druggie boyfriend is dead!" I said, and I laughed awkwardly. Bliss took my hand and looked as if she might cry, suddenly the guys were on the floor with us and the groupies had disappeared.

I turned to them, smiling and nodding as I repeated my mantra to them, "He was a junkie. Junkie's die."

Fray took my hand in his. He didn't say anything; he just held my hand as I stared at it like it was some foreign object.

"You don't have to pretend, Cas," Fray said. "It's ok to be sad."

I laughed. "I know that. And I am sad. What is weird is that I don't....you know how when someone dies you wish they were with you? I don't wish he was still around. Isn't that fucked up? He left this world and no one really wishes he was still here."

Fray squeezed my hand. I laughed again and tried my best not to look awkward.

"That is not entirely true. Rollo will miss him. That makes me feel a bit better," I said with a big sigh. "It least someone will miss him. I don't even know if his parents are still around....they were out of the picture for so long."

I banged my glass and Bliss and I took another shot.

"Thank God for booze. I don't know why I don't drink more," I mumbled, the alcohol already making the world warm and fuzzy around the edges. I felt better, more relaxed. I knew immediately that I couldn't make this a habit or I would end up being an alcoholic.

Bliss pet my arm. "And my idiot brother got mixed up in it all. I swear he was hatched from an egg. How do we have the same parents?"

"I think that about Poppy, but more that she must have been pulled out of some hell hole somewhere. You've seen that movie Drag Me to Hell? They dragged Poppy out. How can we put her back in?"

Bliss laughed. "Maybe if we sent her looking for Bucky they will fall into a hole together."

We both laughed, a weird chuckle that made us both sound like angry chickens. The boys just sat and watched, I didn't look directly at them to see if they were uncomfortable. And frankly I didn't care.

Bliss and I kept drinking and laughing about stupidness until we were drunk enough that we were lying on the floor. It was the most fun I had had in years.

And Fray stayed with us. Even after the boys left, even after he got us blankets and pillows. When Bliss passed out I pulled Fray over, and he spooned me as I cried myself to sleep.

My back hurt the next morning when I woke up, but luckily I wasn't hung over. Before I stood up I grabbed my phone out of my purse to text Ted, just to let him know Bliss and I went drinking and I was ok and would be home later. He sent me back a winking emoji.

"Everything ok?" Fray asked from behind me.

"My Uncle sent me an emoji," I replied, clearing my throat.

Fray chuckled. "From what I remember of Ted that's kind of random."

"I'm surprised you remember him," I replied, rubbing my finger around the outline of the bishop chess piece tattoo on his arm.

"I should have chosen you," I said. "I should have split from Jesse the first time he fucked me over and moved on. Maybe I would live here. Maybe he wouldn't be...."

"Or none of this would have happened. We could have split and gone our separate ways, and our paths been totally different. And, as you said, he was a junkie. Without you he could have died a lot sooner," Fray replied. "You went above and beyond for him, Cas. This isn't your fault."

I rolled over so we were face to face and kissed him softly.

"I know that. I do. But that doesn't make it any less painful. And you're right about the path thing. Other then the obvious shit things have been going pretty good, right?"

He smiled. "I think so. Sorry about the girls. One extra always shows up when the boys bring girls back."

"That's no problem. I'm not your girlfriend so I don't have the right to say anything."

"Do you want to be?"

"What?"

"My girlfriend."

I smiled. "Really?"

"Yeah, really."

"I do, but not yet. I don't want anyone to think you're just a rebound, or it's something I am doing out of grief."

He stroked my hair. "I can wait. I have waited this long."

"No you haven't. It's not like you have been celibate since high school."

"I know but I have been hoping. I sing that song for you every show hoping you would hear it. And, as fate would have it, you finally did. I will wait until you are ready, because you are the one that I want."

I leaned in and kissed him, and said, "Thank you."

"Now, how about some breakfast? I make a mean hangover special. I'm sure Bee is going to need it, contrary to what she might say she cannot drink like she used to."

Fray was true to his word, he made a massive

breakfast of eggs, bacon and hash browns that was beyond amazing. I ate so much I thought I would pass out. Bliss was very hung over but happily ate and took a handful of aspirin.

I kissed him goodbye and Bliss took me home, she apologised for being so quiet but the hangover was murder on her head.

We parted ways with the promise to call and to keep each other updated. We hugged, and I thanked her.

"For what?" she asked.

"For letting me know that I do have friends," I replied.

She smiled. "Don't you forget it. Call me if you need anything."

When I got inside Ted was hovering like he had been waiting for me.

"We have to go," Ted said when I put my purse down.

"Go where?"

"Kiera just called. She put it off for as long as she could. We have to go."

"But it's only been a day. Does this mean something?"

"It could. They wanted the body ID'd immediately for a reason."

"Do I have time to shower?"

"Of course."

20.

Before we left, I gathered up every random memento of Jesse that I could find and left them in a pile on my bed.

I didn't want his body on a slab in the morgue to be my last memory of him. That was one of the reasons I was so against open casket funerals. Ted had insisted on my parents caskets being closed and at the time I didn't get it, neither did most of my family.

But Grandma Bishop sat me down and explained it to me and afterwards I was grateful. I remembered the funeral but it was just a funeral, my last memory of them remained pure and untainted.

My last memory of Jesse was the drive by break up manoeuvre, and while it wasn't the best it least it was honest and not going to cause me nightmares.

"You ok, kid?" Ted asked as we got out of the car and headed into the morgue.

I was relieved that it was in the separate coroner's complex as opposed to the basement of police headquarters. I didn't want to see anyone I might know, or my Dad's photo, or my cousins have access to his body. I just wanted to go in, identify him, and have my meltdown in peace.

Ted and I wandered through quite the labyrinth before we found Kiera. The building seemed overly complicated and I was surprised that Ted still knew where he was going.

It dawned on me as he chatted briefly with Kiera that the last time he had come here was probably to ID my parents.

Kiera put her hand on my shoulder. "You ok, kid?"

"I don't know. Can we get this shit over with? The anticipation is the worst part," I replied.

Kiera nodded and handed me a nose plug. I stared at it, it took a few minutes for me to realize what it was and when I did the knot in my throat got tighter.

"Hey, so I was thinking, could you just take a photo of him with your phone while I wait in the hall?" I asked, trying to smile.

"Nope, sorry kid," Kiera replied as she opened the doors for us.

"Dammit. Well, you can't blame me for trying," I reached out for Ted's arm as we past the little desk through another set of doors into the room with the metal slabs and the drawers. The knot turned into an ache, the idea that he was alone in this cold, metal place was heart-breaking. Reduced to just a piece of meat on a slab, just like my parents had been.

The coroner came in, a short pudgy little man in a lab coat with glasses. He smiled and nodded at Kiera, walking straight to one of the drawers. I squeezed Ted's arm as my breath caught.

The coroner opened the door and pulled out a slab with a black bag on it. The bile rose in my throat and I had to hold my breath to bite it back.

"Are you okay, kid?" Kiera asked. "You ready?"

I nodded quickly and Kiera motioned for the coroner to open the bag.

The opening of the zipper made me cringe, and when he pulled the bag back from the face I thought I was going to puke all over the body.

Jesse's skin had a bluish tinge and was puffed up from bloating. The veins in his face were dark purplish and so were his lips. His blonde hair was matted to his head and the skin on his eyelids was dark.

"Camille, is this Jesse Garrow?" Kiera asked me. I nodded quickly but didn't say a word; I was trying too hard to swallow my vomit.

"I'm sorry Camille, but I need you to say out loud yes or no," Kiera said.

"Yes, it's him," I said quickly. My tears began to fall and blinded me, and I wailed so loud it echoed in the small room.

Things got fuzzy after that.

The next thing I remembered was sitting in a chair in the hallway and Ted handing me a bottle of water before speaking to a small blonde woman with Kiera. She looked familiar but I couldn't make the connection.

The blonde woman went back in the morgue with Kiera and Ted guided me back out to the car.

"Who was that?" I asked Ted when we got moving.

"Jesse's Mom," he replied.

"Fuck. Should I have....?"

"No. She didn't expect it, either, considering the circumstances. Kiera has been talking to them. They are going to bury him, by the way."

I turned to him. "They are?"

"Yep. Sounds like he had been in touch with his parents in the past few years."

"He never mentioned it. I am glad they are involved. Props to Kiera on that one."

"It's her job. His mother and I exchanged contact info and will let us know about the arrangements. I can talk to them, they don't expect you to talk to them but they would like you to."

I began to laugh. "I didn't even think about the funeral. Oh God! I have to go to his funeral. Oh God! I don't have to pay for it, do I?"

I started to hyperventilate and put my head on my knees. Ted reached out and put his hand on my back.

"I just said no. His parents are covering it. They will contact us with the details," he replied. "Relax Cas.

The really bad part is over."

"Do you think they would be stupid enough to have an open casket?"

He sighed loudly. "Fuck, I hope not."

When we got back to the house Rollo was sitting on the porch. He looked like he hadn't slept in a few days and was high as a kite.

"How long?" he said angrily as we approached. Ted motioned for me to stay behind him.

"I don't know what you're talking about, Rollo," I replied.

"How long have you known he's dead, Camille?" he said through clenched teeth.

I studied his face, trying to decide how I should handle this. "A day and a half."

"A day and a half? Are you fucking serious? You've known for more than 24 hours and you felt no need to call me? Are you that heartless?" he yelled.

"I'm still trying to process this, Rollo. It hasn't even totally sunk in yet."

"I always knew you were an evil bitch, Camille, but I never thought you were so cruel. None of this would have happened if you would have just taken one for the team..."

I shook my head really fast. "Excuse me? Run that by me again?"

"If you weren't such a fucking baby about Amanda

this wouldn't have happened. He always came crawling back to you for some stupid reason and the one time, the one damn time you decide to not be a worthless bag of trash he ends up dead."

"Listen here you fucking moronic asshat, did you ever think that maybe he wouldn't be dead if you, I don't know, *stopped giving him drugs?* This had nothing to do with me, do you understand? Maybe you should go and talk to *Amanda* and find out what really happened to him. Now get the fuck off my porch before I call the cops," Ted kept holding me back as I screamed at Rollo.

After staring blankly at me for about a minute he got up, muttering 'This isn't over' at me as he walked past to his car.

"Text Kiera when he gets inside. You got any photos of this Amanda?" Ted asked as we headed in the house.

"Remember the hooker from the brothel?"

"The blonde? Yep. Got a few good shots of her too," he replied. "I hate to mention it but have you been tested recently?"

"Calling now to try to get an appointment. Forward those shots to Kiera. And some of Bucky if you got."

I got the appointment, and I got every test for every disease I could get.

Better safe than sorry.

I told Dr. Massimino what happened with Jesse, she had been my doctor since I was a child and she knew me very well.

She gave me a prescription for something called Clonazepam. She said it was similar to Valium, and I should take it to help me sleep and if I was having a panic attack. She told me she would put a rush on the tests so I should know everything in three days.

She also reminded me that I had been on the same medication when my parents had passed when I expressed my concern about them. It was something I had hid from Jesse; the pills had helped me go on in those early years.

But grief and I were old friends.

Grief was an emotion that I understood all too well. I had been grieving for him anyhow, a different sort of grief but mourning for the loss of him.

As I headed home from the doctor I couldn't shake what Rollo had said. The realization that any of it could be true was upsetting. The 'could it' stuck to me like a bad smell. I knew in my very core that this was not my fault, but I couldn't shake the idea that if I had stuck around I could have done something. That my influence kept his head above water, kept him from truly sinking into the deep.

I texted Bliss when I got home to make sure she was ok. She texted me back and asked if I wanted to chill with her at Ren tonight. I hadn't gotten a yes or no that I shouldn't go there, and the death in the family excuse would work for why I hadn't come in for a shift, so I decided to go. I could talk to October if she was there and I could use the distraction.

I showered and changed, putting on one of the new outfits I had bought. I told Ted where I was going and he didn't seem to mind.

"Don't let Bliss drive if she has been drinking," Ted said. I saluted him as I headed for the door.

"You don't drive either. I am assuming you will be drinking," he called out to me as I headed outside.

I was happy to see Bliss when she pulled up. I was sitting on the porch waiting for her.

"You look nice," Bliss said when I got in her car. I was wearing black capri pants and a loose fitting white oversize t-shirt that was slightly see through and showed off my white bra. My hair was actually doing a cool bed head thing that hadn't worked so well when my hair was longer.

"Thanks, so do you," I replied. She was glowing in a yellow sundress with her dark hair hanging loose around her shoulders.

"I'm surprised you want to go hang out at Ren," I said.

She shrugged. "I have an ulterior motive."

"Ruh row."

"The Kinkaid's are in the VIP room tonight. You got any audio recording equipment on you?"

I smiled. "You know I do."

"Will it be usable with the noise of the club?"

"I got a techie who can do some amazing things. She got into the webcams in the brothel, that's how I learned about Jesse."

"I also got word that they might know where Bucky is."

"Come again?"

"Don't get your panties in a knot but remember moth face from the meth house? Well that club she talked about is run by the Kinkaid's."

"And because of that they would know where Bucky is?"

"Well, let's see. Jesse and Bucky go out clubbing, one is dead the other is missing. Someone as high profile as Bucky Fiori doesn't disappear from a mob club without the higher ups knowing what the deal is."

"Unless it all happened after they left."

She shrugged. "Right. I also figured you would want to know if they mentioned your client."

"I do. You're starting to think like a P.I. Ever thought about dropping this stripper thing and coming to work with me?"

"You think I could?"

"I do. But we'll have to work on reigning in the bloodthirsty part. I struggle with mine all the time, it's not easy. Not that there is anything wrong with stripping."

"It's not ideal, but its better then waitressing."

"Or being on that site The Dollhouse. My client was doing that. Which reminds me, I should try to get a meeting with them."

"I can do that in the morning."

"Wait. What?"

"You're talking about The Dollhouse dot com? My cousin Nico has his toes dipped in that. I'm sure he'll talk to you. You might have to come to my Mom's house for dinner, though."

I smiled. "I would be happy to. I would never turn down a home cooked meal."

We pulled into the parking lot at Ren and she smiled nervously as she gathered up her things.

"Everything ok?" I asked her.

"Hanging out with the Kinkaid's is always stressful. Lucia Kinkaid is....well....to put it lightly she is a grade A crazy bitch."

"I'd heard. But coming from you that's pretty serious."

"Just be on your guard. She will immediately be suspicious of you. Don't let her get under your skin."

The entire club had a totally different vibe when the Kinkaid's were present. The waitresses were all on edge, looking like deer caught in headlights as they walked in and out of the VIP section. Tor looked like she was vibrating.

She smiled when she saw us, and we had a quick word about my 'death in the family' and she said Chris had told her and she hoped I'd be back soon. I was happy that Chris had maintained my position, it implied to me that he had faith that I would return. Perhaps I was fooling myself but it gave me a false sense of security.

I followed Bee back into the VIP section and tried to appear confident. I wasn't sure if Tobias would recognize me and even if he did it wouldn't be a big deal. I didn't do anything they could trace back to me somehow.

A bleached blonde with an amazing topknot stood just outside the entrance, her dark coloured bandage dress fit like it was her skin. The heels on her gladiator sandals were a minimum of six inches.

She smiled when she saw Bee and I saw the muscles in my friend's arms tense, which was a clear sign to me that this was Lucia Kinkaid.

"Glad you could finally join us," the girl said sarcastically, her nude lip gloss was so shiny I could probably see my face in it. She turned her eyes on me and I shivered.

"Got some shit going on at home, took some time to get away," Bee replied. "This is my girl Camille. She waitresses here sometimes."

"Holy shit it's you!" I heard a male voice exclaim, I guessed Tobias did remember me. "Sorry if I scared you before. I was a goddamn mess."

I smiled sheepishly at him. "It's no problem. Just another day at the office."

He pointed at the blonde. "This is my sister Lucia. Don't mind her; she's just as bitchy as she looks."

Lucia flipped her brother off as I tried to smile at her; she looked me up and down with an expression that would make a weaker person cry. I smiled my best smile at her, hoping she would brush me off as a moron.

Bliss pulled me into the empty end of the booth and I got a good look at the other Kinkaid boys. Where

Tobias may have been considered good looking the one who I picked up in conversation's name was Marcus looked like he had fallen out of the ugly tree and hit every branch on the way down. His skin looked like pock marked leather that had been cooked in the sun. He was scary, and seemed to be a fan of Bliss.

The smallest one, Rufus, looked like the runt of the litter. He was tiny; small hands, small head and small features that were sharp and made him look like a bird. His blue eyes were piercing and so light they looked almost white, giving him an otherworldly ghoulish look.

We sat and had drinks; Bliss was her charming self and mostly ignored me. It gave me the chance to turn on my audio recorder on my phone and put it in the side pocket of my purse where it would be the most effective.

Lucia continued to openly watch me, which made me feel awkward and uncomfortable.

"Lucia, leave the girl alone. She's cool," Tobias finally told her. "You stare at her like she said something bad about the family when she has barely spoke."

Lucia snorted, a menacing smile stretching across her face. "Yeah, and we don't want to forget how I handle people saying things about our family. Have you seen the news lately, Camille?"

I had to suck the bile that rose in my throat back down while maintaining my composure. Bliss put her hand on my leg and dug her nails in as a warning; first swing and

Lucia Kinkaid had already got to me. I was getting too sensitive and I had to stop.

I shrugged. "I don't blame you. Family is important, I know mine is."

"And what did you say your last name was?" Lucia asked. Her eyes sparkled like she was trying to toy with me.

"I didn't. It's LeFaye."

"Oh. Never heard of it," she said with a shrug and turned away. I picked up my glass and stared at the bottom like it contained the mysteries of life.

This might have been a bad idea. I was getting touchy over very small things, and I couldn't be such a wimp around these people.

The ice in my glass caught a flash of light off of something, and I looked up to see a mirror on the ceiling I hadn't noticed before. I glanced quickly at first, just because I didn't want to be the weirdo staring at the damn ceiling, but had to look again when I didn't see the top of Lucia's blonde head.

I didn't see it because it wasn't there.

Lucia and her three brothers *were not there.*

Their companions were there, communicating with nothing, like they were hallucinating.

I spent the next however many hours trying to figure out how to get a photo. It was dark and would take some work to edit so it was visible, but it could be done.

It had to. No one would believe me.

I took out my cell phone and started taking photos of

the ceiling. I didn't give a shit about the audio; it wasn't usable in court anyhow. It was something I would only be able to use as a jumping off point with Ted and Kiera; photos would be much more useful. I pretended to be angrily texting someone and took photos of the Kinkaid children with my flash off.

"Everything ok?" Bliss asked.

"Yep, just idiot old boyfriend," I said, giggling awkwardly and putting my phone back in its side pocket. "I wonder who has to clean the mirror on the damn ceiling. I mean, have you seen that shit? I will have to ask Tor."

I gestured up to get Bliss to look, her eyes widened a little but she brushed it off and went back to being charming.

"So you dancing tonight Bee?" Marcus asked. He smiled and I hoped that he didn't see me cringe. I would have to congratulate Bliss on dealing with creeps like him with such grace. When he looked at me I was entirely convinced my skin actually crawled.

"Nope, it's my day off. That's why your money is going to the waitress and not into my bra," Bee replied with a toothy grin. Slick.

"Are you a dancer putting your way through school too, Camille?" Marcus asked.

"No, I don't have the body for that! I'm just a waitress. Saving up a little money before I think about school," I replied. "I'm not sure what I want to do yet either."

"Oh my God, is that October Daniels? Why is she

coming over here?" Lucia snapped.

"She's looking for Camille," Bliss said, nudging me to go intercept October before she got over to us.

I was happy to leave the table, and I may have rushed a little too quickly over to her. She looked happy that I was so enthusiastic to see her.

"Hey! Sorry I haven't called you back," I began. "But I have had some major drama. Want to have a drink so we can chat?"

She smiled happily as we linked arms and turned back to the main part of the club. "I'd love to."

We sat at her usual table with her thugs, and once our drinks came I leaned in close to her to be sure she heard me.

"They found Jesse's body a few days ago, he had been dead over a week," I began. "I had to go to the morgue to ID him."

She whistled. "For real? That's something heavy, Camille. I'm not so offended you didn't call me back, even though you could've. I have a pretty good shoulder to cry on."

"Not so much crying, lots of drinking. Are you down for drinking?"

She laughed. "I am always down for drinking, sweet girl. I'm surprised you would drink with *them* though."

"They like Bee. Bliss is my homey. Which reminds me, do you know who Bucky Fiori is?"

"Of course. Why? That Bliss's man or something?"

"Not exactly. Have you seen him recently?" I said with

a smile. If October didn't know Bliss was a Fiori I wasn't going to tell her.

"No. He came in here with Jesse a while ago," she began, then paused. "I suppose it could have been shortly before he....sorry."

I shrugged. "No worries. Like I said, let's get to the drinking!"

When my vision started to get blurry I excused myself and went back to Bliss, promising October dinner later this week.

I liked talking to her. I wasn't going to pass up a chance to chill with her somewhere new.

Bliss was drunk, to put it mildly. Lucia was a little too close to her for my taste, but so was Tobias for that matter. She had said the Kinkaid's liked her but she didn't say how much. It made me wonder if Lucia was in to women, and if she had some weird kink with her brother's that I couldn't begin to understand.

Bliss jumped up when she saw me, returning to her seat at my side.

"How's October?" she asked with a smirk.

"Good. We should ask about security footage," I whispered to her. She laughed, diverting Lucia's attention for a few moments. Bliss took a sip of her drink, her hand shook.

"Should I find us a ride?" I asked.

She smiled wider. "Wanna see if Fray will come get us?"

"He might think I'm stalking him," I said and she

laughed again.

"I can guarantee he does not give a shit, and do you really? He's a rock star for Christ's sake."

Lucia's ears perked up. "Who's a rock star?"

"Long story. We're just trying to decide who should be our designated driver tonight," Bee replied.

"We could drop you off," Lucia said with a smile.

"No, no, hun. It's ok. I have to get someone to drive my car too so it's cool," Bee grabbed her phone and started texting someone. I assumed it was Fray. My stomach started to flutter with excitement. I felt myself randomly smile.

"Why don't you come home with us?" Lucia asked Bliss.

Bliss shook her head a little too quickly. I wondered if she was dizzy afterwards.

"Sorry doll. You know how this goes," she checked her phone. "But we're going to go to the ladies then our ride should be here. So thanks for the laughs and we will see you chickens later."

She grabbed my arm and pulled me away as I said my goodbyes. We were in the bathroom before I even realized what was going on.

"What just happened?" I asked, holding out my arms to try to balance as the room began to sway.

"She's starting to get a little too aggressive for my taste," Bliss said as she ducked into a bathroom stall to pee.

"What happened when I was gone?"

She finished, washed up and pulled me out of the club. "I'll tell you later."

Eamon was waiting outside with Fray. Bliss threw her keys at him before crawling into the back of Fray's Jag.

Fray raised his eyebrows and smiled before he said, "Should I ask?"

"No. You got Photoshop on your computer at home? I need to do something."

I texted Ted that Bee and I were ok and I might not be back, and emailed Q the photos and explained what to look for. I thought I would take a look at them when we got to Fray's but Bliss and I both ended up falling asleep on the way there. We had drunk more than I thought.

21.

"Tell me the story about how the sun loved the moon so much he died every night to let her breathe," my young voice almost twinkled.

My mother's sandalwood perfume washed over me, and I turned my head slightly to see her sitting beside me on my childhood bed. My smile grew bigger, and warmth spread through my body as her hand touched my head. I instantly felt calmer and relaxed, part of my Mother's personal magic.

"Enough stories, sweetheart," she said softly. *She seemed distant, as if her thoughts were somewhere else.*

"But they help me not be afraid when I am going to sleep," I replied.

She smiled down at me, curling around my small body. "You have nothing to be afraid of, Camille. I am always with you. And you are more powerful than you could ever imagine. You just need to learn how to harness it."

I woke up in Fray's bed the next morning, fully clothed and alone I might add, to my phone going ballistic.

I didn't know how long it had been ringing for, or where anyone else was, or who would be blowing up my phone in the first place.

It was Q.

"Hello?" I tried not to sound too fucked up when I answered.

"Dude, what the fuck did you send me?" Q asked.

"Good morning to you too. I sent you some pictures of the Kinkaid kids. I said that in my email. Why?"

"That email was barely readable. Didn't anyone ever tell you not to drink and email? No one else is in those photos other than you and your friend Bliss."

I couldn't help but laugh. This all seemed a little too simple, but maybe that was the point. You can throw crap at a wall but it doesn't mean it will stick.

"Can you clean them up and send them back? I will need them," I replied.

"Of course. Are you for real that there were other people there?" she asked.

"Yeppers. Five for sure, may have been seven. My hangover is clouding my thoughts. But there were only four Kinkaid kids."

"I have to be totally honest with you Cas. This is tech I have never even dreamed of. I'm not sure it even exists, something that can remove people from pictures like that. And only certain people too, picking out specific people like that is what is fucking with my head. If there was some sort of sensor it would give off a radius and anyone close to it....."

"What are you saying, Q?"

"I cannot explain this, Camille. There is no logical explanation."

"What is an illogical explanation?"

"Some insane tech I have never heard of. And vampires."

"Come again?"

"Vampires don't show up in photos."

I laughed. "Ok, let me get on top of this hangover and we'll talk more. I'm going to go talk to the people at Dollhouse dot com, anything I should look out for?"

"Well, how do I put this? I have personally tried to hack their server and could not."

"Why would you hack The Dollhouse server?"

"Long story. But I could not get in. I actually tried. No half ass or nothing. They are smart and very good. So watch your back."

"Thanks man," we agreed to talk later and hung up.

Fray's bed was comfortable. Warm. Had that wonderful musky scent of him that was mouth watering.

I noticed when I got out of the bed and stood up there was a bucket on the floor beside the nightstand. It was empty but it was there.

I would have considered it thoughtful until I opened

the door and saw him sneaking a blonde out the front door. I paused.

My scrambled brain wasn't sure how to process this information. A part of me wanted to be hurt, but this other part of me wasn't. This other part felt darker, cold, and cared very little. It was the hole that Jesse created, not just by his death but by all the hell he put me through over the years.

Not that I didn't like Fray. Not that I wasn't attracted to Fray. But the idea that an uber hot rock star would want a hot mess like me as any more than a fuck buddy.... well, if I bought into such a romantic dream then I am dumber than I thought. He probably has so many women he can't keep track. I bet there are codes in his phone to keep their names straight, if he bothers at all.

I closed the door softly and stood and waited, listening carefully to see if he saw me. All I could hear was a soft shift from somewhere in the room with me, when I turned all the pictures on the wall were crooked. The photos that were framed on his dresser were all tilted to one side.

"What the fuck?" I said out loud, a knock at the door making me jump. I was about to open the door when my phone started ringing again.

I didn't bother looking at the number, assuming it was Q I answered, "Word up."

The person on the other end cleared their throat and said, "May I speak to Camille Bishop please?"

"Shit, yes hi. I'm Camille. Sorry, it's been a weird morning."

"That's not a problem. I'm calling because Dr. Massimino would like you to come in and talk about your test results. Do you have time to come today?" the receptionist asked.

"Is everything alright?"

"I'm sorry. I can't discuss results over the phone. Are you available today?"

"Yes, of course. Is there a specific time or can I just come?"

"Do you have a general idea of what time you will be here?"

"I will be there within the hour."

"Great! See you soon."

I stumbled out of Fray's room, clutching my purse and my phone like my life depended on it. I debated asking Bliss for a ride but I wasn't sure I wanted to explain.

I wasn't used to having friends. I never had anyone I had to explain things to until they were already done, not even Ted. The idea of telling Fray and Bee that I had to go back to the doctor made me want to vomit.

It least I hadn't slept with Fray. That would have been so much worse.

Fray was in his kitchen making coffee, Bliss was perched on a stool with her head on the kitchen counter.

"Good morning," Fray said with a smile. "Everything

alright? I heard your phone going crazy this morning."

"Yeah. But I have to go. I got to meet my tech, and got a pile of stuff to do at the office," I said quickly. I smiled and prayed I didn't look too awkward.

Bee shifted so she could see me. "You need a ride?"

"No. No I'm good. You nurse that hangover," I replied.

"I was volunteering Fray but thank you," she said with a smirk. I kissed both her and Fray on the cheek as I headed towards the door.

"I'm curious about what your tech says. Call me later, k?" Bliss said as I opened the door.

I smiled as wide as I could. "You got it."

I got in a cab and went straight to the doctors. I didn't even bother to look in the mirror, and clearly the receptionist was confused when I walked in the door.

She smiled brightly. "Can I get you an aspirin? Some water?"

"No, I'm good. Just get this over with."

Dr. Massimino was frowning when she came in and I almost burst into tears.

"Camille, I'm sorry to bring you down here but there is something we must discuss," she sat down and turned to me, crossing her legs and putting on her glasses. She rested a file folder on her knee.

"So what have I got? Syphilis? Super syphilis?" I asked. She smiled an expression I could only categorise as a 'mom smile'.

"No, dear. You have no sexually transmitted diseases. You are totally clean," she began. "But when the lab was conducting the testing they found an anomaly."

"What now?"

Oh God.

"There is an anomaly in your blood. Something that confused the lab technicians, the one I spoke to on the phone was quite adamant that it had to be genetic. To the point that I had them look up your old blood tests just to prove it. Did Jesse have any disorders that you are aware of?"

"No. But he didn't go to the doctor much, unless it was to get tested for STD's."

She smiled nervously. "I have to ask you this and I am pretty sure I already know the answer. Are you using intravenous drugs? Sharing needles? Ingesting blood somehow?"

I stared at her blankly for a few minutes, my hangover brain not fully processing the situation. "Fuck no! Can you explain this anomaly at all?"

"It's like nothing I have ever seen before. I will be consulting with some colleagues to figure out the right course if treatment. But I am going to have to remind you to be diligent about having protected sex. Until we figure out what this thing is we have to narrow down the chances of it being transmitted," Dr. Massimino kept talking but I only got bits and pieces.

I was already in this.

But now.

Now I was down the rabbit hole with no way of going back.

I stumbled out of the doctor's office with her promises that she would get me appointments with specialists and that we were 'on it'. I didn't know who to talk to, who to call. Only one name really came to mind.

"Yo," Q answered on the fifth ring when I was about to hang up.

"Yo, you and Lemme busy? I need to talk. To both of you," I began. "Can you guys come meet me?"

"We gotta...."

"Now would be better."

She paused. "What's cracking, Bond? You good?"

"No. Not quite."

"Alright. We'll meet you at the Starbucks by your place. We got exams to cram for when we're done."

I bought us all the biggest most heavily whipped cream Frappuccino's they had and had them armed and ready when the girls arrived.

Q's eyebrows rose. "Wow. This must be serious for that level of caffeine and sugar."

"She's hung over, dude," Lemme said, sitting down and grabbing her drink.

"It's more complicated than that," I began. "I just got back from the doctor and it turns out Jesse had this anomaly too. It's being passed through sex and drug use, or both."

Lemme's ears perked up as Q asked. "So do you think we can get access to his blood? Cuz girlie's will run out eventually and if we can't get a live sample...."

Lemme cocked her head to one side and squinted her eyes like she was examining my face.

"That's not going to be a problem," I replied, sipping my drink and looking away from them.

"Oh yeah? Cops let next of kin do that shit? That's kind of fucked up, for real, but if it works in our favour I'm not complaining," Q said.

"They don't, actually. And I don't have to," I told her.

"Then how the hell...?"

Lemme stared at me and smiled as she said, "Because he gave it to her, dumbass."

"NO!" Q exclaimed, slamming her fist on the table. "Shut up. Are you for real?"

"Yep. Doctor just told me."

Q chuckled. "I don't know what shocks me more, the fact that you didn't duct tape a condom to that dude or that you have it. Did you tell the boss man yet?"

"God no. I only told you two. Not sure if I am going to even tell Ted. It's too fucked up in this extra big ball of fucked up," I said. "What do we do now? What do I do now?"

Lemme grabbed my hand. "Hey. Camille, take a breath. We'll figure it out. I have access to the best medical minds in the country. You're not alone. We're here for you."

"Of course. Shit, sorry dude. I'm such a knob. We got your back Bond," Q added. "So you got any idea how

Jesse picked this up?"

"There was something about a Kinkaid club with moths drawn on their face. Other than that I don't know. I could ask his buddy; see if I can get his phone."

"Do that. And come to the lab so we can take blood. Meet Rory Woo. She's my number two on this project," Lemme began. I grabbed my phone and dialled Rollo.

"Ya'll are coming with me if I have to go meet this clown," I pointed at them both with the phone to my ear.

"What do you want?" Rollo snapped, answering on the second ring.

"Watch your tone, butt munch. I'm looking into what happened to Jesse but I need a few things. Any chance you got his phone?" I asked.

"Finally. I told her you would come around...."

"Told who?"

"Amanda. She had her panties in a wad about it, wanted to talk to you herself...."

I couldn't help but laugh. "That's cute. Did she mention our first meeting? So you got his phone?"

"Actually, you're in luck. I picked it up from whoever found it in the garbage can."

"Awesome. You need to write down and email me all that info. Also anything you know about a club where they paint moths on your face. And bring me the phone."

"What about Amanda?"

"What about her?"

"Do you want me to give her your number?"

I laughed. "No. She can email me the info like you do.

It's easier, saves me writing it down."

"Should we meet so we can talk?"

"Unless you want to pay me by the hour, no. This is off book on my own time and, frankly, I don't have a lot of it."

"Ok. I'm down the street. Can I put the phone in Ted's mailbox?"

"That would be amazing. I can get Ted to bring it to me. You'll do that now?"

"I'm pulling up now. Text me your email."

"Awesome. Thanks Rollo," I hung up before I had to make small talk. I sighed loudly then texted Ted to let him know Rollo was dropping a phone and not to kick his ass. He sent me thumbs up and a smiley face and said it would be on top of the fridge.

I growled. "I forgot about her."

"Who?" Q asked.

"Remember the whore from the brothel? Jesse was banging her."

"Well isn't that peachy! So this shit is spreading like a prostatot after a few wine coolers."

"What the hell is a prostatot?"

"A preteen who dresses like a hooker."

I laughed a little too hard. They both watched me with complete confusion. The longer I sat with them the more comfortable I got, and I slowly started to unravel.

"Fuck, I need a drink. You guys want to go get a drink?" I asked. "I think I need a flask or a purse mickey or something. How am I supposed to function without liquid courage?"

"Like the rest of us. You just do," Q said. "You want to be like him? You're talking like an addict and you're better than that."

"I know! It just makes things so much less chaotic in my head. How sad is that?"

"It's not sad. You have a lot going on. The world just kind of decided to screw with you for a while. Don't let it take you down," Q continued. "Wanna go smoke a bowl? Pot's a better plan than booze. It'll calm you down."

"Pot makes me sad and paranoid. Not my thing," I replied. "Weren't you just lecturing me about addiction and now you are offering me pot?"

She snorted. "Pot is not addictive. It's good for you."

"It's cute that you think that way, but you are wrong my friend," I pat her hand lightly. "So what now?"

"We got to cram today but come by the lab tomorrow. See what you can get off Jesse's phone then I will take over. We'll start with blood work," Lemme said with a smile. "But we're going to jet. Exams are kicking my ass. Don't worry though, I got your back. Science will be my bitch when this is over."

"Dammit! I almost forgot!" Q exclaimed. "I cleaned up those photos for you. It's a total mind fuck, dude. How many other people did you say were there?"

I smiled. "Five. Is it something I can show Ted?"

"Have at it. And tell the boss man that I am gobsmacked."

"You're what? Did you get a word of the day calendar or something?"

"I am totally confused. I have no idea what kind of tech could have done that. Use whatever word you want."

"I actually kind of like gobsmacked. I will try to use that in a sentence myself today."

Q smiled. "Can we drop you at home?"

"Sure."

Ted was hovering when I got back. He clearly had to leave but was trying to decide if it was more important to talk to me first.

I grabbed a glass of juice when I got in the kitchen. "You okay, Ted? You seem a bit on edge."

He handed me Jesse's phone. I could tell by the look on his face that he knew whose it was.

"Anything you want to tell me Cas?" he asked.

"In regards to what exactly?"

"Why did Rollo bring you Jesse's phone?"

"Because I need it to help Bliss find Bucky."

He sighed. "Crap. Still no sign of him?"

"No. And his phone popped up in a meth house on the other side of town."

"Bucky was into meth?"

"No, but Jesse could be. Could've been. Some junkie with a moth drawn on her face said they went to a new club and something about a new drug, which was a Kinkaid club by the way. And, *and,* Bee and I had drinks with the Kinkaid spawn and I took some pictures."

"There is photographic evidence of your drunken escapade? Not cool, Cas."

"That's not it! The Kinkaid kids don't show up in pictures!"

His head cocked to one side. "What?"

"I took photos. Of them. And they are just not there, like I am talking to the invisible man. Q said she was gobsmacked."

He chuckled. "I see she is using that word of the day calendar I bought her."

"My point is that *I have these photos!* We can take them to Kiera. We can take them to the press! We can blow this thing up!" I was almost to the point of jumping up and down.

"Have you looked in that box I gave you?"

I stopped and groaned loudly. "Oh boo! Why do you have to rain on my parade?"

"Because if you look in that box you would know that your old man scheduled *the exact same parade,*" Ted began. "Did you think you were the first? I'm sure I have a few of these invisible man photos somewhere that I took myself."

"So how do you explain it? Why has this never caught fire?"

"I can't explain it. It should catch fire. It's weird and makes no sense. But the Kinkaid's are too big and powerful and their network will crush it before it goes anywhere."

"But...."

"But then. *Then they will come after you. They will come after you like they came after him.*"

I paused and stared at him before saying, "I can't just let this go."

"I never said you had to. I'm saying you need more."

"More than this? This is pretty big."

He smiled. "I know it is. I am sorry that it's not enough. There will be something else, I'm sure."

Ted left a short time later, and I was so deflated that I flopped down on the living room couch, my back on the seat, feet in the air, and head over the side.

Just like I had when I was a kid. It used to clear my head and I had hopes it would again.

My phone beeped that I had a text. It was Bliss, she had spoken to her cousin who worked for The Dollhouse and he would see us this afternoon. I tried Jesse's phone and it was dead, luckily I had his spare charger that he made me keep for emergencies. I plugged it in and hopped in the shower, texting Bliss that I would be ready shortly.

It would be good to do some proper work with a clear head.

Jesse's phone was taking a charge, thankfully, and I kept glancing at it as I got ready. Like it would start ringing and magically be him, like he had left it in my purse again.

I pushed the power button and the screen lit up, my own face stared back at me. A knot began to form in my stomach.

The phone was password protected, and unless he had randomly changed it I knew it. He never knew that I knew it but I did. 6969.

It worked. His wallpaper was lingerie clad Amanda posing on a bed. I couldn't help but sigh, and being the jackass I am I went straight to his pictures.

Not that I was surprised, but there was a whole file full of different girls doing a similar pose on the same bed. Some of them looked young. Really young. One girl even looked like Bliss in profile.

No. She wouldn't.

My phone rang before I could do more. It was Bliss and she was outside. I put the phone down and gathered up my things.

I debated on telling her about the phone. I didn't want to get her hopes up that this might help find Bucky. There was always the chance that the two incidents were not connected.

But there was also a good chance that Bucky was dead, or that he killed Jesse and was in the wind. Of the two, death was the better option.

22.

Bliss and I drove downtown to Toronto's entertainment district, which was gross in the daytime. All of the glamour and mystery was lost in the sunlight.

The Dollhouse's offices were in the upper floors of a defunked nightclub. Bliss had changed into a pair of black fitted ankle pants, a black t-shirt and a denim blazer so we kind of matched, only my t-shirt was blue and my blazer was dark purple.

She banged on the door like she owned the place and I tried my best not to look nervous.

A dude in a light grey suit answered, smiling at Bee in a way that made me want to slap him.

"Hi! We're looking for Nico?" she asked. She was alarmingly peppy; I had to wonder if she had some hangover cure that I didn't know about.

"Hey gorgeous, come on in," he replied, ushering us inside. "Are you guys here to audition?"

"I'm Nico's cousin," she said. Something flickered in the guy's eyes, he must have known who the Fiori's were, and the pervy smile dropped.

"Have a seat," he motioned to the little couch in the entryway then disappeared back into the offices.

We sat and looked around. It was just as seedy as I had expected. The paint was peeling; the vinyl furniture had been repaired with duct tape. There was no receptionist, and once you went past the little sitting area it was a bunch of grey false walls forming cubicles.

"Huh," was all I could think of to say.

"What were you expecting?" Bliss whispered as someone came towards us. Nico Fiori looked a lot like Bucky so I spotted him easily, and Mr Grey Suit had felt the need to walk him to us. Nico was in dark blue jeans and a white button down, with his hair spiked straight up in a way that kind of resembled a helmet.

"Nico!" exclaimed Bliss, hopping up and hugging him. I followed along behind her as he escorted us back to a private office with real walls and a door.

"Nico, this is my friend Camille," Bliss said as he closed the door behind us. I smiled brightly and shook Nico's hand. Maybe he wasn't used to women shaking hands.

"Hey, so Bee said you were a friend of Jane's?" Nico motioned for us to take seats at the desk across from him.

"Yeah and I was wondering if I could ask you a few

questions," I began.

"You a cop or something?"

I glanced at Bee and she nodded that it was ok. "No, I'm a P.I. I'd helped her out with a few things and I just wanted to try to find out what might have happened to her."

"Are you the one who stirred up the Kinkaid bullshit?"

"No. Not at all. As far as I know she did that on her own."

"Good. Well, Jane had her fair share of stalkers as Bella. Twilight fans, vamp enthusiasts, and this weird ass old dude that claimed she stole his credit card info. He even brought a paralegal here," he began, and my throat tightened. "I think the guy even tried to hack our system to find her."

"Did he get anything?"

Nico chuckled. "You're adorable! No. Our system is too advanced for that."

Bliss smiled. "Are you sure or are you just being cocky?"

"No. No I'm not," he continued. "As soon as she started posting those rants we got complaints, and when the cease and desist showed up we had to shut her down. She was livid. Said she was going to explore other options. Two days later she was dead."

I grabbed my notepad from my purse. "The guy who brought the paralegal. You got a name? The paralegal's name?"

He smiled, opened the top drawer of the desk, and

pulled out a business card that he handed to me. I didn't need to see it to know who it was.

I didn't want to burst Nico's bubble that they had been hacked. And by a dude that I was pretty sure was an old drunk in disguise.

When we got back in the car my throat felt like it was in a vice grip.

"You know this dude he was talking about, don't you?" Bliss asked.

I nodded.

"You can't send the cops to Nico. You know that, right?"

I nodded again.

"Too bad this didn't help us with any clues to find Bucky."

I tried to swallow. "I may have a lead."

"Does this have anything to do with where you ran off to this morning?"

I made a so-so sign with my hand. I wasn't going to tell her all of it. I wasn't going to try to explain something to someone that I didn't understand myself.

"I have Jesse's phone. Not on me. It's charging at my place, but it's mine now. Once I go through it I will give it to my tech and she will go through it. I'm not making any promises so don't get your hopes up.'

She smiled. "How did you swing that? The cops release it to you?"

"No, they didn't have it. His idiot buddy Rollo had it, said he recovered it when he called and some random person answered and said they had found it in a garbage can."

"Rollo, huh?" she said, laughing so hard she thumped on the steering wheel. "That guy should not be allowed out on his own after dark. I always figured Jesse kept him around to take the rap if something big went down."

"Jesse adored him. I don't know how Rollo is going to survive without him. He blames me, you know. For what happened to Jesse. He only gave me the phone because I promised him I would find out what happened."

"You can't take that on. You're not Nancy Drew."

"No but my cousin Kiera is a damn good detective. I'll hand her whatever I....we find and she will figure it out I am sure. I have absolute faith in her."

"What about your uncle and his partner? They're good, aren't they?"

"Yeah but this is police territory. They will let the cops do their thing and won't step in unless they fail. It's kind of how the P.I thing works. It sucks sometimes, but the P.I game sucks sometimes."

"Ok. Well, keep me posted. I'm hoping Bucky is on my Mother's doorstep when I get there."

"Me too. I have to ask, how are you so chipper? This hangover is mushing up my brain."

"Watered down screwdriver with two aspirin and Fray's hangover breakfast. It works wonders. You should have stuck around."

I cringed. "Is he mad?"

"No. Just confused. You'll need to spend time clarifying things with him."

"I will. But right now I have to hand my cousin a suspect."

Bliss dropped me back at home, and the first thing I did was call the office and ask Ramona to tell me anything about the client I was now referring to as McDrunk. I didn't explain why and she didn't ask. She gave me his name and any personal details she had so I could do some legwork from home.

I also texted Q to ask how hard it would genuinely be to hack The Dollhouse server. She had said before that they had tried and failed, I didn't want her to elaborate on the circumstances just the difficulty.

McDrunk's actual name was Morris Ludlow and he had a drunk and disorderly rap sheet that would make a board starlet cry. He was a janitor for an agency that cleaned a bunch of office buildings downtown.

I looked around at his internet presence and it seemed mostly isolated to porn sites. He had no Facebook or social media in general. No family of record. He was a typical sounding single man who hadn't caught up with technology. There was nothing to connect him to Jane Lowry except that Dollhouse subscription.

But something didn't sit right with me about it. It all seemed a little too cut and paste for my liking. I knew that crime often had a simple explanation but this, *this* was just too neat.

My next step was looking into the company he worked for, Ace Industrial Cleaning Services. Apparently they specialized in all sorts of cleaning, including chemical spills and crime scenes. The corporate division, which specializes in cleaning office buildings, boasted on their site that they were the number one agency and references were available upon request.

I debated asking Ramona to make the call but I didn't. Since I was technically not supposed to be working I couldn't do that without getting shit on. I already had to explain to Ted why I needed the info from the file.

I grabbed the cordless house phone and a notepad and dialled the number.

"Ace Cleaning, how may I help you?" a bubbly female voice answered.

"Hi-ee, my name is Natalie and I am calling from L and B Investigations," I began in my best super perky voice. "I am looking for a cleaning company for our offices and I read on your site that you have references?"

"Yes we do!" she was a bit too excited.

"But I also noticed that you guys don't have a price list. Why is that?"

"We prefer to send our price list directly to a potential client. If you give me an email address I would be happy to send you our current price list along with a list of references."

"That would be awesome! Can I get your name, so I

have a contact person?"

"My name is Cynthia. You can ask for me directly when you call back."

"Great! My email is landbinvestigate@gmail.com," I gave her one of several working emails I used when I didn't want things to go to my business email. My real name was on it when emails were sent out; I would have to switch it to Natalie if I ever emailed her back.

"Awesome! I will get that out to you right now."

"Thanks so much for your help Cynthia! Have a fantastic day!"

I sighed loudly when I hung up. Being that perky was exhausting.

Twenty minutes later I had my list. I almost choked on my coffee when I saw their price list, but that wasn't as important.

I cross referenced the names and three out of the five were owned by Labelle Waterford Technologies.

Ted came in before I had a chance to look further, dropping his bag on the kitchen table where I had stationed myself.

"Should I ask?" Ted said as he grabbed a drink and sat beside me.

"Ever heard of Labelle Waterford Technologies?"

"Yep. A division of The Kinkaid Group. Why do you ask?"

I huffed. "This just gets weirder and weirder."

"What do you mean?"

"Well, do you remember, right around the time I first

met with Jane Lowry and an old drunk dude came in? Wanted me to talk to Dollhouse dot com?"

"Yep. You sent him to a paralegal."

"I did. Turns out that he came to me because he was stalking Jane, a performer on that site."

He paused. "Oh. Well then."

My phone beeped, it was a message from Q saying it would take some serious high level hacking steez to hack The Dollhouse server.

"And it appears that he hacked their server to get info on Jane, but Q says it would take some 'serious high level skills' to do so. So, I did a little looking, and he is a janitor for a company that cleans office buildings."

"Buildings run by Labelle Waterford Technologies, a division of The Kinkaid Group," Ted replied.

"I know it's circumstantial. We could probably never find a paper trail but it's something, isn't it. Isn't it?" I asked. "A man who works in a Kinkaid building murders a girl who called out the Kinkaid's?"

"Who he also happens to be stalking? That seems a bit too convenient. I'm guessing you have confirmation of a hack from The Dollhouse?"

"I have confirmation that this particular dude was stalking Jane and showed up at their office with the paralegal whose name I gave him. Dollhouse would never admit they had been hacked."

"So the Fiori's got their toes dipped in that too, huh?"

"Apparently. But no one can find Bucky. It's bizarre."

"That's not good, Cas."

"I know. I don't have the heart to tell Bliss that. Which is one of the reasons I got Jesse's phone from Rollo."

"Any luck with it?"

"It's plugged in; I haven't touched it since I got back. I don't know if I even want to look through it, it's too upsetting."

"Which reminds me, his mother called this morning. The funeral is the day after tomorrow."

"What about that visitation crap?"

"Not necessary. You should send all this to Kiera. See what she can pull together from it. Also spend some time mentally preparing yourself for the funeral. But count your blessings his mother has the casket closed."

23.

"Babe!"

Fingers ran softly through my hair and across my forehead.

A kiss on my cheek. "Babe!"

I opened one eye and Jesse lay in my bed beside me.

"I finally get you out of my life and now you're haunting my dreams too?"

He looked stunned. "You mean you meant all that?"

"Of course I did. I'm tired of your shit. I'm done. I need someone who is there for me and wants me, not what I can do for them. I'm a real person. I deserve more."

He stroked my cheek. "You do. And I am sorry I couldn't give it to you. I'm sorry I couldn't be who you needed me to be."

"I needed you to behave like a human being, not just float in and out of my life as you saw fit. Not just say

pretty things then disappear and ignore me like I'm some kind of hated stepchild. That's not fair. I loved you with a part of my being that I thought no longer existed. But you destroyed it. I will never feel for someone the way I felt about you. You cannot even begin to understand how you hurt me. I know you think I am overreacting but all that does is trivialize how hurt I am. It doesn't make it go away."

He paused for a minute and shook his head. "How did I get here?"

"What do you mean?"

"I was out at....then it all went....and I closed my eyes and then I was here. I don't understand."

I looked at the panic in his eyes and the tension in his body and couldn't help but feel a little confused.

This was a weird ass dream.

He was dead. The conversation made no sense.

"I was sick," he continued. "Bucky and I went out and we....then I got sick. I went to this bar that Amanda works at to get some food."

I put my hand on his cheek, cupping his face in my hands. I smiled and tried to be calm and warm to soothe him. There didn't seem a point in trying to explain it to him. My mind was presenting him like this for a reason. I needed to see him like this for a reason.

"It's ok. You're ok. Just relax and stay with me. You'll be fine," I replied.

"Really? I can stay?"

"Yeah but we've got to sleep. I got a long day tomorrow

and I need to get some rest. You should rest too. You're clearly upset. You'll feel better once you've calmed down and got some perspective."

He put his head down on the pillow and I got a flash of his body in the morgue.

"You're too good to me, Camille. I love you."

I tore apart my room trying to find something to wear. I wanted to be comfortable but respectful, not just to his family but to our years together. I put on the bracelet I had found at the meth house, something about it was comforting.

While I was looking for my sensible shoes that I wore with skirts in the bottom of my closet I came across a wood box I didn't recognise.

It was stained black and had odd markings carved into the surface that was accented with gold leaf. Printed right near the edge of the lid was 'Marie LeFaye' in elegant script.

How did I not see this box?

I opened it and my fingers started to hum, like electricity was coursing through the box. There were some random items that I had never seen before inside; a deck of tarot cards, a big silver ring that looked like intertwined snakes in some sort of Celtic knot, a smaller black box with a gold hieroglyph on the lid, some small satchels of herbs, stones, crystals, and feathers were neatly organized inside.

So it looked as if my Mother had some interesting hobbies I didn't know about.

I picked up the ring, it was heavier then I had expected. I slipped it on my right hand and that hum continued, sending the vibrations up my arm and through my body. It was oddly calming, as if it somehow carried my Mother's energy with it.

I decided against a skirt, instead opting for slim fit black pants and a black v neck top with a black cardigan. When I went to do my hair and my makeup I began to question my judgement about the new hairstyle. One of the reasons I had always dyed my hair black was because it made me look like my mom, I thought.

In that moment I so desperately wanted to see her that her image flashed in the mirror like she was standing with me, her short dark hair perfectly framing her face. She smiled at me, that same knowing Mom smile that put my mind and body at ease.

I often felt guilty that I didn't think about my Dad that way. I couldn't help but wonder if it was because I had Ted. I missed my Dad, I did, but I had Ted to help ease the pain. I didn't have that with my Mother.

A knock at the bathroom door brought me back to reality.

"You ok, kid?" Ted called to me through the door.

"Got any Valium?" I called back. I should have filled that prescription the doctor gave me.

"Better. I got a flask of whiskey."

"The same one you had when my parents died?"

"That's the one. Now we got to go."

I was genuinely surprised at the amount of people who came out for Jesse's service. People we went to high school with that I am confident didn't like him in life decided to show their faces, I supposed he would be a topic of conversation in their little cliques for years to come.

Rollo nodded at me from the back row, and I thought we might sit with him until his companion turned her head and Amanda and I made eye contact.

Before my anger could bubble over someone tapped my shoulder. I was relieved to see Bliss's face.

"Is that her?" she whispered, moving her eyes in Amanda's direction. "She's got some serious balls showing up here."

"I'm still trying to figure out when this became a high school reunion. How did they all know?" I asked.

Bliss shrugged. "Facebook is my best guess. Where are we sitting?"

Ted dragged us in the direction of Jesse's mom, who was waving at us. A young man stood beside her with Jesse's boyhood face staring back at me.

I knew he had a little brother that he hadn't seen in a long time. That was one of the 'last straw' issues with his parents; they didn't want Jesse corrupting the younger Garrow so he had to go. Not that they were saints, but it was easier for them to blame Jesse than admit their failures.

There were three empty seats in the front row with his family.

Two feet away from the casket.

I was pretty sure I had stopped breathing when we had entered the room but now as we got closer to the front I was sure my heart was going to stop too.

I fiddled with my mother's ring as we sat down and tried to centre myself. I hadn't even entertained the idea that I might have to speak to the crowd.

The lights flickered, and I felt a cool breeze on my face. When I looked around I noticed that the handles on the casket were flapping up and down and the flowers were blowing around as if in a windstorm.

The lights flickered again, this time faster, and when I took my hand off the ring it all stopped.

What the hell?

A pastor got up and spoke about peace, about the soul being tormented and about the struggles of addiction and some shit.

Were they really going to make Jesse's death a teaching moment?

His father got up and told delightful stories of a young, happy boy. It was funny that it all seemed to occur before I met him.

There was a moment of no talking where it seemed like the room collectively turned to me. It was a natural time for me to step up. His father ended his stories around the time I came into Jesse's life, it made sense.

I stood up, and Ted grabbed my hand.

"You don't have to do this," he said loud enough that I am sure the whole room could hear.

"Yes I do," I replied. "Someone has to. It should be me. It's supposed to be me."

I walked over to the podium and turned and looked out to the room. The casket loomed like a dark cloud, Amanda's stupid head grated on my nerves.

"I'm not going to stand here and talk about him like he was a saint. I think that's a mistake and dishonest to his memory," I began. "We had a long and complicated relationship, that actually ended a few weeks before....He tried so hard to please people, thinking he wasn't good enough just as he was. I admit that I tried to change him, but it was because I was so desperate to save him from himself. And I'm sorry. I'm sorry, Mr and Mrs Garrow. I'm sorry Rollo. I'm sorry little brother. I remember now, your name is Mark. I'm sorry I couldn't save him. I'm sorry I wasn't enough to save him."

The tears started, big and hot and heavy. I put my hands on the podium and put my head down, and when my hand touched the ring again it was like we were in a wind tunnel. The lights started flickering rapidly and the furniture shaking, people started freaking out and bolted for the door. The funeral director ran in and ushered everyone out, yelling about a ventilation problem. I kept my hand firmly planted on the ring until we stepped into the hallway, and then took it off as I stared into the room, watching as it all went away like magic.

Ted handed me the flask. "I wonder how many of your high school chums are going to say that was his ghost."

"All of them. I will too," I said, taking a swig. "It's the only logical explanation."

Ted had to pick up some things from the office before we headed back, and Bliss had to go to school so I stayed with Ted.

He handed me a twenty dollar bill when we parked out front of the office. "Go grab us some food from the Whistlestop. I won't be long."

"Hi Camille!" Mille smiled brightly when she saw me. "Good to see you!"

"Hey Millie, can I have the usual for me and Ted?" I asked. She got to work and I stood by the counter and stared at the ring on my finger.

"You ok, Camille?" Millie asked as she bagged up our food. She looked at me and stumbled back like she had seen something frightening.

"Yeah, it's just been a rough few weeks. What do I owe you?"

I handed her the twenty and she pointed at my hand.

"That's an interesting ring. Where did you get it?" she stuttered.

"It was my mother's."

She swallowed hard. "Did Marie give it to you herself?"

"No, I....wait. How do you know my mother's name?"

"I was waiting for the right time to tell you. My last

name is LeFaye; I am your mother's cousin. But before I tell you more I am going to need you to take the ring off."

24.

Millie was, in fact, Millie LeFaye.

I am that sort of asshole that made her show me her identification.

She had a box under the counter, not unlike my mother's, that had an envelope full of photos of faces I did not know alongside my mother. I kept the ring on and Millie kept a measured distance.

"I'm embarrassed I don't know any of these people," I told Millie as I looked at the photos. "She didn't talk about her family much after her parents died."

"You never met her sisters? Her brother?" Millie asked. "She told you her parents were dead?"

My eyes filled with tears. "I didn't even know she had sisters. I think I met her brother once. Where are they?"

"It's a long and complicated story. She really told you nothing? This may be a lot to process. I don't even know if you will believe me."

I smiled. "I can't imagine you could shock me any further than I have been shocked lately."

She chuckled, shrugging her shoulders and smiling at me like *don't be so sure!*

"Do you know the story of King Arthur?"

"Yeah, my Mom used to read it to me. Why?"

She took a deep breath, then said, "Well, the Vita Merlini was the most accurate. There were nine sisters who ruled Avalon. Morgan le Fay was their leader. Some even took on the role of Lady of the Lake, which was an office, title, whatever you want to call it."

"Mom mentioned that. Why are you telling me this?"

"Because we are descended from those nine sisters. We are the ruling blood of Avalon. We are their heirs."

"So does that mean we....?" I looked down at the ring again, not able to fully grasp what I was trying to ask. "That would explain *a lot*."

"I wish she would have told you. You were old enough that you should have been told."

"I'm sure she had a reason. But why don't I have...?"

"Have what?"

"Do we have....powers? Was that all true? Was Morgan really a sorceress?"

"Yes she was, but she was also so much more. Her, Vivienne and Nimue. They were all ladies of Avalon. As you are, through them."

I exhaled loudly. "You were right. This is a lot to process."

"There should be a book. We all have a written history of our family. Your mother's should be around," Millie said. The bell over her door rang and Ted came in, Millie gathered the contents of her box and it suddenly disappeared.

"You ready, kid?" Ted asked. 'Hey Millie, how are you?"

"I'm great. Got your food ready for you," Millie handed me the food bag off the counter. "Here you go, Camille. Let's talk again soon."

I smiled and nodded, grabbing the bag and following Ted out.

"Everything alright Cas?" Ted asked as we drove.

"Yes. No. I don't know how to answer that anymore," I began. "I am keeping it together. I got a random question."

"Ruh row."

"Do we have any of my mom's books around?"

"Funny you mention that, I actually found a box of her stuff in the attic yesterday. I'll put it in your room."

"Bitchin. Now, when are we going to talk about me going back to work?"

I could not help but wonder if some higher power made sure that I found all this stuff of my Mother's when I did. My closet wasn't *that* messy. The idea that I just didn't notice it itched at my brain in the most horrible way.

Same thing with Ted randomly finding a box of my Mom's stuff in the attic. That place was insanely organized, like Fort freaking Knox.

I sat on my bed and stared at the box, I was terrified of what was inside it.

What did all this mean?

I wished I had someone to talk to. I had always known in the back of my mind that if Jesse was gone I would be cast out adrift. This crate of my Mother's things was like a life preserver keeping my head above water.

So much was going on already; did I really want to know everything?

I raised my hand to brush my hair off my face and the lid flipped off the box.

I debated taking the ring off. I would have to find a way to control whatever *this* was. But if the power was contained to the ring then it shouldn't be such an issue.

But *I had power.* I had never had real power in my life.

I knew I should have been scared.

But I wasn't.

I liked it.

I put the lid back on the box, took off the ring, lifted my hand and thought 'come off'. The lid flew up and slammed into the ceiling, flaking off some of the white stucco before floating down.

Well. Alright.

I spent some time using this new found power to move random shit around my room. I was so preoccupied that the actual contents of the box slipped my mind, and

I wasn't pulled away from it until Jesse's phone lit up to tell me it was charged.

I typed in his stupid password and that girl's annoying blonde face showed up. Something inside my brain twitched a bit.

I knew she had the anomaly, just like I did. I wanted to say that I felt something for her because of it, but I didn't. I knew I was supposed to feel something, anything, even if it was disgust or anger. But when I looked at her I felt absolutely nothing.

I hoped that the anomaly killed her.

That was something.

I had never openly wished for someone's death before. I didn't want to ruin my karma but for her I could make an exception.

I started going through his photos, there were hundreds. So before I really sat down and went through them I went into his billing app and had the detailed billing logs from the last three months sent to my email. With that I would have every call in and out. Going through his texts and email browser history was a project for another day.

Back in the photos, the last ten pictures were the most telling. The most recent was a selfie in a bathroom mirror at a bar. His face was gaunt, dark shadows rimmed his eyes like a raccoon. He looked like a reflection of the person I knew, and my heart thumped when I remembered that I probably didn't know him at all. One more photo in the bar, a dark haired young woman in the background with penetrating eyes looked familiar even though her face was partially blurred.

Moth face from the meth house showed up in the fifth photo. She was sleeping. I'm pretty sure the photo was taken where I had found her. She was wearing his bracelet that I took from her.

This must have been an after sex photo. He had wanted to remember her. That twitch in my brain happened again, only this time I felt pity.

Not enough pity to tell her about the anomaly, but pity nonetheless.

The pictures after that were of the club. Outside photos that would help pinpoint a location once I uploaded them to my computer and did a search, a few interiors, and one of Jesse and a super wasted Bucky Fiori. I emailed it to myself and the details from the time stamp.

I kind of knew I should copy the contents of the phone and hand it to Kiera but I couldn't. It didn't feel right. She would already have her hands full with what I sent her about Morris Ludlow, and if there was nothing useful on the phone it would just be a big waste of her time.

I zoomed in on Bucky's face. He did not look well, his eyes glazed over and his pupils so dilated his iris was consumed by black. He was never a big drug person, living by the 'don't get high on your own supply' mantra, but maybe Jesse had changed him. Maybe things had changed since we were teenagers.

I plugged the phone into my laptop and started

downloading its contents. I turned back to the book box, using my mind and hand to pull the contents out and neatly place it on my bed.

Sure enough there was a leather bound book, small and brown bound in soft material with gold edging on the pages. It looked old and well used. I immediately felt drawn to it but was intimidated by its presence.

As soon as I picked it up, the moment I opened it, everything in my life would change.

Before I could think any further my phone started ringing. I used my power to lift it off my desk and bring it to me on my bed, smiling happily to myself.

"Hello?" I said without checking the call display.

"Hey kid, it's me," Kiera sounded tired. "I wanted to be the one to tell you that we got him."

"Who?"

"Morris Ludlow," she replied. "Your intel was good; he all out confessed when we picked him up for questioning."

"Shut up. For real?"

"You bet. We just went and searched his house. Grabbed his computer, there was a whole room full of photos of Jane Lowry. It was like something from a movie."

"Wow."

"Wow? I thought you would be happy. You caught a murderer."

"It's all tied up a bit too neat. Can't you sense it too? My bullshit radar is spiking."

"It happens. Not everything is perfect. Sometimes you just have to go with the evidence."

"That's why you're the detective."

"Which reminds me, the next time that fucker Dorien Reid calls me two I am going to break his goddamn nose," she snapped. "Sorry. My bad. Also, just a heads up, a body came in today that is looking like Bucky Fiori. We're trying to ID it through dental records. Don't get your friend in a twist yet but she is going to need you if it is."

"Dental records? How fucked up is he?"

Pause. "How much do you understand about tissue decomposition?"

"A whole lotta nothing."

"Right. So I will keep you posted. But I gotta go, kid. We'll chat again soon," Kiera hung up quickly before I could say more. As soon as she hung up I called Q.

It went straight to voicemail. I briefly explained that a decomposed body that they think is Bucky Fiori has showed up in the morgue, and it would be useful if we had access to the lab reports for our tests in case he's infected. And if Jesse's autopsy report appears too it could come in handy. I added at the end that I would see what I can do, in case it came back to bite me in the ass later.

While I had my phone I messaged Fray, letting him know I was thinking of him and I wanted to see him soon. Before I could push send my phone started ringing. It was Bliss.

"Hey Bee. What's up?" I asked.

"I need to talk to you. It's important," she sounded like she was walking somewhere. "Are you free?"

"Is everything ok?"

"I can talk more when I see you. Are you at home?"

"You're freaking me out, Bee. What's going on?"

She exhaled loudly. "For fucks sake, Cas. You had a doctor's appointment when you ran out of Fray's, didn't you?"

"Uh...."

"Cut the crap. Did you know before Jesse infected you?"

"I'm at home. Come over."

About twenty minutes later my doorbell rang. I was so nervous I thought I might barf on Bliss when she came in the door.

She pushed passed me. "Are we alone?"

"Yeah. Why?"

"Are you 100% sure? You guys don't have the house bugged? No recording devices?"

I chuckled. "No. Ted's not *that* paranoid. What the hell is going on?"

She sat me down in the living room. "I have to be honest with you about something. I have wanted to tell you for a long time but I was advised not to, but now with the latest body...."

"Is it Bucky?"

"I don't know yet. How do you know?"

"Kiera wanted to warn me so I could be supportive."

"I always forget there is a Bishop in homicide. Is Reid still calling her Two?"

I smiled. "You're a cop?"

"Yeah. Deep cover. Fray doesn't know either."

"Who are you watching? The people that run Ren? October?"

She chuckled. "No. October Daniels is small fish. Hot, but small."

"So it's the Kinkaid's," it was a statement not a question.

"You should have been a cop!" she replied with a laugh.

"Well, its common sense considering the circumstances. You know about the anomaly?"

"I have been calling it a virus, but yes I do. How do you know?"

"It came up on Jane Lowry's paternity test. I had some of her blood sent to a friend at U of T for further testing."

"Ah. I understand. Was what happened at the funeral because of it? A side effect?"

I looked away from her. "Why would you think that was me?"

"Camille. Please. Give me some credit."

I looked down. "No. That's a whole different bag of snakes. What do you know about the virus as you call it?"

"This will have to be an 'I'll show you mine if you

show me yours' scenario, Camille. My name will have to stay out of it. I am so deep in that Kiera wouldn't even be able to find me."

"How do I know you're not lying? That you're not in with the Kinkaid's and using this as a way to find out what I know?"

She smiled at me. "C'mon. You have Spidey sense, don't you? Concentrate on what I am saying, and if I set off your internal radar I will go and we never have to talk about it again."

I looked her in the eye and concentrated, and I immediately knew she was telling the truth. So I had to ask the first question that came to mind, just to clear the air.

"If you are investigating the Kinkaid's, do you know if they killed my parents?"

"No. I am truly sorry for that," I knew she was going to lie before she even opened her mouth. "The whole Kinkaid web is so much more complicated then you could possibly understand."

I shrugged my shoulders. "I have a box of my Dad's files that I haven't even opened. I am well aware that I don't even know the half of it. Do you think the body is Bucky?"

She sighed loudly and ran her hand through her hair. Her expression sank.

"Knowing my luck? Probably. Fucking asshole. Why couldn't he just grow out of his criminal phase like normal people?" she said angrily.

"You know I have a crazy amount of questions, right?"

"I figured. Coles notes version is that I got tired of being a statistic. I wanted to prove to the world that *a Fiori could be someone.* When I met with that horrible excuse for a guidance councillor we had in high school," she continued as I chuckled and nodded in agreement, "I was so pissed off with how she treated me just because my name was Fiori. So I applied to the police academy on my own, and while doing that I did a psychology degree at York University."

I couldn't help but smile. "You are not fucking around."

"No! One day I want to meet the great Kiera Bishop, the fastest woman promoted to detective in the history of Toronto Police Services. She's a legend among the rookies."

"I knew it was fast but I didn't know it was *that* fast. She is a cool chick. You'll like her. So, where do we go from here?"

"I was about to ask you the same question. Through me you will have the connections you need to figure this out. And if we crack the Kinkaid cabal open it'll be you and me."

"Can you get me lab work, samples, that sort of shit? So I can give it to my lab geeks at U of T and we can figure this virus out?"

"If you share any and all info with me, abso-fucking-lutely."

"Ok. In the interest of honesty and openness, my lab tech said that infected blood obliterated cancer in a rat."

"Huh. Well, in that same interest we have found that the infected either don't last long or thrive with weird vampire like symptoms."

"Don't last long?"

"Yeah. Sorry. I'm pretty sure that's what happened to Jesse. Our guys are analysing tissue samples. Sounds like it happened to Bucky too. How long ago did you have sex with Jesse?"

"More than a month."

"Good. So you passed the usual gestation period. You are good. Good. And you are sure what happened at the funeral had nothing to do with the virus?"

I chuckled. "Yeah I am pretty confident on that."

"What was that anyways?'

That seemed to be the ten million dollar question.

"I don't know. But when I do I will try my best to explain."

She studied my face, then said with a clap of her hands. "Well alright then! Let's get a drink, shall we?"

When Bliss dropped me back at home later that black car was parked out front. I had forgotten all about it, and considering my current situation I had no time to dance around anymore. I needed to know what the hell this was about.

I quickly crossed the street, walked up to the driver side window and knocked.

The window rolled down with a swish, an older

man with kind eyes smiled at me. A black hat sat on the passenger seat; this was the same man who was outside the house weeks ago.

"Can I help you?" I asked with my best menacing face.

"Wow. You look so much like your Mother," he said.

"Who are you exactly?"

He chuckled. "I figured this would happen. I have my ID."

He handed me his driver's license.

"Harold LeFaye?" I croaked. My throat went dry. I swallowed hard and tried to keep calm. I handed him back his ID.

"That doesn't help me. I don't know that name."

"Millie told me you would be suspicious. That's ok I understand. I would be too if I were you," he continued. "I am your grandfather, Camille."

I started laughing. "No you're not. My grandfather is dead. He died when I was a little kid."

"We had a disagreement with your mother years ago and never reconciled. But when I found out that you had talked to Millie I knew it was time."

"Time? You have been stalking me for weeks. If you thought I didn't notice you're a moron."

"Yeah. I would come by and watch periodically. See if you had...."

"You know that's fucking creepy right?"

"I know. And I am sorry. I just wanted to see you."

"Why not come to the door? Call? Text? Email?"

"I was worried how you would react."

"How I would react? To having my grandfather back? To having family? To having a piece of my mother? This is seriously fucked up. And Millie....wait. Wait! I know why you're here. It's about the stupid powers, isn't it?"

I rubbed my face with the hand the ring was on, making sure he got a clear view of it. His pupils dilated and he tried to hide his discomfort.

He clearly knew nothing about my job.

"No! No it's not like that at all, Camille. I don't care at all about your powers. Your grandmother is not well and she wants to see you. I thought seeing you might lift her spirits and bring back some fight in her," he said with a sigh, handing me a business card. "Here is my contact info. Look me up to see if I am legit, I would expect nothing less from a Bishop. Please consider coming to see us."

I took the card and put it in my pocket. I noticed a bunch of white lines that looked like veins running up my hand towards the ring.

"What the hell?" I said out loud.

"Your mother didn't tell you anything, did she?" he asked.

"No. And I have no idea why."

"I do. You need to call us, Camille. You can't do this on your own. At the very least talk to Millie first. Let us help you."

I rolled my eyes. "I totally don't need this right now."

"No. You don't. Your mother should have told you about all of this. Like her mother and I did. I am the

LeFaye blood, the one with the blood link is obligated to teach the next generation."

"Well she's not fucking here to teach me, now is she?"

"I know, Camille, and I am so sorry that you had to go through that."

"Where the fuck were you if you're so damn sorry? She's been dead for ten goddamn years!"

"I don't have anything I can say that could...."

"No! You don't! Whatever your stupidness with her was about should have faded away when *she died and I needed you!*" my voice got louder and angrier. "I have your number. Don't come back unless I call. If you do I will call the cops. Are we clear?"

I turned and headed into the house. I didn't look back. Didn't flip him off. Didn't throw rocks. Didn't use my powers to flip his car over. I thought for a moment about checking to see if he drove away once I got inside but I changed my mind.

I'd had enough for one day.

When I got inside the damn book sat in the middle of my bed. I used my power to move it to my desk, lay down and curled up into a ball. It wasn't long before I felt sleep coming, and I didn't fight it.

I hoped it would give me some much needed clarity.

25.

When I woke up the first thing that was on my mind was Fray. I texted him immediately and asked what his plans were for the day. I put my phone aside and decided to finally open the LeFaye book.

Some of it I already knew, some I did not. The legend of King Arthur had been done and redone so many times it was hard to figure out what might be fact or fiction.

Nine sisters ruled Avalon, Morgan le Fay was one of them. The book briefly touched on their stories, but the one that had the most interest to me was Nimue.

In some stories Nimue is the bad one, she imprisons Merlin or in the latest version I saw on television she is responsible for the death of Ygraine, Arthur's mother.

In this story Nimue is the youngest of Morgan's sisters, and she also has powers. While Morgan had a balance of light and dark, Nimue only had what would be referred to as dark powers. Telekinesis, necromancy, element manipulation, and something that was described as 'reaping', haunted Nimue and drove her to the brink of madness. After the death of the man she loved her power surged and she became unstoppable and feared by everyone. It also described her hands turning white and they began referring to her affliction as *blanchmains*. She retired to Avalon to hide from the world. As one of the Nine and a Lady of Avalon she was safe there, its magic stopped the madness from consuming her.

But she did not want to be feared. All Nimue wanted was to love and be loved in return, and have friends.

Sounds familiar.

Shit.

On a separate page they spoke of a prophecy, of others that would possess the same powers as Nimue. That after the death of a loved one she would become a powerful and unstoppable force. But there would be one, one more that would possess the level of ability that Nimue had.

A few other pages contained family trees. If this was accurate I wasn't just related to Morgan le Fay but Anne Boleyn. There was a note written in the margin that it is believed by the Le Fay that Anne was truly killed because she had Nimue's powers. People were so terrified of what she could do that they killed her rather than see if she could learn to control it.

I heard myself mumble "That's fucked up," before I closed the book and put it down.

That's when it hit me.

They think it's me.

They think I am the prophecy girl.

That is the only logical explanation for Harold LeFaye's behaviour. He must think that I have Nimue's powers, and that I am the girl they speak of. That's probably why my Mom kept me away from them.

But now that someone I love has died, there really is no escaping this.

My phone started ringing. I got all excited, thinking it was Fray but it was only Lemme.

I tried not to sound too bummed when I answered. "Hello?"

"Hi Camille? Hey, it's Lemme."

"Hey girl. What's shaking?"

"Nothing. We got some free lab time today if you want to come by. It'll give you a chance to meet Rory."

I paused for a minute. "Ok. Sure. I can come by now if you want. But it will take a bit because I will be on transit."

"Awesome. I will text you the address."

When I got out of the subway and started walking the two blocks to Lemme's lab I got a phone call from Kiera. I decided to wait until I was done with Lemme before I talked to her so I let it go to voicemail.

It was a good thing Lemme texted me the instructions because it was an absolute maze to get to her lab. She grabbed me when I wandered by the door, confused if I was actually in the right place.

"Good! You're here. Let's get started. Are you scared of needles?" Lemme asked, linking arms with me and pulling me along past different stations. My phone started vibrating in my pocket and it did not stop. I was worried that it had malfunctioned so I pulled it out of my bag to check it.

It was Bliss. Which meant something bad.

"Something wrong?" Lemme asked.

"I'm not sure. Do you mind if I make a call before we get started?" I asked.

"Not at all. I'm going to go gather up what I need," she picked up a tray and disappeared.

I pushed the button to answer. "Hello? Hello, Bee? I'm here."

"It's fucking Bucky," she began. "The son of a bitch got his goddamn face bashed in."

"Dude, I am so sorry. I don't even know what to say."

"I know who did it. I know who did it and I am going after that little bitch and I need to know if you are in or not."

I paused. "What? Who did....?"

"I am not saying on the phone but you damn well know. She killed that girl too and you know it. Are you in?"

"Of course. Let me just finish at the lab."

She paused this time. "The lab? What's going on?"

"They need samples. Which reminds me, can you get some sent over?"

"Yeah, yeah. A deal is a deal. Text me the deets. I'll pick

you up in an hour."

"Will do," she hung up before I could say more.

"Everything ok?" Lemme asked when she returned.

"Yep. Just a work thing."

"Which reminds me, I am going to put together a kit for you so you can take samples. Hair, saliva, whatever you can grab with a DNA sample will be helpful," Lemme began while she moved around getting needles and other stuff organized. She motioned for me to sit on the small stool beside a long desk table thing. Everything was white, glass, and stainless steel. It was stunning.

"I am completely shocked how much this looks just like the movies," I said as she tied off my arm to prepare to take blood. She smiled at me, my breath caught when she wiped my arm with alcohol.

"You good, Bond?" Lemme asked with a big toothy grin. I took a deep breath and nodded.

"Does anyone actually like needles?" I asked.

"Of course not. But they are really not that big of a deal. If you are good and you distract the patient it works well. Like I just did. You're all done," she said, and I looked down to her pressing cotton on my arm.

"Done?" I could not hide my confusion.

"With the blood. But I want some hair, a throat swab, and some nail clippings. That's all at the moment," Lemme replied. A girl with dark brown hair in long dreadlocks that were up in a ponytail and cute glasses came up beside us, grinning ear to ear.

"So this is our girl?" she asked Lemme.

"Yep. Rory Woo, this is codename Janet Bond. Bond, this is my T.A and lab buddy Rory Woo," I stuck out my hand and we shook hands. I would thank Lemme later for the codename.

"Hi! And welcome," Rory said.

"Thank you. Nice to meet you. I also wanted to mention before I forget that a contact with the police will be sending over some samples and lab data for you guys to check out. Another body showed up today," I replied. "This is a new contact so there may be some things you guys get that I don't know about."

"Does this person have the anomaly also?" Rory asked.

"I believe so. And this contact refers to it as a virus."

Rory cocked her head to one side. "Really? I don't see it that way. It doesn't behave like a virus scientifically. But they may know something we don't."

"That could go both ways. You guys have the best lab in the country don't you?" I asked.

"That is up for debate compared to the police force but hey, thank you for saying that. I will leave you to it, it was very nice to meet you Bond," she pat Lemme on the shoulder before walking away.

"I'm going to pull a few strands of your hair," Lemme said as she leaned over my head. "This will probably hurt. I need the root though. Sorry. Keep it in mind when you are collecting samples."

"Ok I will. Thanks for the heads up," I flinched when she pulled, but it was over quickly.

She clipped a few of my nails and took a cheek swab. I thought she was going to do more but she only handed me a large makeup bag.

"Your kit. If you run out of items please call me so I can refill," Lemme said.

"I will. How did you and Q's exams go?"

"Oh they went. Not done yet. But you know how it is; it hasn't been that long since you were in school."

"My schooling was a bit different."

"I kind of imagined your exams to be cool shit, like you have to follow someone and find out info without getting 'made'. Or who can take the best stalker pictures," she said with a big smile.

"I wish! The job is really not that exciting. It's a lot of sitting around waiting for stuff to happen and doing paperwork. This is the most exciting thing that has happened to me, to be honest."

My phone started vibrating. Bliss was outside.

"Duty calls?" Lemme said. I looked into her kind, hopeful eyes and I wanted to keep talking to her. I wanted to stay here with her and Rory Woo and have them teach me science and forget that someone else was dead and this bizarre web had got even more interwoven and complex in a split second.

"Yeah. I gotta go. I'm sorry. I'm going to come back. I want to hang out and have you guys teach me science," I gathered up my things and headed for the door.

"That would be cool. I can teach you science and you can teach me the P.I game."

"That sounds like a plan!"

Bliss had parked on the curb out front of a university building on one of the busiest streets in Toronto.

Oh this is bad.

I broke into a jog and slipped in the passenger side, her car was still on so she took off as soon as I closed the door.

"I found out where the bitch is. You are gonna have to pretend like you want to have a three way," Bee said without looking at me as we sped through the night.

I shook my head quick. "Huh? Run that by me again? Which bitch are we talking about?"

"Lucia fucking Kinkaid. Who did you think I meant? She did this to make a point, that she has the fucking control or some shit. Like I am her property. I am going to get her to confess and bring her in. Are you ready if things go sideways?"

"Sideways as in?"

"If someone gets shot or some shit are you going to turn into a puddle? Jesus you're a Bishop I figured you knew the lingo."

"I would not be in this car if I wasn't ready."

"Ok good. Because I guarantee she won't go down without a fight."

We pulled into the circle driveway of a super posh condo right in the middle of downtown. A valet walked towards the driver door, when he saw Bliss he turned and walked back the other way.

"If things go sideways *he saw us pick her up*," I said, pointing directly at him.

She glanced up quickly from her phone and brushed him off with a wave. "He is a C.I and a meth addict. Not a problem."

"Oh. Well."

"Can you go in the back, by the way? Miss Priss might get her shit in a knot," she asked. I didn't mind at all. I happily got out and climbed in the back. Logistically it worked because I could get in between them easily if something happened.

Just like that she appeared. She looked like a Barbie; a little pink dress and a white fur coat, her hair in a ponytail, I couldn't help but wonder if she had a pink corvette.

She sauntered over to the car, and then I remembered that Bee had told her something about a threesome. I tried my best to smile and look interested.

"Hey ladies," Lucia said as she got in the car. "Are you ready to party?"

She held out her palm to the both of us, producing three pink pills. She smiled; her capped teeth reminded me of a lion. She nodded to us both, we each took one. I put mine under my tongue and pretended to take it, taking it out of my mouth as soon as she turned away and wrapping it in Kleenex and hiding it in my bag. Bliss very casually spat it out of her mouth and I didn't see what she did with it after that.

Lucia either didn't notice or didn't care, popping the pill like it was a tic tac and smiling like the Cheshire cat. This girl was unreal.

"So where are we headed?" Lucia asked once we got rolling.

"I made some arrangements. Don't worry," Bee said with a smile.

"Cool. Once we get there we should be off to the races," Lucia turned her head to Bliss. "I knew you would see things my way. This doesn't have to be a fight. As long as you understand that you're mine we'll be good."

The hair on the back of my neck stood up.

This was going to be a crazy night.

We drove for almost an hour. Bliss was cagey when Lucia asked her questions; I said little to nothing and tried to pretend I was high. Which wasn't easy since I had never taken pills for that purpose.

We pulled off the highway and Bee finally said to Lucia, "You remember what my last name is, right?"

"Huh?" Lucia replied. "I'm confused."

Bliss pulled into the parking lot of a motel but kept driving into the wooded area behind it. It was like something out of a horror movie.

"My mom got a phone call last night. My brother Bucky's body was found. His face is barely recognizable. They could only ID him by his tattoos and dental records," Bliss said. Lucia looked at her, didn't flinch, didn't even look surprised. Her pupils didn't dilate.

Then, Lucia Kinkaid did the dumbest thing I ever thought possible.

She smiled.

The bitch actually fucking smiled.

"That's horrible, Bliss. I am so sorry. If there is anything my brother's and I can do, let us know."

Bee stopped the car, took the keys out of the ignition, and pulled a gun from under her seat.

"You can get out of my car and start fucking walking."

26.

Lucia wasn't getting far, tromping down the dirt road in her heels.

It was almost funny.

Bliss had the gun pointed at her back; I was about three paces behind them. I was pretty sure it was her police issue pistol, I wanted to say something but I figured she had already thought this through.

"Where we going? Do you have some weird outside kink I don't know about?" Lucia asked. She was still smiling.

"I know you did it," Bee told her.

"Did what?"

"I know you killed my brother. Or, I know you got someone else to kill my brother because you're too big of a princess to get your hands dirty."

Lucia scowled. "Do you know who the fuck you're

talking to? You can't talk to me like that."

"You killed my brother. You killed an innocent girl because she told the world she was one of you and you couldn't take it. You have been infecting the population with this....this....*shit* and why?

"I have no idea what you are talking about," Lucia said flatly. She kept hobbling along like a baby deer learning how to walk.

Why do women insist on wearing stupid shoes they can't walk in?

"You think your name is going to protect you? You think being a goddamn Kinkaid makes you untouchable?" Bliss continued.

"Why don't you tell me what you want, Bee?" Lucia said, turning around and holding up her hands. "And put the damn gun away. It won't hurt me anyhow."

"Why me? Out of all the girls in that club, why me?"

Lucia smiled. "Why not you? A beautiful girl falls into my lap, a Fiori falls into my lap and you think I'm not going to claim you? You're mine now. You just need to learn to accept it. I own you."

"You don't own me! I am a person! Why don't you just admit what you did?"

"Fine. You want me to say it? We dealt with your brother. And why? *Because I fucking could, that's why.* To let you know that you are mine now. And that *girl*? That stupid little girl who told the world that we were vampires? She had to die. She talked too much."

Bee sighed and shook her head. "I knew it. I fucking

knew it. I should turn your stupid ass in."

"Why? She will be out in an hour," I said, not really thinking about what I was saying. "We don't have nearly enough to hold her."

"You know, you're right," Bliss cocked her head to one side.

"You don't have the balls," Lucia said with a laugh.

Bliss raised her pistol and shot Lucia in the forehead.

All I could do was stare with my mouth open. Her body sunk down, her blonde hair splattered with pink.

"She infected me," Bliss said without looking at me.

"Come again?" I asked, what had just happened overshadowing the seriousness of her statement.

"The virus. That stupid twat gave it to me. I have been living with this crap for the last eight months, not knowing if I am going to never wake up every time I go to sleep. Then she kills my brother," she burst into tears. "I couldn't fucking take it anymore, Cas. I couldn't deal with the idea that she wouldn't pay for what she has done. All the terrible shit. Look what she did to that girl....your client. That poor girl was her sister for Christ's sake. And your parents."

I put my hand on Bee's shoulder; she lowered the gun and breathed deeply in and out.

"You ok, Cas?" she asked me.

I paused for a minute. "Weirdly enough, I am. My biggest concern is how we're going to deal with the....

clean up."

"Don't worry about that. That's what The Wild Boys are for," she pulled a little red flip phone out of the pocket of her windbreaker.

"A burner? Did you know this was going to happen?"

"Not exactly. But I always prepare for things to go south. Programming from having an unpredictable family."

She put the gun in her pocket and dialled the number. She chatted briefly and gave our location, swapping the phone for a pack of cigarettes when she hung up.

"Can I ask how she infected you?" I said, taking the cigarette she offered me and lighting it. I didn't smoke but I thought now seemed like an appropriate time to try one.

Bliss took a drag of her smoke. "She bit me and drew blood. Luckily I don't have a scar."

"She bit you?"

"Yeah. At first I thought she was just being affectionate or whatever but then I felt the blood. I started going through these weird changes almost immediately. I think Fray thinks I am a cokehead."

"Well, we're in this together now. I have to show you something."

I held out my hand and used my powers to lift Lucia's body a few feet off the ground then put it back down again.

"Dude," Bee said.

"I know. I don't even know the full extent of what I

can do. Apparently I am a descendant of the nine sisters who ruled Avalon. I just found out. My Mom never told me."

"Dude. That is the coolest thing I have ever seen! And I have seen some shit. I just shot a wannabe vampire princess in the head, for Christ's sake."

My phone started going crazy in my pocket, I pulled it out and saw a number I did not recognise but the name LeFaye clearly displayed on the caller ID.

"Speak of the devil," I said.

"Take it. It will help establish our alibi," she replied. I shrugged and answered.

"Hi Camille? It's your Grandfather....I mean, it's Harold LeFaye," he began, speaking rather quickly.

"Oh. Hi. I didn't expect to hear from you. But I can't say that I am surprised."

"I know. I know. But it's your grandmother, Camille. She has taken a turn for the worse. I am afraid that she isn't going to last even through the night," he continued. "I hate to beg, but if you could just come by even for five minutes it would mean the world to her. Her dying wish is to see you one more time. Would you please? I know you don't owe us anything, but I hope you understand that whatever happened between us and Marie has nothing to do with you...."

"Can I bring a friend with me?"

Silence. "What? Really? Of course."

"Ok. Text me your address and we'll be by soon."

More silence, then, "Ok. Ok! We'll see you later."

"We have to go by my Mom's parent's house," I said, putting the phone back in my pocket. "And before your people show up we need to get my kit from my bag and take samples for my science peeps."

"Back up. What kind of samples?" Bee asked.

"Dude, you just shot a girl in the head, almost at point blank range, and you're getting squirrely about samples?" I said with a laugh. "Nothing extreme. Hair, nails, saliva, that sort of shit."

"Ok, ok, let's just get this shit done before The Wild Boys show up."

We were able to get a decent amount of stuff before the black 'to catch a predator' van showed up. Two guys who looked a bit like Tweedle Dum and Tweedle Dee in black leather got out, bagged up the body and cleaned the surrounding area, and cleaned Bliss's gun in some strange contraption that they had in the back of their van.

The freaky part was that there was clearly another bagged up body in the back of the van. I didn't want to ask too many questions but I was intrigued by the whole scenario.

They came over to us when they were done, handing Bliss back her service revolver. She dug into her pocket and handed them a wad of cash that was half an inch thick.

She was a bit too well prepared for this for my taste.

"Anything else, boss?" the larger of the two asked her.

"Yeah. I don't mind if she is found, just fuck her up bad," Bliss told them. "Which is exactly what she did to my brother."

It was then that I noticed someone sitting in the driver seat of the van smoking a cigarette, and I did a double take.

"October is a fucking Wild Boy? How does that work?" I exclaimed. October got out and came over to us; she walked up to Bee and ran her hand through her hair, kissing her passionately on the mouth.

They both laughed when they pulled away from each other, then October came to me and pulled me to her. She kissed me, putting a hand on the back of my neck to pull me in closer.

Her lips were soft, she smelt like smoke and vanilla.

"I am *so confused,*" I said when she pulled away from me. October laughed again, winking at Bliss before heading back to the van. She got in and they drove away without another word.

"So you're into women?" I asked Bliss.

"Nope, just that one," she proclaimed, and she started walking back to her car.

I got in the front seat this time, and had to move Lucia's purse.

"Fuck, I forgot about her phone! Hopefully the GPS and Bluetooth are off," I started digging in her bag, her florescent pink IPhone was easy to spot.

"I'm sure it is. Don't worry; we'll toss it on our way to

your grandparents."

Her phone had no password, so we wiped it. Took the SIM card and the SD card out and smashed them both, then tossed the phone off a bridge.

It all seemed a little too simple. The ducks lined up a little too neatly for my taste.

Somehow I was alright with it. The Kinkaid's got away with so much stuff, they shouldn't be allowed to anymore.

We pulled into the driveway of an older home with a white picket fence.

"Ten goddamn minutes," I said.

Bliss looked confused. "What now?"

"This whole time. They have been ten minutes away the whole damn time," I began. "I thought they were dead. What a goddamn piss off."

"I don't have a response that doesn't sound idiotic. Tell them that when we get inside," Bee said.

"I will. Let's fucking get this over with. Are you ready if this shit goes south? This is the side of the family that has actual magic powers."

She pulled her gun out of her pocket and showed it to me. "Bullet to the brain kills most things. I think we're good."

It was exactly like you would think the inside of a grandparent's house would look like. Cosy and with too many fake flowers.

Harold had also not warned me that a bunch of other LeFaye family would be there. So a bombardment of cousins, aunts and uncles came at me and I didn't register most of their names. They all had this stupid bordering psychotic smile that made the hair on the back of my neck stand up. I tried to hang onto Bliss's arm but everyone wanted to hug me so she just kept as close behind me as she could.

They brought me into a bedroom at the back of the house that was full of candles and incense and herbs and crystals, typical witchcraft stereotypes, with a hospital bed in one corner. Harold motioned me over slowly, and I felt like I tiptoed across the room to the bed.

"Honey?" Harold said to the woman wrapped in blankets. "Honey she's here. Camille is here."

I tried to smile as her eyes turned to me. I was so focused on her that I didn't notice Harold pick up two crystals off the dresser until he touched me with both of them at once.

I turned and looked at him as the pulse went through my body. He said quite calmly to me, "I unbind you," then everything went dark.

27.

"What the hell did you just do to me?" I asked, looking down at myself as I felt the power course through me. My hands had turned white, with thin white lines running up through my arms.

"I unbound your powers. Successfully it seems," he replied. "Your mother bound your powers years ago. I am surprised it held after her death."

"Why would she do that?"

"That would be a question for her. Now that you have your full powers, you can ask her."

"How would I do that?"

He laughed. "Oh, poor naive child."

The rest of the family started coming in, forcing Bliss and I back into the far corner of the room. They all had that smile, and a glowing white crystal in their hands.

"You are the *blanchmains*, Camille. You are lucky

enough to possess the powers of Nimue. You can do things, cross the border between life and death," he began. "You should feel honoured. *You* will make this family powerful. With you, we can be our own cabal. We will no longer have to pay tribute to anyone!"

"Why would I want to do anything for this family? My mother has been dead *for ten years!* You have lived ten minutes away the *entire* damn *time.* I have probably passed all of you on the street dozens of times and had no idea! Why would I do anything for any of you when you abandoned me?!"

"We needed to be sure. We needed to know for sure that you...."

"For sure that what? That I am the chosen one? That I am the goddamn prophecy girl? And if I wasn't, what would you have done? If I was actually some low level piece of shit witch, then what?" I yelled at him. My anger surged through me like a wave, the pictures on the walls started to shake.

Energy began to pulse inside me. Little pieces began to flow out of me like threads. I felt them stream out of my hands and attach themselves to the other people in the room like a parasite, including Bliss, but when I said her name in my mind it detached.

"No. No. This is not how this is going to work," I said, waving a hand in the air. "You don't get to decide when a prophecy happens. That doesn't....wait....holy shit. You killed him."

"What are you talking about?" Harold said with an

uncomfortable laugh.

"You just said you wanted to unbind my powers. The death of a loved one is part of the Nimue prophecy, it was what kicked her powers into high gear," I spoke slowly to work through my thoughts. "You killed my boyfriend as a way to jumpstart my powers."

"I can't arrest anyone without physical proof, Cas," Bliss reminded me.

"I don't need it. I don't need you to arrest them," I replied. "You want me to use my powers? I will enact my own justice."

I mentally wrapped the thread that was attached to the woman in the bed around my hand and yanked. I didn't even yank hard, and a white shadow like smoke came out of her and floated away, dissipating into the air as smoke would. The body half gasped then collapsed on the bed like an empty husk.

"Holy Mary, mother of God," Bliss proclaimed. I watched out of the corner of my eye to see if she had any physical reaction, to see if she pulled her gun on me in fear.

Nope. She stood her ground.

Even if she was scared she didn't show it.

"You killed your Grandmother," Harold said, his voice sounded confused.

"No. I killed your wife. My Grandmother has been dead since I was a kid," I told him. I gently tugged on his thread, causing him to gasp.

"Now that you have a taste of what I can do, this is

how this is going to go. I am going to walk out of here with my friend and I will never see or hear from any of you again. Is that clear?" I continued.

One of the younger women laughed. "Oh, I don't think so. If you are not going to join us we are going to take your powers."

I laughed. "Oh really? And how exactly are you going to do that?"

I tugged on her thread just a little, she sputtered and coughed. She righted herself and a glowing light orb appeared in the palm of her hand. She raised her hand like she was going to throw it at me so I yanked hard on her thread and her body crumpled into what looked like a pile of wet laundry.

"How can you be so callus about human life? Especially your family?" a middle aged woman, I'm guessing an aunt, asked. She stared at the heap on the floor that I assumed was her daughter.

"Jesse was my family!" I screamed. "When my parents died *he* was there! When I had no one *I had him! And you took him from me for what? For some stupid powers? How dare you!*"

The woman tried to continue but I raised my hand to silence her. "Why do you think you get to talk? Who the fuck are you anyhow?"

"I am your mother's older sister Maylee," she proclaimed.

"Oh, you mean one of the sisters I knew nothing about until a few days ago?" I snapped. "Right. You think you get an opinion because....?"

"Stop it! Stop this right now!" Harold yelled. "Camille if you want no part of this you should give us...."

I laughed. I couldn't help it. The laughter just exploded from me. These people were ridiculous.

"I should give you what? Please, humour me with your amazing suggestions of what *I* should give *you*! Can you give me my boyfriend back?" I asked. I concentrated on the inanimate objects in the room and began lifting them with my power, preparing for the fight. I couldn't kill them all, could I?

"Listen Camille. If you want nothing to do with this, you should give us your powers. Then you will be free. You can move on with your life like we never existed," Harold said.

"So, let me get this straight. You just randomly show up, after stalking me for years. You have lived ten goddamn minutes from my house all this time and you haven't bothered to contact me. You killed my boyfriend for nothing, really, let's be honest. You go to great lengths to make me the prophecy girl. You do understand you killed a person, right? You have the balls to think that I am going to hand you my powers?" I replied, and I began to laugh. I laughed probably harder than I should have.

"We could just take them from you. I was trying to be courteous and give you the option."

"The fact that you think that you can take them, just like that, is unbelievably arrogant. You may succeed but you can bet your ass that I am going to kill as many of you as I can before you do. Bee, get behind me. If you hurt her I will kill you with my bare hands, is that clear?"

Harold smiled. "That homicidal streak? You are your Mother's daughter."

He raised his hands and I sent as many things flying at him as I could. While they were distracted I started pulling on threads as hard as I could, one after another. Some of them dropped, other's didn't.

The lights fixtures began to flicker and pull off the wall, dragging the wiring with it. Sparks flew and the bed caught fire, one of the dressers with it.

Harold turned his head and looked at his family in pieces then looked at me. He opened and closed his hand and a glowing orb appeared, just like the younger girl's. I used my power to slam him up against the wall, pushing him up towards the ceiling as he flailed. The few left standing cowered around the bodies, staring up at me in fear.

In that moment I felt powerful.

Now when something bad happened to me I was actually intimidating, scary even.

No one would fuck with me again.

"Are we good here or would you like me to continue?" I yelled.

"Put him down," Maylee said from the ground. She sat beside her daughter and a woman probably in her late 30's. I guessed another aunt.

Well, what was left of them.

"So he can kill me? Nope. Sorry," I replied. "I will only

put him down if you give me your word this is done, we can walk out of here and never see any of you again."

"You have my word. It's done. Now put him down!" Maylee snapped.

I dropped Harold and he fell into a choking heap. I grabbed Bliss's arm and we headed for the door.

"If I ever see any of you again I will kill you all and burn this fucking house down. Am I clear?" I bent down and growled into Maylee's face. She nodded quickly and Bliss and I walked out.

"What the *fuck* just happened?" Bliss exclaimed when we got in the car.

I took a deep breath. "Are you scared of me now?"

"What? No! Are you scared of me? I shot a girl in the head like four hours ago," she asked.

"No. I guess we're really in this together now."

"Did you know you could do any of that stuff?"

"No. This is all new. Like I said, I just found out and what I had discovered was parlour tricks compared to that. It all hasn't really sunk in yet."

"Do you think....?"

"What?"

"Do you think they could have killed Bucky too? If he was with Jesse?"

I turned and put my hand on her shoulder. "No. He didn't serve their purpose. Lucia had Bucky killed. You were justified."

She shrugged. "I don't know about that."

"Anyway, did you happen to notice my body count? I think we're pretty even."

She laughed. "After tonight I think I am going to start calling you 'Prophecy Girl'."

"I don't know about that either, but I do know I need a drink."

28.

My phone rang about twenty minutes later from a number I didn't recognise.

"Hello?" I answered on the second ring. The phone dropped on the other end, and I heard a scuffle. Through the crackle and the noise I heard Millie's voice.

Then the screams.

"Can we stop somewhere on the way back?" I asked. "This place by my office. I think my friend is in trouble."

Bliss shrugged. "Sure. It's just around the corner."

When we pulled up out front of The Whistlestop the door was falling off its hinges.

"I should bring my gun?" Bliss asked.

"Please," I replied, even though I was sure that we needed a different kind of help.

We pushed in the front door and the restaurant was turned upside down. There was blood on the floor and Millie was cowering in the corner, a large man standing over her.

"Hey fuckface!" I yelled. The man turned and I was shocked to see Mr. Gray.

"What the hell?" Bliss said behind me. She was as confused as I was. She would know him too.

But there was no time to ask questions. He was going to kill Millie if I hesitated. I used my power to grab him and throw him up at the ceiling, then off to one side, crashing into the wall.

He got back up like a goddamn bouncy ball and lunged for me, reciting something that was followed with me being pushed over like he had physically touched me.

I wanted to laugh as I stood up but instead said, "Dude, are you kidding me? That was beyond lame."

"You're stronger than I expected. I won't be so naive next time," he said with a grin. I let out one of my threads towards him and he cut it off with a quick snap of his fingers.

"What the hell are you?" I asked. I pushed back at him, flinging him back into the wall and smashing some things. I didn't know what exactly; I just heard it hit the ground.

"Witch hunter," I heard Millie growl from behind me. "Don't let him touch you and watch the knife."

I thought really hard about his throat and began to squeeze. He started to cough and choke. He pulled something out of his pocket and threw it towards me. I stepped out of the way as a cloud of smoke appeared, releasing him for a split second. It was enough time for him to get away and he disappeared out the back.

"You ok, Millie?" I asked as I approached her. I flipped a chair and table right side up using my power and pulled her up into it.

"I will be alright. How did you get here so fast?" she asked.

"You mean you don't know? He said he had spoken to you."

"No. Sorry. I have been otherwise occupied. What happened?"

"We went to Harold's because apparently his wife was about to die and it was actually a trick to break my Mom's spell to unbind my powers or whatever. When I wouldn't be their leader they tried to take my powers and I might have killed a few of them. I shouldn't say might. I did. It was this thread thing that came from my hands that when I pulled they went poof, for lack of a better explanation. Apparently I am the prophecy girl or whatever."

Millie stared blankly at me for a few minutes, blinked, then said, "Oh. Well ok."

"You're not angry at me?" I asked.

"No. I wish I had known so I could have warned you. Please know that we are not all like that."

I smiled. "I do. So why are witch hunters after you?"

"Long story. How exactly do you know him?"

"I met him through Chris Lewis on a job. Why?"

"Gray knows Lewis, huh? Does Lewis know anything about your mother?"

"He knew my mother. And my father. Ted and him were partners for like 20 years or something before my parents were killed and that was 10 years ago. I have known him my whole life," a light bulb went off on my mind. "Could Mr. Gray have killed my parents?"

Millie shrugged. "The idea does have merit but the family has been looking into it since it happened. Unless we're really lost it's not witch hunters."

Bliss shuffled her feet and cleared her throat.

"Shit! I'm an asshole. Millie, this is my friend Bliss. Bee, this is my mom's cousin Millie," I said.

Bliss smiled and waved. "Nice to meet you, and thank you for not trying to kill us. It's been a long night."

"Nice to meet you too. I must say, you have a strange glow about you. Do you have any magic?"

"No. This girl gave me a virus....it's a long story."

"Does this have anything to do with the Kinkaid's virus?"

"It does, actually. What can you tell us about it?" I asked.

"Can you fix it?" Bliss added.

"Let me make you guys something to eat and we'll chat. Seems we have some things to discuss."

"So the Kinkaid's used magic and science to create

a new breed of vampire? Is that what you are saying?" Bliss asked Millie as we ate. We had been talking mostly about what happened with the LeFaye's but had moved on.

"That is the simplest explanation I can give you. We don't know everything though, and we could be totally off," Millie said, reaching out a hand to mine. "That poor dead boy infected you?"

"Yeah. But I will be ok I think. I passed the initial bad period, right Bee?"

"Yep, and I am about eight months along. We'll be ok I think," Bliss added.

"We will find something to treat it. Between me and your scientists we will figure it out. You guys don't need to worry," Millie replied.

"Do I need to worry about the cops and the body count?"

"No. The family will deal with it. We cannot risk exposing magic to the world. And if it comes up I will make sure you guys are safe."

I smiled. "Thank you."

"So can I ask the million dollar question?" Bliss asked.

"Sure," Millie replied. "What's on your mind?"

"Going off what we know now, does that mean other *things* exist as well?"

Millie smiled. "What sort of *things*?"

"Well, you guys are witches, right? Is that an acceptable word to use?" Millie nodded and Bliss continued. "Does that mean that werewolves and vampires and demons and mermaids and that sort of stuff exist too?"

"Mermaids I don't know about for sure. But the cabals that run the city at the moment are run by vampire families. There is one werewolf cabal who tries to make a play for power every so often but Elliot Kinkaid shuts that down pretty fast. Or he has until recently, and that is one of the reasons why he created the virus. It not only kills off unworthy humans, but werewolves."

I was going to say something but she continued. "We as witches have never had enough power to have any weight as a cabal. That's why Harold wanted your powers. You have to be very careful. What you did in front of Gray is nothing, but you cannot do anything more than that."

"Would they kill me?" I asked.

"It's not that simple. There is no proof either way that necromancy can be used to control vampires. They would test that first, anyone would. Then they would use you as a weapon."

"What is necromancy?"

"The basic explanation is that it is the power to control the dead. Whether it is summoning spirits, zombies, that sort of thing."

"I'm a necromancer?"

"That is one of many things you can do. We will discuss it further another day, which is when we will also talk about demons."

"Can I talk to my mother? Harold mentioned something...."

Millie looked confused. "What do you mean?"

"Necromancers deal with all things dead, right? If I can do that, does that mean I can communicate with my mother? With either of my parents?"

"Eventually you may be able to. But it takes time. You may have already done so in your dreams, which many aren't aware of in the beginning and is one of the early stages of being able to communicate with the dead."

I stared at her in silence for what seemed like an eternity. The realization of what this could mean, what all the insanity I had experienced since the night my parents died really was washed over me like a wave and I was completely overwhelmed.

"So tell me about these werewolves," Bliss broke the silence. "Are they cute? I always wanted to bang a werewolf."

Millie smiled, and I saw a little twinkle in her eye. She laughed; actually it was more like a girlish giggle.

"Millie!" I exclaimed. "For real?"

"They are wonderful in many ways, Bliss," Millie said. "The Fitzpatrick's and I have a good relationship. One day I will introduce you, if you'd like."

"Wait till I get this virus in check, then we can have at it," Bliss replied.

"Speaking of virus, what will it do, if anything, to my powers?" I asked.

"I don't know. Hopefully nothing. We don't want things getting any weirder for you, Camille," Millie said.

"Not sure if they could, but thank you. And please, call me Cas."

29.

Waking up the next day I felt renewed. Refreshed. Like someone had hit my reboot button and I had restarted somehow.

I felt better than I had in years.

When I came down for breakfast everyone was all smiles. Ted was making pancakes.

"Good morning," Ted said, handing me a cup of coffee. "You seem chipper this morning."

"Feeling good today," I replied, taking the coffee.

"Well, put a cork in it and save it for later. Get your work shit together; Chris has called us into the office."

"Me too? Ruh row."

"I don't think it's anything major. But eat up and caffeinate in case it is."

We ate well and got ready like it was any other day. It felt good to return to some form of normalcy. The colour in my hands had returned to normal, but I had my sleeves pulled down to cover them just in case. It would be a hard thing to explain.

I wanted to ask Ted if he knew anything about my mother's family, about magic. I was pretty confident he didn't, and I didn't want to bring it up and try to explain something that I did not understand myself yet. I also didn't want him to think I was returning to the state I was in when I was first sent into therapy.

While I felt fantastic my mother was at the forefront of my thoughts. I wanted to know why she made so many of the decisions she did. The prospect that I may be able to communicate with her was incredible.

Ramona was all smiles when we came in. She hugged me tightly and her eyes sparkled a bit when she looked at me, there were no clear signs that anything nefarious was going on. Which meant all was well or she was just that good.

Ted and I put down our gear and headed for the boardroom. I hoped I didn't look as nervous as I felt, I loved my job and I would fight to keep it if I had to.

A guy in his mid thirties sat having coffee and doughnuts with Chris, they were both smiling and laughing. The guy turned to me when we came in the room and my heart jumped in my throat.

They both stood when we came in, the guy was in khaki's and a sweater with a bird on the front with a collared shirt underneath.

"Eric Sadler, this is Ted Bishop, my partner and our new detective, Ted's niece Camille," Chris began. "Guys, I would like you to meet Eric Sadler."

Ted shook his hand, and I wanted to ask when we were holding auditions for the Abercrombie and Fitch catalogue but decided that might not be the first impression I wanted to give so I smiled and extended my hand. He smiled back.

Good Lord he was cute.

Our hands touched and there was a spark, not the whole romantic business but an actual spark that shocked us both and caused us to pull our hands away quickly.

"Everything ok?" Chris asked.

"Yeah. All good. Nice to meet you Eric," I said, sitting down on the opposite side of Ted. They both sandwiched Eric. I felt a bit out of the loop but I tried to focus on the moment.

"So I have called this meeting and am introducing you all because I have decided to take Eric on as my protégée," Chris began. "Things have been going so well with Camille I thought we could take on another young associate."

Ted smiled. "Welcome Eric! Please let me know if you need anything, and I will happily answer any questions that I can. If I have a case I think that you can come in on I will run it by you and see if you're interested, ok?"

I must have frowned, because Eric said, "You mean if

you're not taking Camille?"

"Not at all! It would be good for you two to work together actually. Camille has done this for a long time, first as my assistant and now a full fledged investigator in her own right. She has her own caseload."

I chuckled. "Not at the moment, but...."

Chris laughed. "As I had mentioned earlier Camille had taken a little break but she has a few appointments later today if she's ready."

I looked to Ted for some confirmation. No one had told me that they had cleared me to come back. Ted didn't mention it this morning.

He also didn't mention that he had known about this guy beforehand, but that was another issue altogether.

"Awesome. Looking forward to it," I said with a smile. And I was. It would be a welcome distraction from the explosion that just happened in my life.

I wanted to interrogate Ted but I knew that I couldn't. It was like an itch I couldn't scratch and it was frustrating.

I ate while the men chatted, keeping my mouth full so I wouldn't have to talk. I felt Eric watching me, I wanted to ask if Chris had told him the details of my chaotic life but then I remembered.

We're private investigators. If he was any good, he vetted me a long time ago.

True to Chris's statement, I had case files and appointments. I had a full day of work, which I was not expecting, so I filled myself up with as much caffeine as possible.

I had brought Jesse's phone with me so I could plug it into my laptop and copy the rest of the info, that way if Q appeared I could hand it off to her immediately. When I had a minute I texted Bliss to check in and Fray to see if he wanted to meet up later. I hadn't heard from him in a few days and I wanted to make sure things were still good.

I didn't see Eric again until lunchtime. With The Whistlestop in shambles I figured it wasn't open, and I was going to talk Ted into ordering a pizza until I found the spread that was in the lunchroom.

Eric was putting himself together a plate when I walked in, we smiled at each other and I grabbed a plate for myself.

"Chris must love you," I mumbled, not realizing it was loud enough that Eric heard.

"So this layout isn't normal?" he asked. "That's disappointing."

I shook my head quickly. "Sorry! Sarcasm is my default setting. I am actually a nice person; I just seem to stick my foot in my mouth a lot."

"No worries," he replied. His voice was husky like he had smoked a pack of cigarettes a day for the past 10 years. He reminded me of everyone's favourite crossbow wielding zombie hunter from that TV show.

"I think most people in our generation are like that," he said, smiling.

I chuckled. "Which is probably in the top five reasons why we're all doomed."

He laughed, and I could tell it was genuine by the way his entire face lit up. Something about him made me feel safe and comfortable. I had this weird urge to hold his hand.

When I really looked at him I realized his clothes were just an outfit. His short dark hair was cut unevenly, like he had done it himself, but it worked with his scruffy moustache and goatee. His hands were callused but strong.

I smiled and started to pile food on my plate. I noticed the skin on my finger around my ring was glowing white. I'd have to ask Millie if that was like magic radar or something because it was weird.

Ramona came by like ten minutes later to tell me my next client was here so I didn't have a chance to talk to Eric more.

I wanted to say something smart and witty but all I could manage was, "Back to the old salt mines."

I hung my head and went back to my office, hoping that Eric didn't think I was a complete moron just yet.

Ramona brought a young woman into my office; she was probably twenty one, tops. She had baby fine extra light blonde hair that hung around her shoulders and tiny features like she was really a pixie.

She smiled; her perfect white teeth looked like they

had just been polished.

"Hi, Miss Bishop?" her voice was soft and tinkling like chimes.

I stood up from behind my desk and shook her hand. "Yes, I am Camille Bishop. Nice to meet you. And you are?"

"Are you the same Bishop who met with Jane Lowry?" she asked.

My heart sank, turning into an aching knot in my chest. I'd wondered if this would happen eventually.

"Look, if you are trying to get a news story this is a really shitty way to...."

"Story?" she asked. "No! No! You misunderstand me. I am not a reporter. My name is Leena Rose. I am.... was....sorry, it's still so weird. I am a friend of Jane's. She referred you to me. I would have been here sooner but your receptionist said you had to take some time off....?"

My aching knot of a heart started to thump in my chest and I wasn't sure I could speak.

"Oh. Oh ok. Yeah, I took some time off after what happened," I said.

"I don't blame you. I took some time off from everything myself."

I grabbed my notepad and a pen. "So what can I do for you Leena?"

"Well, I think I have a stalker. Jane said you are really good at what you do, and I can trust you even if it's weird," a tear rolled down Leena's cheek. "She did not deserve what happened to her."

I swallowed hard. "No she didn't. I wish I could have done more for her. Now what can you tell me about this possible stalker?"

****

The screams were so loud they echoed through my mind as if they came from my own mouth.

But I knew it wasn't me. I was in a strange place, if it had been me it surely would have woken me up.

This had to be what Millie had been talking about.

I had gone home from the office and fallen into a deep sleep, exhausted from a long day. I did not remember falling asleep but I was confident I had arrived home safely.

I was hopeful when I saw the silhouette of a person, then immediately annoyed when the dishevelled blonde hair came into full view. She turned to me, her eyes wild and feral, her teeth barred like an angry beast on the attack.

With fangs. She had actual fangs.

"You!" she yelled. "You did this to me!"

"Actually I didn't. I was just there when it happened."

"Right, that bitch Bliss did this. She will get hers. Then you will too!"

"You're pretty cocky for a dead girl."

"I'm going to rip you to shreds!"

She came at me and I used my powers to push her back.

"Yeah, no. I control things here sweet pea."

She cackled like a crazy old woman.

"You think you are in control, necromancer? That is a fucking joke. When my family finds you they are going to make you their personal slave! You think your magic can save you?"

"You have absolutely no regard for anyone else, do you? Like you can just do whatever you want with no repercussions. That poor girl did nothing to you. How can you have so little regard for human life?"

"Human life? Humans are just toys and food, put on this earth for our amusement. We are the superior species. That 'poor girl' thought she could mess with my family...."

"She just wanted to know the truth of who she was, who her family really was. You killed her for it."

She laughed. "We killed people for a lot less than that. You think your magic can protect you? My family will come for you as well. You'll see!"

I pulled her to me and grabbed her throat, squeezing tight with my actual hand.

"I am Camille Bishop. I am a descendant of the Nine Sisters of Avalon. I am blanchmains, like Nimue before me," I said in her ear, my breath hot on her cheek.

Repeating my own prophecy, my truth, gave me strength.

"Let them come. I am not afraid."

My phone ringing was loud and obnoxious. I was

immediately offended when I had to open my eyes. Through my clouded vision I couldn't read the call display and I fumbled for the answer button.

"Yeah," I growled. I didn't care at this point who it was.

"Cas?" Bliss whispered loudly. "Cas? Can you hear me? Cas?"

"Yep. Sorry I had fallen asleep. What's up?"

"The Kinkaid boys. They came to Ren and grabbed me. I think they are going to...."

I sat up quickly. "Going to what? Bliss? Bliss, are you there?"

"I have the GPS and Bluetooth turned on on my phone. Track it and find me. But they may come after you too so watch your back. If I don't make it promise me you'll run, Cas."

"What? Fuck that! I am coming for you Bliss. I will call in the cavalry."

I heard yelling in the background. There was some shuffling, Bliss screamed, then the phone falling.

"Are you that retarded that you didn't check her for a phone?" a male voice yelled. There was a loud crunch just before the phone went dead.

"Bliss?! Bee?!! Hello?"

Fuck.

ACKNOWLEDGMENTS

This project would not be what it is without the few people I have in my corner.

It is hard for me to express in words how grateful I am to my book bitches, as I call them. Thank you for allowing me to be part of your world. I am proud and honoured to be part of this incredible group of people who share this amazing dream with me and I feel so lucky to be part of it.

Tara Dawn, thank you for your kindness and friendship. Thank you for listening to my ramblings and for not thinking I am insane. And thank you for believing in Prophecy Girl even when I wasn't sure I did. I look forward to our conversations, our sprints, and our future collaborations together.

RM Gilmore, thank you for allowing me to be part of your world. Thank you for helping me even when I wasn't sure I needed it, and for being one of the greatest people I know. Thank you for believing in Prophecy Girl, and in me. You're my hero.

Thank you Becky Johnson and the girls at Bex 'n' Books and Hot Tree. You guys are fucking awesome and I appreciate the support.

I also wanted to thank Laurell K Hamilton for writing Anita Blake. I consider Anita a dear friend. She has got me through some tough times. And I wouldn't have gone on this incredible journey with Camille if Anita had not paved the way. She absolutely changed my life for the better and I thank you every time I look at my bookshelf and I am reminded that she is always there.

Thank you to my father, Lawrence, for helping me whip this story into shape. I really appreciate your keen eye and our plot conversations.

Thank you to Michael, as always, for helping keep me sane. Being a writing spouse is not easy and I appreciate you putting up with my randomness.

To Khaleesi, as always.

To my Mother, may she rest peacefully.

To you, dear reader – I hope you have enjoyed reading about the beginning of Camille's journey as much as I have enjoyed writing it. And there is much more to come.